I wondered, for the very first time, if maybe I was doing this whole thing wrong. If maybe I'd allowed myself to be blinded by my own anger to the exclusion of all else. If maybe, just maybe, I'd been so determined not to be stereotyped that I'd begun to stereotype everyone around me.

It made me think about Ocean.

He kept trying to be nice to me and, in an unexpected turn of events, his kindness left me angry and confused. I pushed him away because I was afraid to be even remotely close to someone who, I was certain, would one day hurt me. I trusted no one anymore. I was so raw from repeated exposure to cruelty that now even the most minor abrasions left a mark. The check-out lady at the grocery store would be rude to me and her simple unkindness would unnerve me for the rest of the day because I never knew—I had no way of knowing—

Are you racist? Or are you just having a bad day?

I could no longer distinguish people from monsters.

I looked out at the world around me and no longer saw nuance. I saw nothing but the potential for pain and the subsequent need to protect myself, constantly.

Damn, I thought.

This really was exhausting.

A VERY LARGE EXPANSE OF SEA

TAHEREH MAFI

HARPER

An Imprint of HarperCollinsPublishers

MAFI

A Very Large Expanse of Sea

Copyright © 2018 by Tahereh Mafi

All rights reserved. Printed in the United States of America. No part of this book may be
used or reproduced in any manner whatsoever without written permission except in the
case of brief quotations embodied in critical articles and reviews. For information address
HarperCollins Children's Books, a division of HarperCollins Publishers,
195 Broadway, New York, NY 10007.

www.epicreads.com

Library of Congress Control Number: 2018945999

ISBN 978-0-06-286657-8

Typography by Jenna Stempel-Lobell

19 20 21 22 23 PC/LSCC 10 9 8 7 6 5 4 3

❖

First paperback edition, 2019

ONE

We always seemed to be moving, always for the better, always to make our lives better, whatever. I couldn't keep up with the emotional whiplash. I'd attended so many elementary schools and middle schools I couldn't keep their names straight anymore but this, this switching high schools all the time thing was really starting to make me want to die. This was my third high school in less than two years and my life seemed suddenly to comprise such a jumble of bullshit every day that sometimes I could hardly move my lips. I worried that if I spoke or screamed my anger would grip both sides of my open mouth and rip me in half.

So I said nothing.

It was the end of August, all volatile heat and the occasional breeze. I was surrounded by starched backpacks and stiff denim and kids who smelled like fresh plastic. They seemed happy.

I sighed and slammed my locker shut.

For me, today was just another first day of school in another new city, so I did what I always did when I showed up at a new school: I didn't look at people. People were always looking at me, and when I looked back they often took it as an invitation to speak to me, and when they spoke to me they nearly always said something offensive or stupid or both and I'd decided a long time ago that it was easier to pretend they just didn't exist.

I'd managed to survive the first three classes of the day without major incident, but I was still struggling to navigate the school itself. My next class seemed to be on the other side of campus, and I was trying to figure out where I was—cross-checking room numbers against my new class schedule—when the final bell rang. In the time it took my stunned self to glance up at the clock, the masses of students around me had disappeared. I was suddenly alone in a long, empty hallway, my printed schedule now crumpled in one fist. I squeezed my eyes shut and swore under my breath.

When I finally found my next class I was seven minutes late. I pushed open the door, the hinges slightly squeaking, and students turned around in their seats. The teacher stopped talking, his mouth still caught around a sound, his face frozen between expressions.

He blinked at me.

I averted my eyes, even as I felt the room contract around me. I slid into the nearest empty seat and said nothing. I took a notebook out of my bag. Grabbed a pen. I was hardly breathing, waiting for the moment to pass, waiting for people to turn away, waiting for my teacher to start talking again when he suddenly cleared his throat and said—

"Anyway, as I was saying: our syllabus includes quite a bit of required reading, and those of you who are new here"—he hesitated, glanced at the roster in his hands—"might be unaccustomed to our school's intense and, ah, highly demanding curriculum." He stopped. Hesitated again. Squinted at the paper in his hands.

And then, as if out of nowhere, he said, "Now—forgive me if I'm saying this incorrectly—but is it—*Sharon*?" He looked up, looked me directly in the eye.

I said, "It's Shirin."

Students turned to look at me again.

"Ah." My teacher, Mr. Webber, didn't try to pronounce my name again. "Welcome."

I didn't answer him.

"So." He smiled. "You understand that this is an honors English class."

I hesitated. I wasn't sure what he was expecting me to say to such an obvious statement. Finally, I said, "Yes?"

He nodded, then laughed, and said, "Sweetheart, I think you might be in the wrong class."

I wanted to tell him not to call me *sweetheart*. I wanted to tell him not to talk to me, ever, as a general rule. Instead, I said, "I'm in the right class," and held up my crumpled schedule.

Mr. Webber shook his head, even as he kept smiling. "Don't worry—this isn't your fault. It happens sometimes with new students. But the ESL office is actually just down the—"

"I'm in the right class, okay?" I said the words more forcefully than I'd intended. "I'm in the right class."

This shit was always happening to me.

It didn't matter how unaccented my English was. It didn't matter that I told people, over and over again, that I was born here, *in America*, that English was my first language, that my cousins in Iran made fun of me for speaking mediocre Farsi with an American accent—it didn't matter. Everyone assumed I was fresh off the boat from a foreign land.

Mr. Webber's smile faltered. "Oh," he said. "Okay."

The kids around me started laughing and I felt my face getting hot. I looked down and opened my blank notebook to a random page, hoping the action would inspire an end to the conversation.

Instead, Mr. Webber held up his hands and said, "Listen—me, personally? I want you to stay, okay? But this is a really advanced class, and even though I'm sure your English is really good, it's still—"

"My English," I said, "isn't *really good*. My English is fucking perfect."

I spent the rest of the hour in the principal's office.

I was given a stern talking-to about the kind of behavior expected of students at this school and warned that, if I was going to be deliberately hostile and uncooperative, maybe this wasn't the school for me. And then I was given detention for using vulgar language in class. The lunch bell rang while the principal was yelling at me, so when he finally let me go I grabbed my things and bolted.

I wasn't in a hurry to get anywhere; I was only looking forward to being away from people. I had two more classes to get through after lunch but I wasn't sure my head could take it; I'd already surpassed my threshold for stupidity for the day.

I was balancing my lunch tray on my lap in a bathroom stall, my head in a viselike grip between my hands, when my phone buzzed. It was my brother.

> what are you doing?
> **eating lunch**
> bullshit. where are you hiding?
> **in the bathroom**
> what? why?
> **what else am i supposed to do for 37 minutes?**
> **stare at people?**

And then he told me to get the hell out of the bathroom and come have lunch with him, apparently the school had already sent out a welcome wagon full of brand-new friends in celebration of his pretty face, and I should join him instead of hiding.

no thanks, I typed.

And then I threw my lunch in the trash and hid in the library until the bell rang.

My brother is two years older than me; we'd almost always been in the same school at the same time. But he didn't hate moving like I did; he didn't always suffer when we got to a new city. There were two big differences between me and my brother: first, that he was extremely handsome, and second, that he didn't walk around wearing a metaphorical neon sign nailed to his forehead flashing CAUTION, TERRORIST APPROACHING.

I shit you not, girls lined up to show my brother around the school. He was the good-looking new guy. The interesting boy with an interesting past and an interesting name. The handsome exotic boy all these pretty girls would inevitably use to satisfy their need to experiment and one day rebel against their parents. I'd learned the hard way that I couldn't eat lunch with him and his friends. Every time I showed up, tail between my legs and my pride in the trash, it took all of five seconds for me to realize that the only reason his new lady friends were being nice to me was because they wanted to use me to get to my brother.

I'd rather eat in the toilet.

I told myself I didn't care, but obviously I did. I had to. The news cycle never let me breathe anymore. 9/11 happened last fall, two weeks into my freshman year, and a couple of weeks later two dudes attacked me while I was walking home from school and the worst part—the worst part—was that it took me days to shake off the denial; it took me days to fathom the *why*. I kept hoping the explanation would turn out to be more complex, that there'd turn out to be more than pure, blind hatred to motivate their actions. I wanted there to be some other reason why two strangers would follow me home, some other reason why they'd yank my scarf off my head and try to choke me with it. I didn't understand how anyone could be so violently angry with me for something I hadn't done, so much so that they'd feel justified in assaulting me in broad daylight as I walked down the street.

I didn't *want* to understand it.

But there it was.

I hadn't expected much when we moved here, but I was still sorry to discover that this school seemed no better than my last one. I was stuck in another small town, trapped in another universe populated by the kind of people who'd only ever seen faces like mine on their evening news, and I hated it. I hated the exhausting, lonely months it took to settle into a new school; I hated how long it took for the kids around me to realize I was neither terrifying nor dangerous; I hated the pathetic, soul-sucking effort it took to finally make a single friend brave enough to sit next to me in public. I'd had to relive this awful cycle so many times, at so many different schools, that sometimes I really wanted to put my head through a wall.

All I wanted from the world anymore was to be perfectly unre-markable. I wanted to know what it was like to walk through a room and be stared at by no one. But a single glance around campus deflated any hopes I might've had for blending in.

The student body was, for the most part, a homogenous mass of about two thousand people who were apparently in love with basketball. I'd already walked past dozens of posters—and a massive banner hung over the front doors—celebrating a team that wasn't even in season yet. There were oversize black-and-white numbers taped to hallway walls, signs screaming at passersby to count down the days until the first game of the season.

I had no interest in basketball.

Instead, I'd been counting the number of dipshit things people had said to me today. I'd been holding strong at four-teen until I made my way to my next class and some kid passing me in the hall asked if I wore that thing on my head because I was hiding bombs underneath and I ignored him, and then his friend said that maybe I was secretly bald and I ignored him, and then a third one said that I was probably, actually, a man, and just trying to hide it and finally I told them all to fuck off, even as they congratulated one another on having drummed up these excellent hypotheses. I had no idea what these ass-wipes looked like because I never glanced in their direction, but I was thinking seventeen, *seventeen*, as I got to my next class way too early and waited, in the dark, for everyone else to show up.

These, the regular injections of poison I was gifted from strangers, were definitely the worst things about wearing a headscarf. But the best thing about it was that my teachers couldn't see me listening to music.

It gave me the perfect cover for my earbuds.

Music made my day so much easier. Walking through the halls at school was somehow easier; sitting alone all the time was easier. I loved that no one could tell I was listening to music and that, because no one knew, I was never asked to turn it off. I'd had multiple conversations with teachers who had no idea I was only half hearing whatever they were saying to me, and for some reason this made me happy. Music seemed to steady me like a second skeleton; I leaned on it when my own bones were too shaken to stand. I always listened to music on the iPod I'd stolen from my brother and, here—as I did last year, when he first bought the thing—I walked to class like I was listening to the soundtrack of my own shitty movie. It gave me an inexplicable kind of hope.

When my last class of the day had finally assembled, I was already watching my teacher on mute. My mind wandered; I kept checking the clock, desperate to escape. Today, the Fugees were filling the holes in my head, and I stared at my pencil case, turning it over and over in my hands. I was really into mechanical pencils. Like, nice ones. I had a small collection, actually, that I'd gotten from an old friend from four moves ago; she'd brought them back for me from Japan and I was mildly obsessed. The pencils were delicate and colorful and glittery and they'd come with a set of adorable erasers and this really cute case with a cartoon picture of a sheep on it, and the sheep said *Do not make light of me just because I am a sheep*, and I'd always thought it was so funny and strange and I was remembering this now, smiling a little, when someone tapped me on the shoulder. Hard.

"What?" I turned around as I said it, speaking too loudly by accident.

Some dude. He looked startled.

"What?" I said quietly, irritated now.

He said something but I couldn't hear him. I tugged the iPod out of my pocket and hit pause.

"Uh." He blinked at me. Smiled, but seemed confused about it. "You're listening to music under there?"

"Can I help you?"

"Oh. No. No, I just bumped your shoulder with my book. By accident. I was trying to say sorry."

"Okay." I turned back around. I hit play on my music again.

The day passed.

People had butchered my name, teachers hadn't known what the hell to do with me, my math teacher looked at my face and gave a five-minute speech to the class about how people who don't love this country should just go back to where they came from and I stared at my textbook so hard it was days before I could get the quadratic equation out of my head.

Not one of my classmates spoke to me, no one but the kid who accidentally assaulted my shoulder with his bio book.

I wished I didn't care.

I walked home that day feeling both relieved and dejected. It took a lot out of me to put up the walls that kept me safe from heartbreak, and at the end of every day I felt so withered by the emotional exertion that sometimes my whole body felt shaky. I was trying to steady myself as I made my way down the quiet stretch of sidewalk that would carry me home—trying to shake this heavy, sad fog from my head—when a car slowed down just long enough for a lady to shout at me that I was in America now, so I should dress like it, and I was just, I don't know, I was so goddamn tired I couldn't even drum up the enthusiasm to be angry, not even as I offered her a full view of my middle finger as she drove away.

Two and a half more years, was all I could think.

Two and a half more years until I could get free from this panopticon they called high school, these monsters they called people. I was desperate to escape the institution of idiots. I wanted to go to college, make my own life. I just had to survive until then.

TWO

My parents were actually pretty great, as far as human beings went. They were proud Iranian immigrants who worked hard, all day, to make my life—and my brother's life—better. Every move we made was to bring us into a better neighborhood, into a bigger house, into a better school district with better options for our future. They never stopped fighting, my parents. Never stopped striving. I knew they loved me. But you have to know, right up front, that they had zero sympathy for what they considered were my unremarkable struggles.

My parents never talked to my teachers. They never called my school. They never threatened to call some other kid's mother because her son threw a rock at my face. People had been shitting on me for having the wrong name/race/religion and socioeconomic status since as far back as I could remember, but my life had been so easy in comparison to my parents' own upbringing that they genuinely couldn't understand why I didn't wake up singing every morning. My dad's personal story was so insane—he'd left home, all alone, for America when he was sixteen—that the part where he was drafted to go to war in Vietnam actually seemed like a highlight. When I was a kid and would tell my mom that people at school were mean to me, she'd pat me on the head and tell me stories about how she'd lived through war and an actual revolution, and when she was fifteen someone cracked open her skull in the middle of the street while her best friend was gutted like a fish so, hey, why don't you just eat your Cheerios and walk it off, you ungrateful American child.

I ate my Cheerios. I didn't talk about it.

I loved my parents, I really did. But I never talked to them about my own pain. It was impossible to compete for sympathy with a mother and father who thought I was lucky to attend a school where the teachers only *said* mean things to you and didn't *actually* beat the shit out of you.

So I never said much anymore.

I'd come home from school and shrug through my parents' many questions about my day. I'd do my homework; I'd keep myself busy. I read a lot of books. It's such a cliché, I know, the lonely kid and her books, but the day my brother walked into my room and chucked a copy of *Harry Potter* at my head and said, "I won this at school, looks like something you'd enjoy," was one of the best days of my life. The few friends I'd made who didn't live exclusively on paper had collapsed into little more than memories and even those were fading fast. I'd lost a lot in our moves—things, stuff, objects—but nothing hurt as much as losing people.

Anyway, I was usually on my own.

My brother, though, he was always busy. He and I used to be close, used to be best friends, but then one day he woke up to discover he was cool and handsome and I was not, that in fact my very existence scared the crap out of people, and, I don't know, we lost touch. It wasn't on purpose. He just always had people to see, things to do, girls to call, and I didn't. I liked my brother, though. Loved him, even. He was a good guy when he wasn't annoying the shit out of me.

I survived the first three weeks at my new school with very little to report. It was unexciting. Tedious. I interacted with people on only the most basic, perfunctory levels, and otherwise spent most of my time listening to music. Reading. Flipping through *Vogue*. I was really into complicated fashion that I could never afford and I spent my weekends scouring thrift stores, trying to find pieces that were reminiscent of my favorite looks from the runway, looks that I would later, in the quiet of my bedroom, attempt to re-create. But I was only mediocre with a sewing machine; I did my best work by hand. Even so, I kept breaking needles and accidentally stabbing myself and showing up to school with too many Band-Aids on my fingers, prompting my teachers to shoot me even weirder looks than usual. Still, it kept me distracted. It was only the middle of September and I was already struggling to give even the vaguest shit about school.

After another exhilarating day at the panopticon I collapsed onto the couch. My parents weren't home from work yet, and I didn't know where my brother was. I sighed, turned on the television, and tugged my scarf off my head. Pulled the ponytail free and ran a hand through my hair. Settled back onto the couch.

There were *Matlock* reruns on TV every afternoon at exactly this hour, and I was not embarrassed to admit out loud that I loved them. I loved *Matlock*. It was a show that was created even before I was born, about a really old, really expensive lawyer named Matlock who solved criminal cases for a ton of money. These days it was popular only with the geriatric crowd, but this didn't bother me. I often felt like a very old person trapped in a young person's body; Matlock was my people. All I needed was a bowl of prunes or a cup of applesauce to finish off the look, and I was beginning to wonder if maybe we had some stashed somewhere in the fridge when I heard my brother come home.

At first I didn't think anything of it. He shouted a hello to the house and I made a noncommittal noise; Matlock was being awesome and I couldn't be bothered to look away.

"Hey—didn't you hear me?"

I popped my head up. Saw my brother's face.

"I brought some friends over," he was saying, and even then I didn't quite understand, not until one of the guys walked into the living room and I stood up so fast I almost fell over.

"*What the hell*, Navid?" I hissed, and grabbed my scarf. It was a comfortable, pashmina shawl that was normally very easy to wear, but I fumbled in the moment, feeling flustered, and somehow ended up shoving it onto my head. The guy just smiled at me.

"Oh—don't worry," he said quickly. "I'm like eighty percent gay."

"That's nice," I said, irritated, "but this isn't about you."

"This is Bijan," Navid said to me, and he could hardly contain his laughter as he nodded at the new guy, who was so obviously Persian I almost couldn't believe it; I didn't think there were other Middle Eastern people in this town. But Navid was now laughing at my face and I realized then that I must've looked ridiculous, standing there with my scarf bunched awkwardly on my head. "Carlos and Jacobi are—"

"Bye."

I ran upstairs.

I spent a few minutes considering, as I paced the length of my bedroom floor, how embarrassing that incident had been. I felt flustered and stupid, caught off guard like that, but I finally decided that though the whole thing was kind of embarrassing, it was not so embarrassing that I could justify hiding up here for hours without food. So I tied my hair back, carefully reassembled myself—I didn't like pinning my scarf in place, so I usually wrapped it loosely around my head, tossing the longer ends over my shoulders—and reemerged.

When I walked into the living room, I discovered the four boys sitting on the couch and eating, what looked like, everything in our pantry. One of them had actually found a bag of prunes and was currently engaged in stuffing them in his mouth.

"Hey." Navid glanced up.

"Hi."

The boy with the prunes looked at me. "So you're the little sister?"

I crossed my arms.

"This is Carlos," Navid said. He nodded at the other guy I hadn't met, this really tall black dude, and said, "That's Jacobi."

Jacobi waved an unenthusiastic hand without even looking in my direction. He was eating all the rosewater nougat my mom's sister had sent her from Iran. I doubted he even knew what it was.

Not for the first time, I was left in awe of the insatiable appetite of teenage boys. It grossed me out in a way I couldn't really articulate. Navid was the only one who wasn't eating anything at the moment; instead, he was drinking one of those disgusting protein shakes.

Bijan looked me up and down and said, "You look better."

I narrowed my eyes at him. "How long are you guys going to be here?"

"Don't be rude," Navid said without looking up. He was

now on his knees, messing with the VCR. "I wanted to show these guys *Breakin'*."

I was more than a little surprised.

Breakin' was one of my favorite movies.

I couldn't remember how our obsession started, exactly, but my brother and I had always loved breakdancing videos. Movies about breakdancing; hours-long breakdancing competitions from around the world; whatever, anything. It was a thing we shared—a love of this forgotten sport—that had often brought us together at the end of the day. We'd found this movie, *Breakin'*, at a flea market a few years ago, and we'd watched it at least twenty times already.

"Why?" I said. I sat down in an armchair, curled my legs up underneath me. I wasn't going anywhere. *Breakin'* was one of the few things I enjoyed more than *Matlock*. "What's the occasion?"

Navid turned back. Smiled at me. "I want to start a break-dancing crew."

I stared at him. "Are you serious?"

Navid and I had talked about this so many times before: what it would be like to breakdance—to really learn and perform—but we'd never actually done anything about it. It was something I'd thought about for years.

Navid stood up then. He smiled wider. I knew he could tell I was super excited. "You in?"

"Fuck yeah," I said softly.

My mom walked into the room at that exact moment and whacked me in the back of the head with a wooden spoon.

"*Fosh nadeh*," she snapped. *Don't swear.*

I rubbed the back of my head. "Damn, Ma," I said. "That shit hurt."

She whacked me in the back of the head again.

"*Damn*."

"Who's this?" she said, and nodded at my brother's new friends.

Navid made quick work of the introductions while my mother took inventory of all that they'd eaten. She shook her head. "*Een chiyeh?*" she said. *What's this?* And then, in English: "This isn't food."

"It's all we had," Navid said to her. Which was sort of true. My parents never, ever bought junk food. We never had chips or cookies lying around. When I wanted a snack my mom would hand me a cucumber.

My mother sighed dramatically at Navid's comment and started scrounging up actual food for us. She then said something in Farsi about how she'd spent all these years teaching her kids how to cook and if she came home from work tomorrow and someone hadn't already made dinner for her we were both going to get our asses kicked—and I was only forty percent sure she was joking.

Navid looked annoyed and I almost started laughing when my mom turned on me and said, "How's school?"

That wiped the smile off my face pretty quickly. But I knew she wasn't asking about my social life. My mom wanted to know about my grades. I'd been in school for less than a month and she was already asking about my grades.

"School's fine," I said.

She nodded, and then she was gone. Always moving, doing, surviving.

I turned to my brother. "So?"

"Tomorrow," he said, "we're going to meet after school."

"And if we get a teacher to supervise," Carlos said, "we could make it an official club on campus."

"Nice." I beamed at my brother.

"I know, right?"

"So, uh, small detail," I said, frowning. "Something I think you might've forgotten—?"

Navid raised an eyebrow.

"Who's going to teach us to breakdance?"

"I am," Navid said, and smiled.

My brother had a bench press in his bedroom that took up half the floor. He found it, disassembled and rusted, next to a dumpster one day, and he hauled it back to one of our old apartments, fixed it, spray-painted it, and slowly amassed a collection of weights to go with it. He dragged that thing around with us everywhere we moved. He loved to train, my brother. To run. To box. He used to take gymnastic classes until they got to be too expensive, and I think he secretly wanted to be a personal trainer. He'd been working out since he was twelve;

he was all muscle and virtually no body fat, and I knew this because he liked to update me on his body-fat percentage on a regular basis. Once, when I'd said, "Good for you," he'd pinched my arm and pursed his lips and said, "Not bad, not bad, but you could stand to build more muscle," and he'd been forcing me to work out with him and his bench press ever since.

So when he said he wanted to teach us how to breakdance, I believed him.

But things were about to get weird.

THREE

It happened a lot, right? In high school? Lab partners. That shit. I *hated* that shit. It was always an ordeal for me, the awkward, agonizing embarrassment of having no one to work with, having to talk to the teacher quietly at the end of class to tell her you don't have a partner, could you work by yourself, would that be possible, and she'd say no, she'd smile beatifically, she'd think she was doing you a favor by making you the third in a pair that had been very excited about working the hell alone, Jesus Christ—

Well, it didn't happen that way this time.

This time God parted the heavens and slapped some sense into my teacher who made us partner off at random, selecting pairs based on our seats, and that was how I found myself in the sudden position of being ordered to skin a dead cat with the guy who hit me in the shoulder with his bio book on the first day of school.

His name was Ocean.

People took one look at my face and they expected my name to be strange, but one look at this dude's very Ken-Barbie face and I had not expected his name to be Ocean.

"My parents are weird," was all he said by way of explanation.

I shrugged.

We skinned the dead cat in silence, mostly because it was disgusting and no one wanted to narrate the experience of cutting into sopping flesh that stank of formaldehyde, and all I could think was that high school was so stupid, and what the hell were we doing, why was this a requirement oh my God this was so sick, so sick, I couldn't believe we had to work on the same dead cat for two months—

"I can't stay long, but I have a little time after school," Ocean said. It felt like a sudden statement, but I realized only then that he'd been talking for a while; I was so focused on this flimsy scalpel in my hand that I hadn't noticed.

I looked up. "Excuse me?"

He was filling out his lab sheet. "We still have to write a report for today's findings," he said, and glanced up at the clock. "But the bell is about to ring. So we should probably finish this after school." He looked at me. "Right?"

"Oh. Well. I can't meet after school."

Ocean went a little pink around the ears. "Oh," he said. "Right. I get it. Are you— I mean, are you not allowed, to, like—"

"Wow," I said, my eyes going wide. "*Wow*." I shook my head, washed my hands, and sighed.

"Wow what?" he said quietly.

I looked at him. "Listen, I don't know what you've already decided about what you think my life is like, but I'm not about to be sold off by my parents for a pile of goats, okay?"

"Herd of goats," he said, clearing his throat. "It's a herd—"

"Whatever the hell kind of goats, I don't care."

He flinched.

"I just happen to have shit to do after school."

"Oh."

"So maybe we can figure this out some other way," I said. "Okay?"

"Oh. Okay. What, uh, what are you doing after school?"

I'd been stuffing my things into my backpack when he asked the question, and I was so caught off guard I dropped my pencil case. I reached down to grab it. When I stood up he was staring at me.

"What?" I said. "Why do you care?"

He looked really uncomfortable now. "I don't know."

I studied him just long enough to analyze the situation. Maybe I was being a little too hard on Ocean with the weird parents. I shoved my pencil case into my backpack and zipped the whole thing away. Adjusted the straps over my shoulders. "I'm joining a breakdancing crew," I said.

Ocean frowned and smiled at the same time. "Is that a joke?"

I rolled my eyes. The bell rang.

"I have to go," I said.

"But what about the lab work?"

I mulled over my options and finally just wrote down my phone number. I handed it to him. "You can text me. We'll work on it tonight."

He stared at the piece of paper.

"But be careful with that," I said, nodding at the paper, "because if you text me too much, you'll have to marry me. It's the rules of my religion."

He blanched. "Wait. What?"

I was almost smiling. "I have to go, Ocean."

"Wait— No, seriously— You're joking, right?"

"Wow," I said, and I shook my head. "Bye."

My brother, as promised, had managed to get a teacher to sign off on the whole breakdancing thing. We'd have paperwork by the end of the week to make the club official, which meant that, for the first time in my life, I'd be involved in an extracurricular activity, which felt strange. Extracurricular activities weren't really my thing.

Still, I was over the goddamn moon.

I'd always wanted to do something like this. Breakdancing was something I'd admired forever and always from afar; I'd watched b-girls perform in competitions and I thought they looked so cool—*so strong*. I wanted to be like them. But breakdancing wasn't like ballet; it wasn't something you could look up in the yellow pages. There weren't breakdancing schools, not where I lived. There weren't retired breakdancers just lying around, waiting for my parents to pay them in Persian food to teach me to perfect a flare. I wasn't sure I'd have been able to do something like this if it weren't for Navid. He'd confessed to me, last night, that he'd been secretly learning and practicing on his own these last couple of years, and I was blown away by how much he'd progressed all by himself. Of the two of us, he was the one who'd really taken our dream seriously—and the realization made me both proud of him and disappointed in myself.

Navid was taking a risk.

We moved around so much that I felt like I could never make plans anymore. I never made commitments, never joined school clubs. Never bought a yearbook. I never memorized phone numbers or street names or learned anything more than was absolutely necessary about the town I lived in. There didn't seem to be a point. Navid had struggled with this, too, in his own way, but he said he was done waiting for the right moment. He would be graduating this year, and he finally wanted to give breakdancing a shot before he went off to college and everything changed. I was proud of him.

I waved when I walked into our first practice.

We were meeting in one of the dance rooms inside the school's gym, and my brother's three new friends looked me up and down again, even though we'd already met. They seemed to be assessing me.

"So," Carlos said. "You break?"

"Not yet," I said, feeling suddenly self-conscious.

"That's not true." My brother stepped forward and smiled at me. "Her uprock isn't bad and she does a decent six-step."

"But I don't know any power moves," I said.

"That's okay. I'm going to teach you."

It was then that I sat down and wondered whether Navid wasn't doing this whole thing just to throw me a bone. Maybe I was imagining it, but for the first time in a long while, my brother seemed to be mine again, and I didn't realize until just that moment how much I'd missed him.

He was dyslexic, my brother. When he started middle school and began failing every subject, I finally realized that he and I hated school for very different reasons. Words and letters never made sense to him like they did to me. And it wasn't until two years ago when he was threatened with expulsion that he finally told me the truth.

Screamed it, actually.

My mom had ordered me to help him with his homework. We couldn't afford a tutor, so I would have to do, and I was pissed. Tutoring my older brother was not how I wanted to spend my free time. So when he refused to do the work, I got angry.

"Just answer the question," I'd snap at him. "It's simple reading comprehension. Read the paragraph and summarize, in a couple of sentences, what it was about. That's it. It's not rocket science."

He refused.

I pushed.

He refused.

I insulted him.

He insulted me back.

I insulted him more.

"Just answer the goddamn question why are you so lazy *what the hell is wrong with you—*"

And finally he just exploded.

That was the day I learned that my brother, my beautiful, brilliant older brother, couldn't make sense of words and letters the way that I could. He'd spend half an hour reading a paragraph over and over again and even then, he didn't know what to do with it. He couldn't craft sentences. He struggled, tremendously, to translate his thoughts into words.

So I started teaching him how.

We worked together every day for hours, late into the night, until one day he could put sentences together by himself. Months later he was writing paragraphs. It took a year, but he finally wrote his own research paper. And the thing no one ever knew was that I did all his schoolwork in the interim. All his writing assignments. I wrote every paper for him until he could do it on his own.

I thought maybe this was his way of saying thanks. I mean, it almost certainly wasn't, but I couldn't help but wonder why else he'd take this chance on me. The other guys he'd collected—Jacobi, Carlos, and Bijan—already had experience in other crews. None of them were experts, but they weren't novices, either. I was the one who needed the most work, and Navid was the only one who didn't seem irritated about it.

Carlos, in particular, wouldn't stop looking at me. He seemed skeptical that I'd end up any good, and he told me so. He wasn't even mean about it, just matter of fact.

"What?" I said. "Why not?"

He shrugged. But he was staring at my outfit.

I'd switched into some of the only gym clothes I owned— a pair of slim sweatpants and a thin hoodie—but I was also wearing a different scarf; it was made of a light, cotton material that I'd tied up into a turban style, and this seemed to distract him.

Finally, he nodded at my head and said, "You can break-dance in that?"

My eyes widened. For some reason I was surprised. I don't know why I'd thought these dudes would be marginally less stupid than all the other ones I'd known.

"Are you for real?" I said. "What a dick thing to say."

He laughed and said, "I'm sorry, I've just never seen anyone try to breakdance like that before."

"Wow," I said, stunned. "I've literally never seen you take off that beanie, but you're giving me shit for *this*?"

Carlos looked surprised. He laughed harder. He tugged the beanie off his head and ran his hand through his hair. He had very black, springy curls that were slightly too long and kept falling in his face. He put the beanie back on. "All right," he said. "All right. Okay. Sorry."

"Whatever."

"I'm sorry," he said, but he was smiling. "Seriously. I'm sorry. That was a dick thing to say. You're right. I'm an asshole."

"Clearly."

Navid was laughing so hard. I suddenly hated everyone.

Jacobi shook his head and said, "Damn."

"Wow," I said. "You all suck."

"*Hey*—" Bijan was in the middle of stretching his legs. He pretended to look hurt. "That's not fair. Jacobi and I didn't even say anything."

"Yeah but you were thinking it, weren't you?"

Bijan grinned.

"Navid," I said, "your friends suck."

"They're a work in progress," he said, and chucked a water bottle at Carlos, who dodged it easily.

Carlos was still laughing. He walked over to where I was sitting on the floor and offered me his hand.

I raised an eyebrow at him.

"I'm sorry," he said again. "Really."

I took his hand. He hauled me to my feet.

"All right," he said. "Let me see that six-step I keep hearing about."

I spent the rest of that day practicing simple skills: doing handstands and push-ups and trying to improve my uprock. An uprock was the dance you did while you were upright. Much of breakdancing was performed on the ground, but an uprock was given its own, special attention; it was what you did first—it was an introduction, an opportunity to set the stage—before you broke your body down, figuratively, into a downrock and the subsequent power moves and poses that generally constituted a single performance.

I knew how to do a very basic uprock. My footwork was simple, my movements fluid but uninspired. I had a natural feel for the beats in the music—could easily sync my movements to the rhythm—but that wasn't enough. The best breakdancers had their own signature styles, and my moves were still generic. I knew this—had always known this—but the guys pointed it out to me anyway. We were talking, as a group, about what we knew and what we wanted to learn, and I was leaning back on my hands when my brother tapped my knuckles and said, "Let me see your wrists."

I held out my hands.

He bent them forward and backward. "You've got really flexible wrists," he said. He pressed my palm backward. "This doesn't hurt?"

I shook my head.

He smiled, his eyes bright with excitement. "We're going to teach you how to do the crab walk. That will be your signature power move."

My eyes widened. The crab walk was exactly as strange as it sounded. It was nothing at all like the sort of thing they taught you in elementary school gym classes; instead, it was a move that, like much of breakdancing, challenged the basic rules of gravity. It required total core strength. You held your body weight up on your hands—your elbows tucked into your torso—and you walked. With your hands.

It was hard. Really hard.

"Cool," I said.

Somehow, it had been the best day of high school I'd ever had.

FOUR

I didn't end up getting home until around five, and by the time I'd finished showering my mom had already shouted at us several times that dinner was ready. I made my way downstairs even though I knew I had a bunch of worried, and later, exasperated, text messages from Ocean waiting for me on my phone, but only because I didn't have the kind of parents who allowed me to ignore dinner—not even for homework. Ocean would have to wait.

Everyone was already assembled when I made it downstairs. My dad had his laptop out—the ethernet cable dragging all across the floor—and his reading glasses on his head; he waved me over when I walked into the room. He was reading an article about pickling cucumbers.

"*Mibini?*" he was saying to me. *Do you see?* "Very easy."

It didn't look particularly easy to me, but I shrugged. My dad was a master of making things, and he was always trying to recruit me to join him in his projects, which I didn't mind at all. In fact, it was kind of our thing.

I was nine the first time my dad took me to a hardware store, and I'd thought the place was so cool my brain just about exploded. I began daydreaming about going back there, about saving up the money I would've otherwise spent on Lisa Frank notebooks and instead purchasing a piece of plywood just to see what I could do with it. Later, my dad was the one who taught me how to work a needle and thread. He'd seen me stapling the cuffs of my jeans to keep them from dragging, and one night he showed me how to properly hem a pair of pants. He also taught me how to swing an ax to split firewood. How to change a flat tire.

But sometimes my dad's mind worked so quickly I almost couldn't keep up. My father's father—my grandfather—had been an architect in Iran, responsible for designing some of the country's most beautiful buildings, and I could see that same kind of brain in my dad. He devoured books even faster than I did; he carried them around with him everywhere. Wherever we'd lived, our garage became his workshop. He'd rebuild car engines, for fun. He built the table we were currently sitting around—it was a re-creation of a mid-century Danish style he'd always loved—and when my mom went back to school and needed a bag, my dad insisted on making one for her. He studied patterns. He bought the leather. And then he pieced it together for her, stitch by stitch. He still has a scar, spanning three of his fingers, where he accidentally sliced his skin open.

It was his idea of a romantic gesture.

Dinner was already on the table, slightly steaming. I'd been able to smell it from upstairs: the scents of buttery basmati rice and *fesenjoon* had flooded the whole house. *Fesenjoon* was a kind of stew made of walnut paste and pomegranate molasses, which sounds weird, I know, but it was so, *so* good. Most people made *fesenjoon* with chicken, but my late aunt had reinvented it with bite-size meatballs, and it had become a family recipe in her honor. There were also little side dishes of pickled vegetables and garlic yogurt and the still-warm disks of fresh bread that my dad baked every evening. There was a plate of fresh herbs and radishes and little towers of feta cheese. A bowl of dates. A cup of fresh, baby walnuts. The samovar, gurgling quietly in the background.

Food was a fixture in our home, and in Persian culture in general. Mealtimes were gathering moments, and my parents never allowed us to break this tradition, no matter how badly we wanted to watch something on TV or had somewhere else we wanted to be. It had only occurred to me a couple of years ago, when a friend of Navid's had come over for dinner, that not everyone cared about food like this. He thought it was kind of crazy. But this—here, on the table tonight—this was the extremely stripped down version of a Persian dinner. This was how we set a table when we were really busy and no one was coming to visit. For us, it was normal.

It was home.

When I finally made it upstairs, it was past eight, and Ocean had hit peak panic.

I cringed as I clicked through his messages.

hey
you there?
this is ocean
i really hope this is the right number
hello?
this is ocean, your lab partner, remember?
it's getting late and now i'm getting worried
we really have to finish this before class tomorrow
are you there?

I'd only gotten a cell phone a few months ago, and it had taken a great deal of begging—everyone I knew got theirs the year prior—before my parents finally, begrudgingly, took me to a T-Mobile store to get my very own Nokia brick. We had a family plan, which meant our limited bundle of minutes and text messages were to be shared by all four of us, and text messaging, though still kind of a brand-new phenomenon, had already caused me a lot of trouble. Somehow, in my excitement to experience the novelty of text messages (I'd once sent Navid thirty messages in a row just to piss him off), I'd gone way over our limit in the span of a single week, racking up a bill that caused my parents to sit me down and threaten to take away my phone. I realized far too late that I was being charged not only for the texts I *sent*, but also for the ones I received.

One glance at Ocean's long string of messages told me a lot about the state of his bank account.

hi, I wrote. **you know these text messages are expensive, right?**

Ocean wrote back immediately.

oh, hey
i nearly gave up on you
sorry about the texts
do you have AIM?

AIM was how I figured we'd do most of our talking tonight. Sometimes kids used MSN Messenger to connect, but mostly we used the tried-and-true, the one and only, the magical portal that was AOL Instant Messenger. Still, I was always a bit behind on the technological front. I knew there were teenagers out there with fancy Apple computers and their own digital cameras, but we'd only just gotten DSL in my house, and it was an actual miracle that I had an old, busted computer in my bedroom that managed to connect to the internet. It took me like fifteen minutes just to turn the thing on, but eventually we were both logged in. Our names now lived in a little square messaging window all our own. I was really impressed Ocean didn't have some kind of douchey screen name.

riversandoceans04: Hey
jujehpolo: Hi

I checked his profile automatically—it was practically a reflex—but I was surprised to find that he'd left it blank. Well, not blank, exactly.

It said *paranoid android* and nothing else.

I almost smiled. I wasn't sure, but I was hoping this was a reference to a Radiohead song. Then again, maybe I was imagining something that wasn't there; I really liked Radiohead. In fact, my AIM profile currently contained a list of songs I was listening to on repeat last week—

1. *Differences*, by Ginuwine
2. *7 Days*, by Craig David
3. *Hate Me Now*, by Nas
4. *No Surprises*, by Radiohead
5. *Whenever, Wherever*, by Shakira
6. *Pardon Me*, by Incubus
7. *Doo Wop*, by Lauryn Hill

—and only then did I realize that Ocean might check my profile, too.

I froze.

For some reason, I quickly deleted the contents. I didn't know why. I couldn't explain why I didn't want him to know what kind of music I listened to. It was just that the whole thing felt suddenly too invasive. Too personal.

riversandoceans04: Where were you today?
jujehpolo: Sorry
jujehpolo: I had a really busy afternoon
jujehpolo: I just saw your messages
riversandoceans04: Were you really breakdancing after school?
jujehpolo: Yeah
riversandoceans04: Wow. That's cool.

I didn't say anything. I didn't really know how to respond. I'd just looked away to grab my backpack when I heard, once again, the soft double ding that indicated I'd received a new message, and I turned down the volume on my computer. I checked to make sure my door was closed. I felt suddenly self-conscious. I was talking to a boy in my bedroom. *I was talking to a boy in my bedroom.* AIM made things feel unexpectedly intimate.

riversandoceans04: Hey I'm sorry for thinking you weren't allowed to do things after school.

double ding

riversandoceans04: I shouldn't have said that

And I sighed.

Ocean was trying to be friendly. He was trying to be a friend, even. *Maybe.* But Ocean was all the traditionally pleasant things a girl might like about a guy, which made his friendliness dangerous to me. I might've been an angry teenager, but I wasn't also blind. I wasn't magically immune to cute guys, and it had not escaped my notice that Ocean was a superlative kind of good-looking. He dressed nicely. He smelled pleasant. He was very polite. But he and I seemed to come from worlds so diametrically opposed that I knew better than to allow his friendship in my life. I didn't want to get to know him. I didn't want to be attracted to him. I didn't want to think about him, period. Not just him, in fact, but anyone like him. I was so good at denying myself this, the simple pleasure of even a secret crush, that the thoughts were never allowed to marinate in my mind.

I'd been here so many times before.

Though for most guys I was little more than an object of ridicule, occasionally I became an object of fascination. For whatever reason, some guys developed an intense, focused interest in me and my life that I used to misunderstand as romantic interest. Instead, I discovered—after a great deal of embarrassment—that it was more like they thought of me as a curiosity; an exotic specimen behind glass. They wanted only to observe me from a comfortable distance, not for me to exist in their lives in any permanent way. I'd experienced this enough times to have learned by now that I was never a real candidate for friendship—and certainly nothing more than that. I knew that Ocean, for example, would never befriend me beyond this school assignment. I knew he wouldn't invite me into his inner circle where I'd fit in as well as a carrot might, when pushed through a juicer.

Ocean was trying to be nice, sure, but I knew that his sudden sympathetic heart was born only of awkward guilt, and that this was a road that would lead to nowhere. I found it exhausting.

jujehpolo: It's okay

riversandoceans04: It's not okay. I've felt terrible about it all afternoon.

riversandoceans04: I'm really sorry

jujehpolo: Okay

riversandoceans04: I've just never actually talked to a girl who wears the headpiece thing before.

jujehpolo: Headpiece thing, wow

riversandoceans04: See? I don't know anything

jujehpolo: You can just call it a scarf

riversandoceans04: Oh

riversandoceans04: That's easy

jujehpolo: Yeah

riversandoceans04: I thought it was called something else.

jujehpolo: Listen, it's really not a big deal. Can we just do the homework?

riversandoceans04: Oh

riversandoceans04: Yeah

riversandoceans04: Okay

And I'd turned away for five seconds to grab the worksheets out of my backpack when there it was again—the soft double ding. Twice.

I looked up.

riversandoceans04: Sorry

riversandoceans04: I didn't mean to make you uncomfortable.

Jesus Christ.

jujehpolo: I'm not uncomfortable.

jujehpolo: I think maybe you're uncomfortable, though.

riversandoceans04: What? No

riversandoceans04: I'm not uncomfortable

riversandoceans04: What do you mean?

jujehpolo: I mean, is this going to be a problem? My
headpiece thing?

jujehpolo: Is my whole situation just too weird for you?

Ocean didn't respond for at least twenty seconds, which,
in the moment, felt like an actual lifetime. I felt bad. Maybe I'd
been too blunt. Maybe I was being mean. But he was trying *so*
hard to be, I don't know? Way too nice to me. It felt unnatural.
And I just, I don't know, it was making me mad.

Still, guilt gnawed at my mind. Maybe I'd hurt his feelings.

I drummed my fingers against the keyboard, wondering
what to say. How to walk this back. We still had to be lab
partners, after all.

Or maybe we didn't. Maybe he'd just ask the teacher for
a new partner. It had happened before. Once, when I'd been
paired at random with another student, she'd just revolted.
She flat out refused to be my partner in front of the entire
class and then demanded to work with her friend. My teacher,
flimsy pancake that she was, panicked and said okay. I ended
up working alone. It was humiliating.

Shit.

Maybe this time I'd brought the humiliation upon myself.
Maybe Ocean would revolt, too. My stomach sank.

And then—

double ding

riversandoceans04: I don't think you're weird.

I blinked at the computer screen.

double ding

riversandoceans04: I'm sorry

Ocean appeared to be a chronic apologizer.

jujehpolo: It's okay
jujehpolo: I'm sorry for putting you on the spot like
that. You were just trying to be nice.
jujehpolo: I get it
jujehpolo: It's fine

Another five seconds dragged on.

riversandoceans04: Okay

I sighed. Dropped my face into my hands. Somehow I'd made things awkward. Everything was fine, totally normal, and then I had to go and make it weird. There was only one way to fix this now. So I took a deep, sad breath, and typed.

jujehpolo: You don't have to be my lab partner if you don't want to be.
jujehpolo: It's okay
jujehpolo: I can tell Mrs. Cho tomorrow.
riversandoceans04: What?
riversandoceans04: Why would you say that?
riversandoceans04: You don't want to be my lab partner?

I frowned.

jujehpolo: Uh, okay, I don't know what's happening.
riversandoceans04: Me neither
riversandoceans04: Do you want to be my lab partner?
jujehpolo: Sure
riversandoceans04: Okay
riversandoceans04: Good
jujehpolo: Okay
riversandoceans04: I'm sorry

I stared at my computer. This conversation was giving me a headache.

jujehpolo: Why are you sorry?

Another couple of seconds.

riversandoceans04: I don't actually know anymore

I almost laughed. I didn't understand what the hell had just happened. I didn't understand his apologies or his confusion and I didn't even think I wanted to know. What I wanted was to go back to not caring about Ocean James, the boy with two first names. I'd spoken to this kid for a total of *maybe* an hour and suddenly his presence was in my bedroom, in my personal space, stressing me out.

I didn't like it. It made me feel weird.

So I tried to keep things simple.

jujehpolo: Why don't we just do the homework?

Another ten seconds.

riversandoceans04: Okay

And we did.

But I felt something change between us, and I had no idea what it was.

FIVE

The next morning, my brother, who had a zero period and always left for school an hour before I did, stopped by my room to borrow the Wu-Tang CD I'd stolen from him. I'd been putting on mascara when he started knocking on my door, and he was now demanding I give him back not only his CD but his iPod, too, and I was shouting back that his iPod was far more useful to me during the school day then it had ever been for him, and I was still making this argument when I opened the door and he suddenly froze. He looked me up and down and his eyes widened, just a little.

"What?" I said.

"Nothing."

I let him inside. I gave him the CD he was looking for. He kept looking at me.

"*What?*" I said again, irritated.

"Nothing," he said, and laughed. "You look nice."

I raised an eyebrow. This was a trick.

"New outfit?"

I looked down at what I was wearing. My sweater wasn't new. But I'd bought these jeans from the thrift store last week and had just finished altering them. They'd been a few sizes too big for me, but the quality of the denim was too good to pass up. Besides, they'd only cost me fifty cents. "Sort of," I said. "The jeans are new."

He nodded. "Well, they're nice."

"Yeah. Okay," I said. "Why are you being weird?"

He shrugged. "I'm not being weird," he said. "The jeans are nice. They're just, uh, really tight. I'm not used to seeing you in pants like that."

"Gross."

"Hey, listen, I don't care. They look good on you."

"Uh-huh."

"No, I mean it. They look nice." He was still smiling.

"Oh my God, *what*?"

"Nothing," he said for the third time. "I just, you know, I don't think Ma is going to like seeing your ass in those jeans."

I rolled my eyes. "Well she doesn't have to look at my ass if she doesn't want to."

Navid laughed. "It's just—sometimes what you wear doesn't really match, you know? It's a little confusing." He gestured, vaguely, at my head, even though I hadn't put on my scarf yet. Still, I knew what he was trying to say. I knew he was trying not to be judgmental. But the conversation irritated me.

People—and often guys—liked to say that Muslim women wore headscarves because they were trying to be demure, or because they were trying to cover up their beauty, and I knew that there were ladies in the world who felt that way. I couldn't speak for all Muslim women—no one could—but it was a sentiment with which I fundamentally disagreed. I didn't believe it was possible to hide a woman's beauty. I thought women were gorgeous no matter what they wore, and I didn't think they owed anyone an explanation for their sartorial choices. Different women felt comfortable in different outfits.

They were all beautiful.

But it was only the monsters who forced women to wear human potato sacks all day that managed to make headline news, and these assholes had somehow set the tone for all of us. No one even asked me the question anymore; people just assumed they knew the answer, and they were nearly always wrong. I dressed the way I did not because I was trying to be a nun, but because it felt good—and because it made me feel less vulnerable in general, like I wore a kind of armor every day. It was a personal preference. I definitely *didn't* do it because I was trying to be modest for the sake of some douchebag who couldn't keep his dick in his pants. People struggled to believe this, because people struggled to believe women in general.

It was one of the greatest frustrations of my life.

So I shoved Navid out of my room and told him it was none of his business what my ass looked like in my jeans and he said, "No, I know—that's not what I meant—"

"Don't make it weird," I said, and closed the door in his face.

After he left, I looked in the mirror.

The jeans were *nice*.

The days continued to dissolve, and quietly.

Aside from breakdancing, pretty much nothing had changed except that Ocean was suddenly different around me in bio. He'd been different ever since that first, and only, AIM conversation we'd had, over two weeks ago.

He talked too much.

He was always saying things like *Wow, the weather is so weird today* and *How was your weekend?* and *Hey, did you study for the quiz on Friday?* and it surprised me, every single time. I'd glance at him for only a second and say *Yeah, the weather is weird* and *Um, my weekend was fine* and *No, I didn't study for the quiz on Friday* and he'd smile and say *I know, right?* and *That's nice* and *Really? I've been studying all week* and I'd usually ignore him. I never asked him a follow-up question.

Maybe I was being rude, but I didn't care.

Ocean was a really good-looking guy, and I know this doesn't sound like a valid reason to dislike someone, but it was reason enough for me. He made me nervous. I didn't want to talk to him. I didn't want to get to know him. I didn't want to *like* him, which was harder than you'd think, because he was very likable. Falling for someone like Ocean, I knew, would only end badly for me. I didn't want to embarrass myself.

Today he'd been trying really hard to make small talk—which I guessed was understandable, as it was otherwise awkward to sit around for an hour saying nothing while you picked apart a dead cat—and he said, "So, are you going to homecoming?"

I'd actually looked up, then. I looked up because I was amazed. I laughed, softly, and turned away. His question was so ridiculous I didn't even answer him. We'd been having pep rallies all week in anticipation of the homecoming game—it was a football thing, I think—and I'd been skipping them. We were also, apparently, having class spirit competitions, whatever that meant. I was supposed to be wearing green or blue or something today, but I wasn't.

People were losing their minds over this shit.

"You don't really do school stuff, huh?" Ocean said, and I wondered why he cared.

"No," I said quietly. "I don't really do school stuff."

"Oh."

There was a part of me that wanted to be friendlier to Ocean, but sometimes it made me really, actually, *physically uncomfortable* when he was nice to me. It felt so fake. Some days our interactions felt like he was trying really hard to overcompensate for that first error, for thinking my parents were about to ship me off to a harem or something. Like he wanted another chance to prove he wasn't close-minded, like he thought I might not notice that he went from thinking I couldn't even meet up after school to thinking I might show up at a homecoming dance, all in the span of two weeks. I didn't like it. I just didn't trust it.

So I cut the heart out of a dead cat and called it a day.

I showed up to practice a little too early that afternoon and the room was still locked; Navid was the one who had the key that would let us in and he hadn't arrived yet, so I slumped down on the ground and waited. I knew that basketball season was starting sometime next month—I knew this, because I saw the posters plastered everywhere—but the gym was, for some reason, already busier than I'd ever seen it. It was loud. Super loud. Lots of shouting. Lots of whistles blowing and sneakers squeaking. I didn't really know what was happening; I didn't know much about sports, in general. All I heard were the thunderous sounds of many feet running across a court. I could hear it through the walls.

When I finally got into the dance room with the other guys, we turned up the music and did our best to drown out the reverberations of the many basketballs hitting the floor. I was working with Jacobi today, who was showing me how to improve my footwork.

I already knew how to do a basic six-step, which was exactly what it sounded like: it was a series of six steps performed on the ground. You held yourself up on your arms while your legs did most of the work, moving you in a sort of circular motion. This served as an introduction to your power move—which was your acrobatic move—the kind of thing that looked, sometimes, like what you saw gymnasts do on a pommel horse, except way cooler. Breakdancing was, in many ways, closer to something like capoeira, an Afro-Brazilian form of martial arts that involves a lot of kicks and spins in midair; capoeira made kicking someone's ass look both scary and beautiful.

Breakdancing was kind of like that.

Jacobi was showing me how to add CCs to my six-step. They were called CCs because they were invented by a group of breakers who called themselves the Crazy Commandos, and not because the move looked anything like a *c*. They were body rotations that made my legwork more complex, and just, overall, made the routine look cooler. I'd been working at it for a while. I'd already learned how to do a double-handed CC, but I was still getting the hang of doing a one-handed CC, and Jacobi was watching me as I tried, over and over again, to get the thing right. When I finally did, he clapped, hard.

He was beaming.

"Nice job," he said.

I just about fell backward. I was on the ground, splayed like a starfish, but I was smiling.

This was nothing; these were *baby steps*. But it felt so good.

Jacobi helped me to my feet and squeezed my shoulder. "Nice," he said. "Seriously."

I smiled at him.

I turned around to find my water bottle and suddenly froze.

Ocean was leaning against the doorframe, not quite in the room and not quite outside of it, a gym bag slung across his chest. He waved at me.

I looked around, confused, like maybe he'd been waving at someone else, but he laughed at me. Finally I just met him at the door, and I realized then that someone had propped it open. It happened, sometimes, when it got really hot in here; one of the guys would wedge the door open to let the room breathe a little.

Still, our open door had never attracted visitors before.

"Uh, hi," I said. "What are you doing here?"

Ocean shook his head. He seemed, somehow, even more surprised than I was. "I was just walking by," he said. "I heard the music. I wanted to know what was happening."

I raised an eyebrow. "You were just walking by."

"Yeah." He smiled. "I, um, spend a lot of time in the gym. Anyway, I honestly didn't know you'd be in here. Your music is just super loud."

"Okay."

"But I figured I should say hi instead of standing here, watching you like a creep."

"Good call," I said, but I was frowning. Still processing. "So you don't, like, need something? For class?"

He shook his head.

I stared at him.

Finally, he took a deep breath. "You really weren't kidding," he said. "About the breakdancing thing."

I laughed. Looked at him incredulously. "You thought I would lie about something like that?"

"No," he said, but he seemed suddenly uncertain. "I just, I don't know. I didn't know."

"Uh-huh."

"Are these your friends?" Ocean said. He was staring at Jacobi, who was shooting me a look that said *Who's the guy?* and *What's going on?* all at the same time.

"Sort of," I said.

"That's cool."

"Yeah." I was so confused. "Um, I should go."

Ocean nodded. Stood up straighter. "Yeah, me too."

We said awkward goodbyes. As soon as he was out of sight, I closed the door.

Jacobi was the only one who noticed me talking to Ocean that day, and when he asked me about it, I said it was nothing, just a kid from class who needed something. I wasn't even sure why I lied about it.

I was totally perplexed.

SIX

Things in my life began to find a rhythm.

I was settling into a new routine in this town, and my anxieties about being friendless at school were beginning to fade. I was no longer a shock to the system; instead, I'd become a regular fixture at school, one that most of my classmates could now comfortably ignore. People still enjoyed referring to me as the Taliban as I walked by, and every once in a while I'd find an anonymous note in my locker telling me to fuck off back to where I came from, and occasionally someone would take the time to point out that towelheads like me didn't deserve to live in their country—but I tried not to let it bother me. I tried to get used to it. I'd heard somewhere that people could get used to anything.

Luckily, breakdancing kept me busy in the best possible way.

I loved everything about it: the music, the moves, even the history. Breakdancing started back in the 1970s in the South Bronx, New York, and slowly, over time, made its way across the country to Los Angeles. It was an iteration, a simultaneous arm and evolution of hip-hop, and, coolest of all—it was originally used as an alternative to physical violence. In their fights over territories, gangs would have breakdancing battles to determine ownership—and that's why the term *battle* still exists today. Breaking crews don't compete; they battle. Each crew member delivers a performance.

Best b-boy—or b-girl—wins.

I threw myself into the work, hitting the gym nearly every day. When we didn't have access to the school's dance studio we'd break down oversize cardboard boxes in abandoned streets and parking lots, set up a boom box, and practice. Navid would drag me out of bed way too early on weekend mornings to do ten-mile runs with him. We started training together, regularly. Breakdancing involved extremely taxing physical work, but it was work that filled me with joy and purpose. In fact, I was so focused on this new life outside of school—and so tired after practice every day—that I hardly had time to be angry about all the assholes littered everywhere.

The educational aspect of school was pretty boring.

I'd figured out a long time ago how to get As without trying; my secret to success was that I genuinely didn't care. I felt no pressure to perform, so I usually did fine. I'd stopped caring about school a few years ago, right around the time I was old enough to realize that caring about a school—its teachers, its students, its walls and doors and many hallways—nearly always ended in heartbreak. So I just stopped. I stopped remembering things. People. Faces. In time, the institutions and their many names all blurred together. Mrs. Someone was my first grade teacher. Mr. Whatsisname taught third grade. Who knew.

I was required by law and the wooden spoon my mom liked to whoop my ass with to show up every day, so I did. I showed up, I did the work, I dealt with the dependable, unrelenting microaggressions from the masses that influenced the emotional weather patterns of my day. I didn't stress about getting into a good college because I already knew I couldn't afford to go to a good college. I didn't stress about AP classes because I didn't think of them as any different from regular classes. I didn't stress about the SATs because who gave a shit about the SATs. Not me.

I don't know, I guess I always thought I'd turn out okay, no matter how badly my many schools tried to mutilate me. And I held on to that feeling every day. *Two and a half more years*, I thought. Just two and a half more years until I could get the hell away from this existence organized by school bells that, let's be honest, didn't even ring.

They beeped.

This was what I was thinking as I peeled another layer of soggy cat flesh away from soggy cat muscle. I was thinking about how much I hated this. How I was already anxious to get into the gym again. I was getting better at holding the crab pose now—I'd almost managed to hold my body weight up on my elbows yesterday—and I wanted to see if I'd make more progress this afternoon. I was headed to my first live break-dancing battle this weekend, and I wanted to feel like I knew something when I got there.

I finished my shift with the cat and peeled off my gloves, tossing them into the trash before washing my hands—for good measure—in our lab station's sink. So far, our discoveries had been underwhelming, which was how I liked them. One of the groups in our class discovered that the cat they'd been dissecting had died pregnant; they'd found a litter of unborn kittens in her uterus.

This was a seriously messed-up school assignment.

"Your turn," I said, glancing at Ocean, whose attitude toward me had changed, rather dramatically, in the last week.

He'd stopped talking to me in class.

He no longer asked me generic questions about my evenings or my weekends. In fact, he'd said no more than a couple of words to me in the last few days, not since that afternoon I saw him in the dance studio. I often caught him looking at me, but then, people were always looking at me. Ocean at least had the decency to pretend he *wasn't* looking at me, and he never said anything about it, for which I was secretly grateful. I much preferred silent stares to the loud assholes who told me, unprompted, exactly what they thought of me.

But I'd be lying if I said I wasn't a little confused.

I thought I'd had Ocean pretty figured out, but suddenly I

wasn't so sure. Aside from the unusual name, he seemed to me like an extremely ordinary boy raised by extremely ordinary parents. The kind of parents who bought canned soup, lied to their kids about Santa Claus, believed everything they read in their history books and didn't really talk about their feelings.

My parents were the exact opposite.

I was fascinated by canned food simply because that miracle of Western invention was never allowed in my house. My parents made everything from scratch, no matter how basic; we never celebrated Christmas, except that sometimes my mom and dad took pity on us—I received a box of envelopes one year—and my parents had taught us about the atrocities of war and colonialism since before I could read. They also had no problem sharing their feelings with me. They relished it. My parents loved telling me what they felt was wrong with me—it was what they called my *unfortunate attitude*—all the time.

Anyway, I couldn't really get a bead on Ocean anymore, and it bothered me that it even bothered me. His silence was what I thought I wanted; it was, in fact, exactly what I'd been working toward. But now that he really had ignored me, I couldn't help but wonder why.

Even so, I thought his silence was for the best.

Today, though, was a little different. Today, after a twenty-minute stretch of perfect quiet, he spoke.

"Hey," he said, "what happened to your hand?"

I'd been trying to tear open a seam in a leather jacket last night and I'd tugged a little too hard; the seam ripper slipped and sliced open the back of my left hand. I had a pretty intense bandage taped over the space between my finger and thumb. I met Ocean's eyes. "Sewing accident," I said.

His eyebrows pulled together. "*Sewing accident?* What's a sewing accident?"

"Sewing," I said. "Like, sewing clothes? I make a lot of my own clothes," I said, when he didn't seem to understand. "Or, I mean, often I'll just buy vintage and do the alterations myself." I lifted my hand as proof. "Either way, I'm not great at it."

"You make your own clothes?" His eyes had widened, just a little.

"Sometimes," I said.

"Why?"

I laughed. It was a reasonable question. "Well, uh, because the clothes I really want are out of my price range."

Ocean only stared at me.

"Do you know anything about fashion?" I asked him.

He shook his head.

"Oh," I said, and tried to smile. "Yeah. I guess it's not for everyone."

But I loved it.

Alexander McQueen's fall line had just hit stores and, after a lot of begging, I'd convinced my mom to drive me to one of the fancy malls around here just so I could see the pieces in person. I didn't even touch them. I just stood near them, staring.

I thought Alexander McQueen was a genius.

"So—did you do that to your shoes?" Ocean said suddenly. "Like, on purpose?"

I glanced down.

I was wearing what used to be a pair of simple white Nikes, but I'd drawn all over them. And my backpack. And my binders. It was just something I did sometimes. I'd lock myself in my room, listen to music, and draw on things. Sometimes it was random doodles, but lately I'd been experimenting with graffiti—tagging, specifically—because some tagging techniques reminded me of highly stylized Persian calligraphy. I wasn't like Navid, though; I'd never graffitied public property. Not more than twice, anyway.

"Yeah," I said slowly. "I did that on purpose."

"Oh. That's cool."

I laughed at the look on his face.

"No, really," he said. "I like it."

Still, I hesitated. "Thanks."

"You have another pair like that, too, huh?"

"Yes." I raised an eyebrow. "How'd you know?"

"You sit in front of me," he said. He looked me right in the eye and he almost smiled, but it looked like a question. "You've been sitting in front of me for two months. I stare at you every day."

My eyes widened. And then I frowned. I didn't even have a chance to say the words before he said—

"I didn't mean"—he shook his head, looked away—"wow,

I didn't mean that, like, I stare at you. I just meant that I *see* you. You know. *Shit*," he said softly, and mostly to himself. "Never mind."

I half laughed, but it sounded weird. "Okay."

And that was it. He didn't say anything else worth remembering for the rest of the period.

SEVEN

I was dropping off my books in my locker after school—and grabbing the workout clothes I'd stashed in there with my gym bag—when I heard a sudden swell of voices. The halls were usually pretty quiet at this hour, and I rarely saw people after school let out, so the sounds were unusual. I turned around before I could think it through.

Cheerleaders.

There were three of them. Very pretty and peppy. They weren't in official cheerleading uniforms—they were wearing matching tracksuits—but somehow it was obvious that they were cheerleaders. Interestingly, cheerleaders had never been mean to me; instead, they ignored me so completely that I found their presence unexpectedly comforting.

I turned back around.

I'd just slung my gym bag over my shoulder when I heard

someone call out a greeting and I was very certain that whoever was talking was not talking to me, and that even if they *were* talking to me, that I'd turn around only to be met with some new creative bullshit, so I ignored it. I slammed my locker closed, spun the combination, and walked away.

"Hey—"

I kept walking, but now I was beginning to feel a little creeped out because the voice *did* seem to be focused in my direction and I didn't think I wanted to know why someone was trying to flag me down right now. All the people I knew at this school were waiting for me, at this exact moment, inside of a dance room in the gym, so whoever this was, they were almost certainly trying to bother me and—

"Shirin!"

I froze. This was an unusual development. Generally, the assholes who harassed me in the hallways didn't know my name.

I turned around, but only halfway.

"Hey." It was Ocean, looking a little exasperated.

I had to make a physical effort to keep from looking too surprised.

"You dropped your phone," he said, and held it out for me to take.

I looked at my phone in his hand. Looked at him. I didn't understand why the world kept throwing him in my path, but I also didn't know how to be mad at him for being a decent person, so I took the phone.

"Thanks," I said.

He looked at me and his expression was somehow both frustrated and amused and still he said nothing, which would've been fine, except that he looked at me for just three seconds too long, and suddenly it was weird.

I took a deep breath. I was about to say goodbye when someone called his name. I looked past him to see that it was one of the cheerleaders.

I was surprised but tried not to show it.

And then I left, without a word.

That night, after a particularly exhausting training session, I felt too wired to sleep, and I couldn't explain why. I was sitting in bed, writing, writing, writing. I'd always kept a pretty intense diary.

I scribbled in that thing every day, multiple times a day. In the middle of class, even. During lunch hours. The thing was so precious to me that I carried it around everywhere I went, because it was the only thing I could think to do—the only way to keep it safe. I worried that one day my mom might get her hands on it, read it, realize her daughter was a complicated, flawed human being—one who often disregarded the dogma of religion—and have an actual aneurysm. So I always kept it close.

But tonight, I couldn't focus my mind.

Every once in a while I'd look up, look at my computer, its dead, dark face gleaming in the dim light, and I'd hesitate. It was really late, maybe one in the morning. Everyone was asleep.

I put my pen down.

The old, hulking computer in my room was a bulky, unwieldy thing. My mother had built it, piece by piece, a couple of years ago when she was getting some new level of certification in computer programming. It was a bit like Frankenstein's monster, except that it was my mother's monster, and I'd been the lucky recipient of its great girth. Quickly, before I could change my mind, I turned the thing on.

It was loud.

The screen lit up, blinding and ostentatious, and its CPU component started whirring like crazy. The fan was working too hard, the hard drive was *click-clicking* away, and I immediately regretted my decision. I'd heard stories of parents who let their kids stay up all night, but I didn't know them. Instead, my parents were always on my case, and always suspicious— though generally for good reason; my brother and I weren't very good at following rules—and I was sure that they would hear me tooling around in here, barge inside, and force me to go to sleep.

I bit my lip and waited.

The damn computer had finally turned on. It took like ten minutes. It took another ten to click around and get the internet to work, because sometimes my computer was just, I don't know, obstinate. I was weirdly nervous. I didn't even know what I was doing. Why I was doing it. Not exactly.

My AIM account logged in automatically, and my short list of buddies were all offline. Except one.

My heart did something weird and I stood up too fast, feeling suddenly stupid and embarrassed. I didn't even know this guy. He was not—would *never* be—even remotely interested in someone like me and I knew this. I already knew this and I was still standing here, being an idiot.

I wasn't going to do it. I wasn't going to make an ass out of myself.

I turned back to my computer, ready to hit the power switch and shut this whole thing down when—

double ding
double ding
double ding

riversandoceans04: Hey
riversandoceans04: You're online
riversandoceans04: You're never online

I stared, finger frozen over the power switch.

double ding

riversandoceans04: Hello?

I sat down at my desk.

jujehpolo: Hey

riversandoceans04: Hey
riversandoceans04: What are you doing up so late?

I started typing, *I don't know*, before I realized my answer might be way too obvious. So I tried for something generic.

jujehpolo: I couldn't sleep.
riversandoceans04: Oh
riversandoceans04: Hey, can I ask you a question?

I stared at the messaging window. Felt a little scared.

jujehpolo: Sure
riversandoceans04: What does jujehpolo mean?

I was so relieved he hadn't asked me something super offensive I almost laughed out loud.

jujehpolo: It's, like, a Persian thing. Jujeh means small, but it's also the word for a baby chicken.
jujehpolo: And polo means rice.
jujehpolo: I realize as I'm typing this that that doesn't make any sense, but it's just, like, an inside joke, I guess. My family calls me jujeh, because I'm small, and jujeh kabab and rice is, like, a kind of food . . .
jujehpolo: Anyway
jujehpolo: It's just a nickname.

riversandoceans04: No, I get it. That's nice.

riversandoceans04: So you're Persian?

jujehpolo: Yeah

riversandoceans04: That's so cool. I really like Persian food.

My eyebrows shot up my forehead. Surprised.

jujehpolo: You do?

riversandoceans04: Yeah. I really like hummus.

riversandoceans04: And falafel.

Ah. Yeah. Okay.

jujehpolo: Neither one of those things is Persian.

riversandoceans04: They're not?

jujehpolo: No

riversandoceans04: Oh

I dropped my head in my hands. I suddenly hated myself. What the hell was I doing? This conversation was so stupid. I was so stupid. I couldn't believe I turned on my computer for this.

jujehpolo: Anyway, I should probably go to bed.

riversandoceans04: Oh, okay

I'd already typed the word *Bye*, was just about to hit enter—

riversandoceans04: Hey, before you go

I hesitated. Deleted. Rewrote.

jujehpolo: Yeah?
riversandoceans04: Maybe some day you can show me what Persian food is.

I stared at my screen for too long. I was confused. My first instinct told me he was asking me out; my second, wiser instinct told me that he would never, ever be stupid enough to do something like that, that he was almost certainly aware of the fact that nice white boys did not presume to ask weird Muslim girls out on dates, but then, barring that, I was mystified.

Did he want me to, like, educate him on Persian food? Teach him about the ways of my people? What the hell?

So I decided to be honest.

jujehpolo: I don't think I understand what you mean.
riversandoceans04: I want to try Persian food
riversandoceans04: Are there any Persian restaurants around here?
jujehpolo: Lol
jujehpolo: Around here? No

jujehpolo: Not unless you count my mom's kitchen

riversandoceans04: Oh

riversandoceans04: Then maybe I can come over for dinner

I nearly fell out of my chair. The balls on this kid, holy shit.

jujehpolo: You want to come into my house and have dinner with my family?

riversandoceans04: Is that weird?

jujehpolo: Um, a little

riversandoceans04: Oh

riversandoceans04: So is that a no?

jujehpolo: I don't know

I frowned at my computer.

jujehpolo: I guess I can ask my parents.

riversandoceans04: Cool

riversandoceans04: Okay, goodnight

jujehpolo: Uh

jujehpolo: Goodnight

I had no idea what the actual hell had just happened.

EIGHT

I spent the weekend ignoring my computer.

It was the middle of October, I'd been in school for a couple of months, and I was still trying to wrap my head around it. I hadn't made any of my own friends, but I wasn't feeling lonely, which was new. Plus, I was busy—also new—and bonus, I suddenly had *plans*. In fact, I was getting ready to head out.

Tonight, I had a breakdancing battle to attend.

We were just going to be in the audience, but the prospect still excited me. We wanted to join the breaking scene in this new city and see where it would take us. Maybe, once we were good enough, we'd start battling other crews. Maybe one day, we dreamed, we'd enter regional and state and maybe, *maybe* international competitions.

We had big dreams. And they had been parent-approved.

My parents were a little conservative, a little traditional, and, in some ways, surprisingly progressive. Generally, they were pretty cool. Still, they had massive double standards. They were terrified that the world would hurt me, as a young girl, far more than it would my brother, and so they were stricter with me, with my curfews, with what I could and could not do. They never tried to cut me off, socially, but they always wanted to know everything about where I was going and who I was going with and exactly when I would be back and on and on and on and they almost never did this with Navid. When Navid came home late they'd only be mildly irritated. Once, I came home an hour late after watching the first Harry Potter movie—I had no idea the thing would be *three hours long*—and my mom was so upset she couldn't decide whether to cry or kill me. This reaction baffled me because my social activities were so mild as to be almost nonexistent. I wasn't out late partying, ever. I wasn't sitting around getting drunk somewhere. I'd do stupid shit with my friends like wander around Target and buy the cheapest stuff we could find and use it to decorate the cars in the parking lot.

My mom did not approve of this.

The upside of breakdancing with my brother was that my parents worried less when they knew he was with me, ready to punch an unsuspecting harasser in the face if necessary. But my brother and I had also learned a long time ago how to game the system; when I wanted to go out somewhere, and I knew my parents wouldn't approve, he'd vouch for me. I'd do the same for him.

But Navid had just turned eighteen. He was older and, as a result, freer. He'd been working odd jobs everywhere we'd lived since he was younger than even me, and he'd saved up long enough to buy himself an iPod *and* a car. It was the teenage dream. He was currently the proud owner of a 1988 Nissan Sentra he would one day use to run over my foot. Until then, my ass was still walking to school every day. Sometimes I'd catch a ride with him, but he had that zero period in the mornings and he usually ditched me after practice to do something with his friends.

Today, we'd be driving that beautiful beast into a new world. A world that would give me a new title and hone a new facet of my identity. I wanted to become a b-girl in the full sense of the word. It would be so much better to be called a b-girl, a breakdancer, than the Girl Who Wore That Thing on Her Head.

The event was even more exciting than I hoped it'd be. I'd seen battles before, of course—we'd been watching old breakdancing competitions on VHS for years—but it was something else entirely to witness these things in person. The space was relatively small—it looked like a converted art gallery—and people were assembled like cigarettes in a pack, pressed up against the walls and doors, squeezing together to leave enough empty space in the center of the room. The energy was palpable. Music was reverberating against the walls and ceilings, the bass pulsing in my eardrums. In here, people didn't seem to care at all about me; no one looked at me, eyes merely glanced off my face and body as they scanned the room. I didn't know why it suddenly didn't matter what I looked like, why my appearance garnered no reactions. Maybe it was because the self-selecting demographic in here was different. I was surrounded by diverse bodies and faces; I was hearing Spanish in one ear and Chinese in the other. We were white and black and brown brought together by a single interest.

I loved it.

Somehow I knew, in that moment, that all that mattered in this particular world was talent. If I were a decent break-dancer, these people would respect me. Here, I could be more than the settings applied to my life by society.

It was all I'd ever wanted.

I came home that night feeling more exhilarated than I'd felt—maybe, ever. I talked my mom's ear off about the whole thing and she smiled, unimpressed, and told me to go do my homework. School would be waiting for me, bright and early the following day, but tonight, I was still aglow. Echoes of the music were dancing around in my head. I got ready for bed and couldn't focus on the schoolwork I'd left unfinished. Instead, I cleared a space in the center of my room and practiced the crab pose for so long the carpet began to burn my palms. I kept falling forward—kissing the floor, as my brother liked to say—and couldn't get it quite right. I still had a long way to go before I'd become even a decent breakdancer, but then, I'd never been afraid of hard work.

9

NINE

My second class of the day was called Global Perspectives. My teacher was one of those wild, creative thinkers, one of those guys determined to make breakthroughs with teenagers. He was cooler than most teachers, but it was obvious, most days, that he was trying a little too hard to convince us of this fact. Still, I didn't hate his class. The only thing he ever required of us was class participation.

There were no exams; no homework assignments.

Instead, he forced us to discuss current events. Politics. Controversial topics. He wanted us to ask each other hard questions—to question ourselves and our ideas about the world—and he wanted us to engage directly with each other in ways we otherwise never would. Those of us who refused to participate—refused to voice aloud our opinions—would fail.

I was into it.

Thus far, the class had been pretty drama-free. He'd started out with softballs. We'd walked in on the second day of class to discover he'd divided all the desks into groups of four. We were supposed to start there, in a smaller group, before he'd change things up.

After thirty minutes of intense discussions, he came by our little cluster and asked us to recap what we'd talked about.

And then, he'd said—

"Great, great. So what are the names of everyone in your group?"

That was the thing that got me to take him seriously. Because wow, we'd been talking for a while and we'd never once asked to know each other's names. I thought maybe this guy was smart. I thought maybe he would be different. I thought, hey, Mr. Jordan might actually know something.

But today was a new Monday. Time for a change.

I'd barely gotten to my seat when he shouted at me.

"Shirin and Travis," he called, "come over here, please."

I looked at him, confused, but he only waved me over. I dropped my backpack on the floor next to my chair and went, reluctantly, to the front of the class. I stared at my feet, at the wall. I was feeling nervous.

I hadn't met Travis yet—he wasn't one of the four people in my group—but Travis was everything television taught you a jock was supposed to look like. He was big, blond, and burly, and he was wearing a letterman jacket. He, too, I noticed, was looking around awkwardly.

Mr. Jordan was smiling.

"A new experiment," he said to the class, clapping his hands together before he turned back to us. "All right, you two," he said, turning our shoulders so that Travis and I were facing each other. "No squirming. I want you to look at each other's faces."

Someone kill me.

I looked at Travis only because I didn't want to fail this class. Travis didn't seem thrilled about staring at my face, either, and I felt bad for him. Neither one of us wanted to be doing whatever the hell my teacher was about to make us do.

"Keep looking," Mr. Jordan said. "I want you two to *see* each other. Really, really see each other. Are you looking?"

I shot a hard glare at Mr. Jordan. I said nothing.

"Okay," he said. He was smiling like a maniac. "Now, Travis," he said, "I want you to tell me exactly what you think when you look at Shirin."

And I lost feeling in my legs.

I felt suddenly faint and somehow still rooted to the ground. I felt panic and outrage—I felt betrayed—and I had no idea what to do. How could I justify turning to my teacher and telling him he was insane? How could I do that without getting into trouble?

Travis had gone bright red. He started sputtering.

"Be honest," Mr. Jordan was saying. "Remember, honesty is everything. Without it, we can never move forward. We can never have productive discussions. So *be honest*. Tell me exactly what you think when you look at her face. First impressions. Off the cuff. Now, *now*."

I'd gone numb. I was paralyzed by an impotence and embarrassment I didn't know how to explain. I stood there, hating myself, while Travis fumbled for the words.

"I don't know," he said. He could barely look at me.

"Bullshit," Mr. Jordan said, his eyes flashing. "That's bullshit, Travis, and you know it. Now be *honest*."

I was breathing too fast. I was staring at Travis, begging him with my eyes to just walk away, to leave me alone, but Travis was lost in his own panic. He couldn't see mine.

"I—I don't know," he said again. "When I look at her I don't see anything."

"What?" Mr. Jordan again. He'd walked up to Travis, was studying him, hard. "What do you mean you don't see anything?"

"I mean, I mean—" Travis sighed. His face had gone blotchy with redness. "I mean she doesn't, like—I just don't see her. It's like she doesn't exist for me. When I look at her I see nothing."

Anger fled my body. I felt suddenly limp. Hollow. Tears pricked my eyes; I fought them back.

I heard Mr. Jordan's vague, distorted sounds of victory. I heard him clap his hands together, excited. I saw him move in my direction, ostensibly to make me take a turn performing his stupid experiment and instead I just stared at him, my face numb.

And I walked away.

I grabbed my backpack from where I'd left it and moved, in what felt like slow motion, straight out the door. I felt blind and deaf at the same time, like I was moving through fog, and I realized then—as I realized every time something like this happened—that I was never as strong as I hoped to be.

I still cared too much. I was still so easily, pathetically, punctured.

I didn't know where I was going. I just knew I had to go. Had to leave, had to get out of there before I cried in front of the class, cussed out Mr. Jordan, and got myself expelled.

I'd charged blindly out the door and down the hall and halfway across the school before I realized I wanted to go home. I wanted to clear my head; I wanted to get away from everything for a little while. So I cut across the quad and through the parking lot and was just about to step off campus when I felt someone grab my arm.

"Holy *shit* you walk fast—"

I spun around, stunned.

Ocean's hand was on my arm, his eyes full of something like fear or concern and he said, "I've been calling your name this whole time. Didn't you hear me?"

I looked around like I was losing my mind. How did this keep happening to me? What the hell was Ocean doing here?

"I'm sorry," I said. I faltered. I realized he was still touching me and I took a sudden, nervous step backward. "I, um, I was kind of lost in my head."

"Yeah, I figured," he said, and sighed. "Mr. Jordan is a dick. What a complete asshole."

My eyes went wide. I was now, somehow, even more confused. "How did you know about Mr. Jordan?"

Ocean stared at me. He looked like he wasn't sure whether or not I was joking. "I'm in your *class*," he said finally.

I blinked.

"Are you serious?" he said. "You didn't know I was in your class?" He laughed, but it sounded sad. He shook his head. "Wow."

I still couldn't process this. It was too much—too much was happening all at once. "Did you just transfer in or something?" I asked. "Or have you always been in my class?"

Ocean looked stunned.

"Oh, wow, I'm really sorry," I said. "I wasn't, like, ignoring you. I just—I don't really look at people most of the time."

"Yeah," he said, and laughed again. "I know."

I raised my eyebrows.

And he sighed. "Hey, really, though—are you okay? I can't believe he did that to you."

"Yeah." I looked away. "I feel kind of bad for Travis."

Ocean made a sound of disbelief. "Travis will be fine."

"Yeah."

"So you're okay? You don't need me to go back in there and kick his ass?"

And I looked up, unable to contain my surprise. When had Ocean become the kind of guy willing to defend my honor?

When had I leveled up to become the kind of person for whom he'd even offer? I barely talked to the guy, and even then, we'd never discussed much. Last week he'd hardly spoken to me in bio. I realized then that I didn't know Ocean at all.

"I'm okay," I said.

I mean, I wasn't, but I didn't know what else to say. I just really wanted to leave. And it only occurred to me that I'd said that last part out loud when he said—

"Good idea. Let's get out of here."

"What?" I accidentally laughed at him. "Are you serious?"

"You were about to cut class," he said. "Weren't you?"

I nodded.

"Well," he said, and shrugged. "I'll come with you."

"You don't need to do that."

"I know I don't *need to do that*," he said. "I just want to. Is that okay?"

I stared at him.

I stared at him and his simple, uncomplicated brown hair. His soft blue sweater and dark jeans. He was wearing very white sneakers. He was also squinting at me in the cold sunlight, waiting for my response, and he finally tugged a pair of sunglasses out of his pocket and put them on. They were nice sunglasses. They looked good on him.

"Yeah," I said quietly. "That's okay."

TEN

We walked to IHOP.

It wasn't far from campus, and it seemed like an innocuous enough destination for cheap food and a little change of scenery. But then we were sitting in a booth, sitting across from each other, and I suddenly had no idea what I was doing. What *we* were doing.

I was trying to think of what to say, how to say it, when Ocean seemed to suddenly remember he was still wearing sunglasses.

He said, "Oh, right—"

And took them off.

It was such a simple thing. It was a quiet, completely unmomentous moment. The world didn't stop turning; birds didn't suddenly start singing. Obviously I'd seen his eyes before. But somehow, suddenly, it was like I was seeing them for the first time. And somehow, suddenly, I couldn't stop staring at his face. Something fluttered against my heart. I felt my armor begin to break.

He had really beautiful eyes.

They were an unusual mix of blue and brown, and together they made a kind of gray. I'd never caught the subtleties before. Maybe because he'd never looked at me like this before. Straight on. Smiling. Really, smiling at me. I only then realized that I'd never gotten a full smile from Ocean before. Most of the time his smiles were confused or scared or a combination of any number of other things. But for some reason, right now, in this extremely ugly booth at IHOP, he was smiling at me like there was something to celebrate.

"What?" he finally said.

I blinked fast, startled. Embarrassed. I looked down at my menu and said, "Nothing," very quietly.

"Why were you staring at me?"

"I wasn't staring at you." I held the menu closer to my face.

No one said anything for a few seconds.

"You never came back online over the weekend," he said.

"Yeah."

"Why not?" He reached forward and gently pushed the menu away from my face.

Oh my God.

I couldn't unsee it. I couldn't unsee it, *oh my God,* someone save me from myself, I couldn't unsee his face. What had happened to me? Why was I suddenly so attracted to him?

Why?

I reached around blindly in my mind for walls, old armor, anything to keep me safe from this—from the danger of all the stupid things that happened to my head around cute boys—but nothing was working because he wouldn't stop looking at me.

"I was busy," I said, but the words came out a little weird.

"Oh," he said, and sat back. His face was inscrutable. He picked up his menu, his eyes scanning its many options.

And then, I just, I don't know. I couldn't take it anymore.

"Why are you hanging out with me?" I said.

The words just kind of happened. They just came out, breathless and a little angry. I didn't understand him, didn't like what was happening to my heart around him, didn't like that I had no idea what he was thinking. I was confused as hell and it made me feel so off-kilter, off my game, and I just needed to break this thing open and be done with it.

I couldn't help it.

Ocean sat up, put down his menu. He looked surprised. "What do you mean?"

"I mean"—I looked at the ceiling, bit my lip—"I mean I don't understand what's happening here. Why are you being so nice to me? Why are you following me out of class? Why are you asking to have dinner at my house—"

"Oh, hey, yeah, did you ask your parents about tha—"

"I don't understand what you're doing," I said, cutting him off. I could feel my face getting hot. "What do you want from me?"

His eyes widened. "I don't want anything from you."

I swallowed, hard. Looked away. "This isn't normal, Ocean."

"What isn't normal?"

"This," I said, gesturing between us. "*This*. This isn't normal. Guys like you don't talk to girls like me."

"Girls like you?"

"Yes," I said. "Girls like me." I narrowed my eyes at him. "Please don't pretend you don't know what I'm talking about, okay? I'm not an idiot."

He stared at me.

"I just want to know what's going on," I said. "I don't understand why you're trying so hard to be my friend. I don't understand why you keep showing up in my life. Do you, like, feel sorry for me or something?"

"Oh." He raised his eyebrows. "Wow."

"Because if you're just being nice to me because you feel sorry for me, please don't."

He smiled, a little, and only to himself. "You don't understand," he said. It wasn't a question.

"No, I don't understand. I'm trying to understand and I don't understand and it's freaking me out."

He laughed, just once. "Why is it freaking you out?"

"It just is."

"Okay."

"You know what?" I shook my head. "Never mind. I think I should go."

"Don't—" He sighed, hard, cutting himself off. "Don't go." He mussed his hair, muttered, *"Jesus Christ,"* under his breath, and finally said, "I just think you seem cool, okay?" He looked at me. "Is that so hard to believe?"

"Kind of."

"I also think you're really goddamn beautiful but you just won't give me a chance to be cool about this, will you?"

I thought, for certain, that my heart had stopped. I knew, rationally, that such a thing was impossible, but for some reason it felt true.

The only time anyone had ever called me anything close to beautiful was when I was in eighth grade. I'd overheard someone say it. She was explaining to another kid that she didn't like me because she thought I was one of those girls who was really pretty and really mean. She'd said it in an unkind, flippant way that made me think she really meant it.

At the time, it had been the nicest thing anyone had ever said about me. I'd often wondered, since that day, if I really was pretty, but no one but my mother had ever bothered to corroborate her statement.

And now, here—

I was stunned.

"Oh," was all I managed to say. My face felt like it had been set on fire.

"Yeah," he said. I wasn't looking at him anymore, but I could tell he was smiling. "Do you understand now?"

"Kind of," I said.

And then we ordered pancakes.

ELEVEN

We spent the rest of our IHOP experience talking about nothing in particular. In fact, we changed gears so quickly from serious to superficial that I actually walked out the door wondering if I'd imagined the part where he told me I was beautiful.

I think it was my fault. I kind of froze. I'd pushed him so hard to give me a straight answer but the one I got wasn't the one I was expecting and it threw me off-balance. I didn't know what to do with it.

It made me feel vulnerable.

So we talked about movies. Things we'd seen; things we hadn't. It was fine, but it was kind of boring. I think we were both relieved when we finally left IHOP behind, like we were trying to shake off something embarrassing.

"Do you know what time it is?" I asked him. We'd been walking in silence, side by side, heading in no particular direction.

He glanced at his watch and said, "Third period is almost over."

I sighed. "I guess we should go back to school."

"Yeah."

"So much for ditching."

He stopped walking and touched my arm. Said my name.

I looked up.

Ocean was quite a bit taller than me, and I'd never looked up at him like this before. I was standing in his shadow. We were on the sidewalk, facing each other, and there wasn't much space between us.

He smelled really nice. My heart was being weird again.

But his eyes were worried. He opened his mouth to say something and then, very suddenly, changed his mind. Looked away.

"What is it?" I said.

He shook his head. Smiled at me out of the corner of his eye, but only briefly. "Nothing. Never mind."

I could tell that something was bothering him, but his reluctance to share made me think I probably didn't want to know what he was thinking. So I changed the subject.

"Hey, how long have you lived here?"

Unexpectedly, Ocean smiled. He seemed both pleased and surprised to be asked the question. "Forever," he said. And then, "I mean, I moved here when I was, like, six, but yeah, basically forever."

"Wow," I said. I almost whispered the word. He'd described in a single sentence something I'd often dreamed about. "Must be nice to live in the same place for so long."

We'd started walking again.

Ocean reached up, plucked a leaf from a tree we were passing, and spun it around in his hands. "It's okay." He shrugged. "Gets kind of boring, actually."

"I don't know," I said. "It sounds really nice. You probably know your neighbors, huh? And you get to go to school with all the same people."

"Same people," he said, nodding. "Yeah. But trust me, it gets old, fast. I'm dying to get the hell out of here."

"Really?" I turned to look at him. "Why?"

He tossed the leaf, shoved his hands into his pockets. "There's so much I want to do," he said. "Things I want to see. I don't want to get stuck here forever. I want to live in a big city. Travel." He glanced at me. "I've never even left the country, you know?"

I smiled at him, kind of. "Not really," I said. "I think I've traveled enough for the both of us. I'm ready to retire. Settle down. Get old."

"You're *sixteen*."

"But in my heart I'm a seventy-five-year-old man."

"Wow, I really hope not."

"You know, when I was eight," I said, "my parents tried

to move back to Iran. They packed up all our shit and sold the house and just, took a leap." I adjusted the backpack on my shoulders. Sighed. "Ultimately, it didn't work out. We were too American. Too much had changed. But I lived in Iran for six months, bouncing between the city and the countryside. I went to this really fancy international school in Tehran for a while, and all my classmates were these horrible, spoiled, dipshit children of diplomats. I'd cry every day. Beg my mom to let me stay home. But then we spent some time farther north, in a part of the country even closer to the Caspian Sea, and I went to class with a bunch of village kids. The entire school was a single room—straight out of *Anne of Green Gables*—and of the twelve schools I've attended in my life, it's still my favorite." I laughed. "The kids used to chase me around at lunchtime and beg me to say things in English. They were obsessed with America," I explained. "I'd never been so popular in my life." I laughed, again, and looked up to meet Ocean's eyes, but he'd slowed down. He was staring at me, and I couldn't read his expression.

"What?" I said. "Too weird?"

The intense look in his eyes evaporated. In fact, he seemed suddenly frustrated. He shook his head and said, "I wish you'd stop saying things like that to me. I don't think you're weird. And I don't know why you think I'm going to have a sudden epiphany that you're weird and start freaking out. I'm not. Okay? I genuinely don't care that you cover your hair. I don't. I mean"—he hesitated—"as long as it's, like, something you actually want to do."

He looked at me. Waited for something.

I looked back, confused.

"I mean," he said, "your parents don't, like, force you to wear a headscarf, do they?"

"What?" I frowned. "No. No, I mean, I don't love the way people *treat* me for wearing it—which often makes me wonder whether I shouldn't just stop—but no," I said. I looked off in the distance. "When I'm not thinking about people harassing me every day, I actually like the way it makes me feel. It's nice."

"Nice how?"

We'd officially stopped walking. We were standing on the sidewalk, next to a sort of busy road, where I was having one of the most personal conversations I'd ever had with a boy.

"I mean, I don't know," I said. "It makes me feel, I don't know. Like I'm in control. I get to choose who gets to see me. How they see me. I don't think it's for everyone," I said, and shrugged. "I've met girls who do feel forced to wear it and they hate it. And I think that's bullshit. Obviously I don't think anyone should wear it if they don't want to. But I like it," I said. "I like that you have to ask for my permission to see my hair."

Ocean's eyes widened suddenly. "Can I see your hair?"

"No."

He laughed out loud. Looked away. He said, "Okay." And then, quietly, "I can already kind of see your hair, though."

I looked at him, surprised.

I wrapped my scarf a little loosely, which made it so that a little of my hair, at the top, sometimes showed, and some people were obsessed with this detail. I wasn't sure why, but they loved pointing out to me that they could already see an inch of my hair, like maybe that would be enough to nullify the whole thing. I found this fixation kind of hilarious.

"Yeah," I said. "Well, I mean, that's usually all it takes. Guys see an inch of my hair and they just, you know"—I mimed an explosion with my hand—"lose their minds. And then it's just, like, marriage proposals, all over the place."

Ocean looked confused.

He didn't say anything for a second, and then—

"Oh. *Oh.* You're joking."

I looked curiously at him. "Yes," I said. "I'm super joking."

He was looking at me just as curiously as I looked at him. We were still standing on the sidewalk, talking. Staring at each other.

Finally, he said: "So you're trying to tell me that what I said was stupid, huh? I only just got that."

"Yeah," I said. "I'm sorry. I'm usually more direct."

And he laughed. He looked away. Looked back at me. "Am I making this weird? Should I stop asking you these questions?"

"No, no." I shook my head. Smiled, even. "No one ever asks me these questions. I like that you ask. Most people just assume they know what I'm thinking."

"Well, I have no idea what you're thinking. Like, ever."

"Right now," I said, "I'm thinking you're so much ballsier than I thought you'd be. I'm kind of impressed."

"Wait, what do you mean, than you *thought* I'd be?"

I couldn't help it, I was suddenly laughing. "Like, I don't know. When I first met you? You seemed really—timid," I said. "Kind of terrified."

"Well, to be fair, you're kind of terrifying."

"Yeah," I said, sobered in an instant. "I know."

"I don't mean"—he shook his head, laughed—"I don't mean because of your scarf or your religion or whatever. I just mean I don't think you see yourself the way other people do."

I raised an eyebrow at him. "I'm pretty sure I know how other people see me."

"Maybe some people," he said. "Yeah. I'm positive there are horrible people in the world. But there are a lot of other people who are looking at you because they think you're interesting."

"Well I don't want to be *interesting*," I said. "I don't exist to fascinate strangers. I'm just trying to live. I just want people to be normal around me."

Ocean wasn't looking at me when he said, quietly, "I have no idea how anyone is supposed to be normal around you. I can't even be normal around you."

"What? Why not?"

"Because you're crazy intimidating," he said. "And you don't even see it. You don't look at people, you don't talk to people, you don't seem to care about anything most kids are obsessed with. I mean, you show up to school looking like you just walked out of a *magazine* and you think people are staring at you because of something they saw on the news."

I went suddenly still.

My heart seemed to speed up and slow down. I didn't know what to say, and Ocean wouldn't meet my eyes.

"Anyway," he said. He cleared his throat. I noticed he'd gone pink around the ears. "So you went to twelve different schools?"

I nodded.

"Damn."

"Yeah," I said. "It sucked. Continues to suck."

"I'm sorry to hear that."

"I mean, it doesn't suck right *now*," I said, staring at our feet. "Right now it's not so bad."

"No?"

I glanced up. He was smiling at me.

"No," I said. "Right now it's not bad at all."

TWELVE

Ocean and I split up for lunch.

I think he might've joined me, if I'd asked, but I didn't ask. I didn't know what he did for lunch, who his friends were, what his social obligations might be, and I wasn't sure I wanted to know yet. At the moment, I just wanted space to process our conversation. I wanted space to figure out what to do about Mr. Jordan's class. I wanted time to get my brain on straight. I was no longer hungry, thanks to the stack of pancakes I'd eaten at IHOP, so I headed straight to my tree.

This had been my solution to the lonely lunchtime problem. I'd grown tired of both the bathroom and the library, and enough time had passed that I no longer felt too self-conscious about eating alone. This school had a couple of green spaces, and I'd picked one at random to make my own. I chose a tree.

I sat under it, leaning against the trunk. I ate food if I was hungry; but mostly I wrote in my journal or read a book.

Today, I was late.

And someone else was sitting under my tree.

I hadn't been looking at people, as was my unfortunate habit, so I hadn't noticed the person sitting under my tree until I nearly stepped on him.

He shouted.

I jumped back. Startled. "Oh," I said, "Oh my God, I'm sorry."

He stood up, frowned, and I took one real look at his face and just about fell over. He was, wow, he was possibly the most good-looking guy I'd ever seen. He had warm brown skin and hazel eyes and he looked distinctly Middle Eastern. I had, like, a Spidey-sense for that sort of thing. He was also clearly not a sophomore, whoever he was; he was maybe my brother's age.

"Hi," I said.

"Hey," he said back. He was looking curiously at me. "You new here?"

"Yeah. I transferred in this year."

"Wow, cool," he said. "We don't get a lot of hijabis in these parts. That's pretty brave," he said, nodding at my head.

But I was distracted. I never thought I'd hear any kid at this school use the word *hijab* so casually. Hijab was the word for a headscarf in Arabic. *Hijabis* was a sort of colloquial term some people used to describe girls who wore hijab. There had to be a reason he knew that.

"Are you Muslim?" I asked.

He nodded. "Hey, why were you about to step on me?"

"Oh," I said, and felt suddenly awkward. "I usually sit here during lunch. I just didn't see you."

"Oh, my bad," he said, looking back at the tree. "I didn't realize this was someone's spot. I was catching up on some homework before class. Needed a quiet place to work."

"The library is pretty reliable for that sort of thing," I said.

He laughed, but didn't offer to explain why he'd bypassed the library. Instead, he said, "Are you Syrian?"

I shook my head.

"Turkish?"

I shook my head again. I got this a lot. There was something about my face, apparently, that made it so people never really knew where to place me on the map. "I'm Persian."

"Oh," he said, his eyebrows high. "Cool, cool. I'm Lebanese."

I nodded, unsurprised. In my experience, the hottest Middle Eastern guys were always Lebanese.

"Anyway," he said, and took a deep breath. "It was nice to meet you."

"You too," I said. "I'm Shirin."

"Shirin," he said, and smiled. "Nice. Well, I hope I see you again sometime. I'm Yusef."

"Okay," I said, which was kind of a stupid thing to say, but I didn't really notice in the moment. "Bye."

He waved and walked away and I was not too proud to

watch him go. He was wearing a tight sweater that did little to hide the fact that he had the body of an athlete.

Damn. I was really beginning to like this school.

Bio was my last class of the day. I was expecting to see Ocean, but he never showed up. I dropped my bag on the floor and looked around the classroom. I sat in my seat and felt distracted. When we were sent to our lab stations, I cut into my soggy cat and couldn't stop wondering where he was. I even worried, for a second, that something bad might've happened. But there was nothing to be done about it.

When the bell rang, I headed to practice.

"So I heard you cut class today," was the first thing my brother said to me.

Shit.

I'd almost forgotten about that. "Who told you I cut class?"

"Mr. Jordan."

"What?" Outrage, again. "Why? How do you two even know each other?"

Navid just shook his head. He almost laughed. "Mr. Jordan is our supervisor for the breakdancing club."

"Of course he is." Cool Teacher Mr. Jordan would've jumped at the chance to supervise a breakdancing club. Of course.

"He said he was worried about you. He said you got upset during class and ran out without a word." Navid paused. Leveled me with a look. "He said you ran off with some dude."

"What?" I frowned. "First of all, I didn't run out of class. And second of all, I didn't leave with *some dude*. He followed me out."

"Whatever," Navid said. "What's going on here? You're ditching class? Running off campus with random guys? Am I going to have to kick the shit out of someone tomorrow?"

I rolled my eyes. Carlos, Bijan, and Jacobi were watching our conversation with great fascination and I was annoyed with all of them. "Mr. Jordan was being an asshole," I said. "He forced me and this other guy to stare at each other in front of the whole class, and then he told the guy to say, out loud, exactly what he was thinking when he looked at me."

"And?" My brother crossed his arms. "So what?"

I looked at him, surprised. "What do you mean, *so what*? What do you think happened? It was humiliating."

Navid dropped his arms. "What do you mean it was humiliating?"

"I mean it was horrible. He said I looked like nothing. That I basically didn't even exist." I waved a frustrated hand. "Whatever. It sounds stupid now, I know, but it really hurt my feelings. So I walked out."

"Damn," Navid said quietly. "So I really *do* have to kick the shit out of someone tomorrow."

"You don't have to kick the shit out of anyone," I said, and slumped down on the floor. "It's fine. I think I might just drop the class. There's still time."

"I don't think so." Navid shook his head at me. "I'm pretty

sure you missed the window. You can still withdraw, but it'll show up on your transcript like that, which m—"

"I don't give a damn about my transcript," I said, irritated.

"Okay," he said, holding up his hands. "Okay." My brother looked at me, genuinely sympathetic, for all of five seconds before he suddenly frowned. "Wait, I don't understand one thing—why would you ditch class with a guy who thinks you don't exist?"

I shook my head. Sighed. "Different guy," I said.

Navid raised his eyebrows. "Different guy?" He glanced at his friends. "You three hearing this shit? She says it was a *different* guy."

Carlos laughed.

"These kids grow up fast," Jacobi said.

Bijan grinned at me and said, "Damn, girl."

"Oh my God," I said, squeezing my eyes closed. "Shut up, all of you. You're being ridiculous."

"So who's the different guy?" Navid asked. "Does he have a name?"

I opened my eyes. Stared at him. "No."

Navid's mouth dropped open. He was half smiling, half surprised. "Wow," he said. "*Wow.* You must really like him."

"I don't like him," I snapped. "I just don't want you bothering him."

"Why would we bother him?" My brother was still smiling.

"Can we just get started on practice? Please?"

"Not until you tell me his name."

I sighed. I knew my evasiveness would only make the situation worse, so I gave in. "His name is Ocean."

Navid frowned. "What the hell kind of a name is Ocean?"

"You know, people wonder the same thing about you."

"Whatever," he said. "My name is awesome."

"Anyway," I said, "Ocean is my lab partner in another class. He just felt bad that Mr. Jordan was being a jerk."

My brother still seemed skeptical, but he didn't push it. I could feel him begin to pull away, to lose interest in the conversation, and it made me suddenly anxious. There was something I still wanted to say. Something that had been bothering me all day. I'd been deliberating for hours whether or not to ask the question—even *how* to ask the question—and, finally, I just gave in and made a mess of it.

"Hey, Navid?" I said quietly.

He'd just turned to grab something out of his bag, and he looked back at me. "Yeah?"

"Do you—" I hesitated. Reconsidered.

"Do I what?"

I took a deep breath. "Do you think I'm pretty?"

Navid's reaction to my question was so absurd I almost don't even know how to describe it. He looked somehow shocked and confused and hysterical all at the same time. Eventually, he laughed. Hard. It sounded strange.

I was mortified.

"Oh my God, never mind," I said quickly. "I'm sorry I even asked. That was so stupid."

I was halfway across the room when Navid jogged—slowly, dragging his sneakers—after me, and said, "Wait, wait, I'm sorry—"

"Forget it," I said angrily. I was blushing past my hairline. I was now standing way too close to Bijan, Carlos, and Jacobi, and I did not want them to hear this conversation. I tried desperately to convey this with my eyes, but Navid seemed incapable of picking up my signals. "I don't want to talk about this, okay? Forget I said anything."

"Hey, listen," Navid said, "I was just surprised. I wasn't expecting you to say something like that."

"Say something like what?" This, from Bijan.

I wanted to die.

"Nothing," I said to Bijan. I glared at Navid. "*Nothing*, okay?"

Navid looked over at the guys and sighed. "Shirin wants to know if I think she's pretty. But, listen," he said, looking at me again, "I don't think I should be answering that question. That feels like a really weird question for a sister to ask her brother, you know? Maybe you should be asking these guys," he said, nodding at the rest of the group.

"*Oh my God*," I said, half whispering the words. I really thought I might murder my brother. I wanted to close my hands around his throat. "What is *wrong* with you?" I shouted.

And then—

"I think you're pretty," Carlos said. He was retying his

shoelaces. He'd said the statement like he was talking about the weather.

I looked at him. I felt slightly stunned.

"I mean, I think you're scary as hell," he said, and shrugged. "But, yeah. I mean, yeah. Very cute."

"You think I'm scary?" I said, and frowned.

Carlos nodded. He wouldn't even look at me.

"Do *you* think I'm scary?" I said to Bijan.

"Oh," he said, and raised his eyebrows. "Definitely."

I actually took a step back, I was so surprised. "Are you serious? Do you all feel this way?"

And they all nodded. Even Navid.

"I think you're beautiful, though," Bijan said. "If that helps."

My mouth fell open. "Why do you all think I'm so scary?"

They collectively shrugged.

"People think you're mean," Navid finally said to me.

"People are assholes," I snapped.

"See?" Navid pointed at me. "This is the thing you do."

"What thing?" I said, frustrated again. "People are flaming pieces of shit to me, like, all day long, and I'm not supposed to be mad about it?"

"You can be mad about it," Jacobi said, and the sound of his voice startled me. He seemed, suddenly, very serious. "But, like, you seem to think *everyone* is horrible."

"That's because everyone *is* horrible."

Jacobi shook his head. "Listen," he said, "I know what it's like to be angry all the time, okay? I do. Your shit—the shit you have to deal with—it's hard, yeah. But you just—you can't do this. You *can't* be angry all the time. Trust me," he said. "I've tried that. It'll kill you."

I looked at him. Really looked at him. There was something in Jacobi's eyes that was sympathetic in a way I'd never experienced before. It wasn't *pity*. It was recognition. He actually seemed to acknowledge me, my pain, and my anger, in a way no one else ever had.

Not my parents. Not even my brother.

I felt suddenly like I'd been pierced in the chest. I felt suddenly like I wanted to cry.

"Just try to be happy," Jacobi finally said to me. "Your happiness is the one thing these assholes can't stand."

THIRTEEN

All afternoon, I'd been thinking about what Jacobi said to me. I got home and I took a shower and I thought about it. All through dinner, I thought about it. I sat at my desk and stared at the wall and listened to music and thought about it and thought about it and thought about it.

I locked myself in my bedroom and thought about it.

It was just past nine o'clock. The house was still. These were the quiet hours before my parents demanded I be asleep—the hours during which all members of my family performed a small mercy and left one another alone for a while. I was sitting in bed, staring at a blank page in my journal.

Thinking.

I wondered, for the very first time, if maybe I was doing this whole thing wrong. If maybe I'd allowed myself to be blinded by my own anger to the exclusion of all else. If maybe, just maybe, I'd been so determined not to be stereotyped that I'd begun to stereotype everyone around me.

It made me think about Ocean.

He kept trying to be nice to me and, in an unexpected turn of events, his kindness left me angry and confused. I pushed him away because I was afraid to be even remotely close to someone who, I was certain, would one day hurt me. I trusted no one anymore. I was so raw from repeated exposure to cruelty that now even the most minor abrasions left a mark. The checkout lady at the grocery store would be rude to me and her simple unkindness would unnerve me for the rest of the day because I never knew—I had no way of knowing—

Are you racist? Or are you just having a bad day?

I could no longer distinguish people from monsters.

I looked out at the world around me and no longer saw nuance. I saw nothing but the potential for pain and the subsequent need to protect myself, constantly.

Damn, I thought.

This really was exhausting.

I sighed and picked up my phone.

hey. why weren't you in class today?

Ocean responded right away.

WOW

i didn't think you'd notice i was gone
can you get online?

I smiled.

jujehpolo: Hey
riversandoceans04: Hi
riversandoceans04: Sorry for bailing on you in bio
riversandoceans04: No one should have to slice into a
dead cat by themselves
jujehpolo: It really is, like, the worst school assignment
I've ever had
riversandoceans04: Same here

And then—

I wasn't sure why, exactly, but I had this sudden, strange
feeling that something was wrong. It was hard to tell from a
few typed words, but I felt it in my gut. Ocean seemed off,
somehow, and I couldn't shake it.

jujehpolo: Hey, is everything okay?
riversandoceans04: Yeah
riversandoceans04: Sort of

I waited.
I waited and nothing happened. He wrote nothing else.

jujehpolo: You don't want to talk about it?

riversandoceans04: Not really

jujehpolo: Did you get in trouble for ditching class?

riversandoceans04: No

jujehpolo: Are you in trouble for something else?

riversandoceans04: Lol

riversandoceans04: You do realize this is the exact opposite of not talking about it, right

jujehpolo: Yes

riversandoceans04: But we're still talking about it

jujehpolo: I'm worried I got you in trouble

And then, our messages crossed paths in the ether:

I wrote my brother didn't bother you, did he? and Ocean wrote don't worry, it has nothing to do with you

And then—

riversandoceans04: What?

riversandoceans04: Why would your brother bother me?

riversandoceans04: I didn't even know you had a brother

riversandoceans04: Wait

riversandoceans04: You told your brother about me?

Shit.

jujehpolo: Apparently Mr. Jordan is supervising our breakdancing club

jujehpolo: He told my brother I ditched class with a guy today

jujehpolo: And my brother was mad

jujehpolo: It's fine now. I told him what happened.

riversandoceans04: Oh

riversandoceans04: So what does that have to do with your brother bothering me

jujehpolo: Nothing

jujehpolo: He just thought we'd ditched class together

riversandoceans04: But we did

jujehpolo: I know

riversandoceans04: So your brother hates me now?

jujehpolo: He doesn't even know you

jujehpolo: He was just being overprotective

riversandoceans04: Wait a second, who's your brother again? He goes to our school?

jujehpolo: Yeah. He's a senior. His name is Navid.

riversandoceans04: Oh

riversandoceans04: I don't think I know him.

jujehpolo: You probably wouldn't

riversandoceans04: So should I be worried?

riversandoceans04: About your brother?

jujehpolo: No

jujehpolo: Lol

jujehpolo: Listen, I'm not trying to freak you out, I'm sorry

riversandoceans04: I'm not freaked out

Sure he wasn't.

I waited a few seconds to see if he'd say anything else, but he didn't. Finally, I wrote:

jujehpolo: So you're really not going to tell me what happened to you today?

riversandoceans04: That depends

riversandoceans04: A lot of things happened to me today

My stomach did a little flip. I couldn't help but wonder if he was talking about us. Our earlier conversations. The lack of physical distance between our bodies as we stood on an unimportant sidewalk in the middle of an unimportant town. I didn't know what any of it meant—or if it would ever mean anything. Maybe I was the only one experiencing these little stomach flips. Maybe I was projecting my own feelings onto his words.

Maybe I was nuts.

I hadn't yet decided what to say when he sent another message.

riversandoceans04: Hey

jujehpolo: Yeah?

riversandoceans04: Can you get on the phone?

jujehpolo: Oh

jujehpolo: You want to talk on the phone?

riversandoceans04: Yeah

jujehpolo: Why?

riversandoceans04: I want to hear your voice

A weird, not exactly unwelcome nervousness flooded through me. My brain felt suddenly warm and like maybe someone had filled my head with fizzy water. I would've vastly preferred to have disappeared in that moment; instead of getting on the phone I wanted to dissect this conversation somewhere else, somewhere by myself. I wanted to pick the whole thing apart and put it back together again. I wanted to understand what seemed inexplicable to me. In fact, I would've been happy if *I want to hear your voice* had been the last thing Ocean ever said to me.

Instead, I wrote, okay

Ocean's voice pressed up against my ear might've been one of the most intense physical experiences I'd ever had. It was strange. It made me surprisingly nervous. I'd talked to him so many times—he was my lab partner, after all—but somehow, this was different. The two of us on the phone felt so private. Like our voices had met in outer space.

He said, "Hey," and I felt the sound wash over me.

"Hi," I said. "This is weird."

He laughed. "I think it's nice. You seem real, like this."

I'd never noticed it in person, with so much else to distract me, but he had a really attractive voice. It sounded different— good, really good—in stereo.

"Oh." My heart was racing. "I guess so."

"So your brother wants to kick my ass, huh?"

"What? No." I hesitated. "I mean, I don't think so. Not really."

He laughed again.

"Do you have any brothers or sisters?" I asked.

"No."

"Oh. Well. That's probably for the best."

"I don't know," he said. "It sounds nice."

"Sometimes it really is nice," I said, considering it. "My brother and I are pretty close. But we also went through a period where we would literally beat the shit out of each other."

"Okay, that sounds bad."

"Yeah." I paused. "But he also taught me how to fight, which was an unexpected fringe benefit."

"Really?" He sounded surprised. "You can fight?"

"Not well."

He said, "Huh," in a thoughtful way, and then went quiet. I waited a couple of seconds before I said,

"So what happened to you today?"

He sighed.

"If you really, *really* don't want to talk about it," I said, "we don't have to talk about it. But if you want to talk about it even a little bit, I'm happy to listen."

"I want to tell you," he said, but his voice sounded suddenly far away. "I just also don't want to tell you."

"Oh," I said. Confused. "Okay."

"It's too heavy, too soon."

"*Oh*," I said.

"Maybe we can talk about my messed-up parental issues after I've learned your middle name, for example."

"I don't have a middle name."

"Huh. Okay, how about—"

"You ask me a lot of questions."

Silence.

"Is that bad?"

"No," I said. "I just—can I ask *you* some questions?"

He said nothing for a second. And then, quietly, "Okay."

He told me why his parents named him Ocean, that the story wasn't that exciting, he said his mom was obsessed with the water and that it was ironic, actually, because he'd always had this strange fear of drowning and was a lousy swimmer and had never really cared for the ocean, actually, and that his middle name was Desmond, so he had not two, but three first names, and I told him I really liked the name Desmond, and he said it had been his grandfather's name, there was nothing special about it, and I asked him if he'd known his grandfather and he said no, he said that his parents had split up when he was five and he'd lost touch with that side of his family, that he'd only seen his dad occasionally since then. I wanted to ask more questions about his parents but I didn't, because I knew he didn't want to talk about it, so instead I asked him where he wanted to go to college and he said he was torn between Columbia and Berkeley, because Berkeley sounded perfect but wasn't in a big city, and he said he really wanted to live in a big city, and I said yes, you said that before, and he said, "Yeah. Sometimes I just feel like I was born into the wrong family."

"What do you mean?"

"I feel like everyone around me is dead," he said, and his anger surprised me. "Like no one *thinks* anymore. Everyone seems satisfied with the most depressing shit. I don't want to be like that."

"I wouldn't want to be like that either."

"Yeah, well, I don't think you're in any danger of that."

"Oh," I said, surprised. "Thanks."

And then he said, "Have you ever had a boyfriend?"

—and I felt the moment freeze all around me.

I had never had a boyfriend, I said to him, no, I had not.

"Why not?"

"Um." I laughed. "Wow, where do I even begin with this? First of all, I'm pretty sure my parents would be horrified if I ever so much as *intimated* that I had feelings for a boy, because I think they still think I'm five.

"Second of all, I've never really lived in one place long enough for something like that to play out, and um, I don't know, Ocean"—I laughed again—"the truth is, guys don't, uh—they don't really ask me out."

"Well what if a guy did ask you out?"

I didn't like where this was going.

I didn't want to act out this scenario. Honestly, I never thought it would get this far. I was so certain Ocean would never be interested in me that I didn't bother to consider how bad it would be if he *were*.

I thought Ocean was a nice guy, but I also thought he was naive.

Maybe I could try letting go of my anger—maybe I could try being kinder for a change—but I knew that even the most optimistic attitude wouldn't change the structure of the world we lived in. Ocean was a nice, handsome, heterosexual white guy, and the world expected great things from him. Those things did not involve falling for a highly controversial Middle Eastern girl in a headscarf. I had to save him from himself.

So I didn't answer his question.

Instead, I said, "I mean, it's not a frequent occurrence in my life, but it actually *has* happened before. When I was in middle school my brother went through a phase where he was a total and complete asshole, and he'd go through my diary and find out about these rare, brave souls and hunt them down. He'd scare the shit out of them." I paused. "It did wonders for my love life, as I'm sure you can imagine."

And I don't know what I was expecting him to say, exactly, but when Ocean said, "You keep a diary?"

I realized I hadn't been expecting him to say *that*.

"Oh," I said. "Yeah."

"That's really cool."

And I knew then, somehow, that I needed to end this conversation. Something was happening; something was changing and it was scaring me.

So I said, a little suddenly, "Hey, I should probably get going. It's late and I still have a lot of homework to do."

"Oh," he said. And I could tell, even in that small word, that he sounded surprised, and maybe—*maybe*—disappointed.

"I'll see you tomorrow?"

"Sure," he said.

"Okay." I tried to smile, even though he couldn't see me. "Bye."

After we hung up, I collapsed onto my bed and closed my eyes. This dizziness was in my marrow, in my mind.

I was being stupid.

I knew better, and I'd texted him anyway, and now I was confusing this poor kid who didn't have a clue what he was wading into. This whole thing probably seemed simple to him: Ocean thought I was pretty and he'd told me so; I hadn't told him to go to hell, so here we were. He was trying, maybe, to ask me out? Asking out a girl he thought was pretty probably seemed like an obvious move to him, but that just wasn't something I wanted to happen. That was drama I didn't want, had no interest in.

Wow, I was stupid.

I'd let my guard down. I did that thing—the thing where I allowed cute boys to get in my head and mess with my common sense—and I'd let my conversation with Jacobi distract me from the bigger picture here.

Nothing had changed.

I'd made a mistake by opening myself up like this. This was a mistake. I had to stop talking to Ocean. I had to dial this back.

Switch gears.

And fast.

FOURTEEN

I bailed on Mr. Jordan's class four days in a row.

I'd gone to my academic counselor and told her I wanted to withdraw from my Global Perspectives class and she asked why and I said I didn't like the class, that I didn't like Mr. Jordan's teaching methods, and she said it was too late to drop the class, that I'd have a *W* on my transcript and that colleges didn't like that, and I shrugged and she frowned and we both stared at each other for a minute. Finally she said she'd have to notify Mr. Jordan that I'd be withdrawing from the class. She said he'd have to approve the action, was I aware of this, and I said, "Yeah, that's fine."

And I just stopped going to Mr. Jordan's class. This worked well enough in the beginning, but on the fourth day—it was now Thursday—he found me at my locker.

He said, "Hey. I haven't seen you in class in a couple of days."

I glanced at him. Slammed my locker shut; spun the combination. "That's because I'm not taking your class anymore."

"I heard."

"Okay." I started walking.

He kept up. "Can I talk to you for a minute?"

"You're talking to me now."

"Shirin," he said, "I'm really sorry. I realize I did something wrong, and I'd really like to discuss it with you."

I stopped in the middle of the hallway. Turned to face him. I was feeling brave, apparently. "What would you like to discuss?"

"Well, obviously I've upset you—"

"*Obviously* you've upset me, yes." I looked at him. "Why would you pull such a dick move, Mr. Jordan? You *knew* Travis was going to say something awful about me, and you wanted him to."

Students were rushing around us, some of them slowing down to stare as they went. Mr. Jordan looked flustered.

"That's not true," he said, his neck going red. "I didn't want him to say anything awful about you. I just wanted us to be able to talk about stereotypes and how harmful they are. How you are more than what he might have assumed about you."

"Whatever," I said. "That's maybe sixty percent true. The other forty percent is that you sacrificed my comfort just to make yourself seem progressive. You put me in that shitty situation because you thought it would be shocking and exciting."

"Can we please talk about this somewhere else?" he said, pleading with his eyes. "Maybe in my classroom?"

I sighed heavily. "Fine."

Honestly, I didn't know why he cared.

I didn't realize it would be such a big deal to drop his class, but then, I didn't know anything about being a teacher. Maybe my complaint got Mr. Jordan in trouble. I had no idea.

But he just wasn't giving this up.

"I'm sorry," he said for the fifth time. "I really am. I never meant to upset you like this. I really didn't think it would hurt you."

"Then you didn't *think*," I said. My voice was shaking a little; some of my bravado had worn off. Here, separated by his desk, I was suddenly very aware of the fact that I was talking to a teacher, and old, deeply ingrained habits were reminding me that I was just a sixteen-year-old kid very much at the mercy of these random, underpaid adults. "It's not much of a leap," I said to him, speaking more calmly now, "to imagine something like that being hurtful. And anyway, this isn't even about you hurting my feelings."

"It's not?"

"No," I said. "It's about the fact that you think you're being helpful. But if you'd stopped to consider for even five seconds what my life was actually like you'd have realized you weren't doing me a favor. I don't need to hear any more people say stupid shit to my face, okay? I don't. I've had enough of that to last me a lifetime. You don't get to make an example out of me," I said. "Not like that."

"I'm sorry."

I shook my head. Looked away.

"What can I do to get you to come back to class?"

I raised an eyebrow at him. "I'm not looking to strike a deal."

"But we need your voice in the classroom," he said. "What you just said to me here, right now—I want to hear you say that in class. You're allowed to tell me when I'm messing up, too, okay? But if you walk away the second it gets hard, how will any of us ever learn? Who will be there to guide us?"

"Maybe you can look it up. Visit a library."

He laughed. Sighed. Sat back in his chair. "I get it," he said, throwing up his hands in defeat. "I do. It's not your job to educate the ignorant."

"No," I said. "It's not. I'm tired as hell, Mr. Jordan. I've been trying to educate people for years and it's *exhausting*. I'm tired of being patient with bigots. I'm tired of trying to explain why I don't deserve to be treated like a piece of shit all the time. I'm tired of begging everyone to understand that people of color aren't all the same, that we don't all believe the same things or feel the same things or experience the world the same way." I shook my head, hard. "I'm just—I'm sick and tired of trying to explain to the world why racism is bad, okay? Why is that my job?"

"It's not."

"You're right," I said. "It's not."

"I know."

"I don't think you do."

He leaned forward. "Come back to class," he said. "Please. I'm sorry."

Mr. Jordan was wearing me down.

I'd never talked to a teacher like this before, and I'd be lying if I said I wasn't surprised I was getting away with it. He also seemed—I don't know? He actually seemed genuine. It made me want to give him another chance.

Still, I said, "Listen, I appreciate your apology, but I don't know if you'd actually want me back in your class."

He seemed surprised. "Why not?"

"Because," I said, "if you pull another stunt like this I'm liable to tell you to go to hell in front of all your students."

He seemed unfazed. "I can accept these terms."

Finally, I said, "Fine."

Mr. Jordan smiled so big I thought it might break his face. "Yeah?"

"Yeah, whatever." I stood up.

"It's going to be a great semester," he said. "You won't regret it."

"Uh-huh."

Mr. Jordan stood up, too. "By the way—I'm really excited to see you guys perform in the talent show. Congratulations."

I froze. "Excuse me?"

"The school talent show," he said. He looked confused. "The breakdancing club—?"

"What about it?"

"Your brother signed you guys up two weeks ago. He didn't tell you? Your application was accepted today. It's a really big deal, actually—"

"Oh, *shit*," I said, and groaned.

"Hey—it'll be great—you guys will do great—"

"Yeah, I have to go," I said. And I had one foot out the door when Mr. Jordan called my name.

I turned back to look at him.

His eyes were suddenly sad. "I really hope you won't let this stuff get you down," he said. "Life gets way better after high school, I swear."

I wanted to say, *Then why are you still here?* But I decided to cut him some slack. Instead, I shot him a half smile and bolted.

FIFTEEN

I walked into practice and Navid clapped his hands together, grinned, and said, "Big news."

"Oh yeah?" I dropped my bag on the ground. I wanted to kill him.

"School talent show," he said, and smiled wider. "It's a couple weeks after we get back from winter break, which means we've got about three months to prepare. And we're going to start now."

"Bullshit, Navid."

His smile disappeared. "Hey," he said, "I thought you were going to be nicer now. What happened to that new plan?"

I rolled my eyes. "Why didn't you tell me you signed us up for the freaking school talent show?"

"I didn't think you'd mind."

"Well I mind, okay? I mind. I have no idea why you'd

think I'd want to perform in front of the whole school. I hate this school."

"Yes, but, to be fair," he said, pointing at me, "you kind of hate everything."

"You guys are okay with this?" I said, spinning around. Jacobi, Carlos, and Bijan had been pretending they couldn't hear our conversation, and they looked up, suddenly. "All three of you want to perform in front of the school?"

Carlos shrugged.

Bijan chose that moment to drink deeply from his water bottle.

Jacobi just laughed at me. "I mean, I'm not mad at it," he said. "It could be cool."

Great. So I was overreacting. I was the only one here who thought this was a stupid idea. That was just great.

I sighed, said, "Whatever," and sat down. I'd changed into my sneakers too quickly today and hadn't yet tied my shoes.

"Hey, it'll be fun," Navid said to me. "I promise."

"I can barely even hold a *pose* right now," I said, and glared at him. "How will that be fun? I'm going to make an ass out of myself."

"Let me worry about that, okay? You're getting better every day. We've still got time."

I grumbled something under my breath.

Bijan came over and sat next to me. I looked up at him out of the corner of my eye. "What?" I said.

"Nothing." He was wearing big, square diamond studs,

one in each ear. His eyebrows were perfect. His teeth were super white. I noticed this last bit because he was suddenly smiling at me.

"*What?*" I said again.

"What is your deal?" he said, and laughed. "Why are you sweatin' this so much?"

I finished tying my shoelaces. "I'm not. It's fine."

"All right," he said. "Get up."

"What? Why?"

"I'm going to teach you to do a backflip."

My eyes widened.

He waved a hand. "Up, please."

"Why?" I said.

Bijan laughed. "Because it's fun. You're small, but you look strong. Shouldn't be too hard for you."

It *was* hard.

In fact, I was pretty sure I nearly broke both my arms. And my back. But yeah, it turned out to be fun, too. Bijan had been, in a former life, a gymnast. His moves were so clean and strong I couldn't help but be surprised he was willing to waste his time here, with our little club. Still, I was grateful. Bijan seemed to feel sorry for me in a way that I found only a little demeaning, so I didn't mind his company. And it didn't bother me too much that he spent the rest of the hour basically making fun of me.

After what felt like my hundredth failed attempt at

a backflip, I finally fell down and didn't get back up. I was breathing hard. My arms and legs were shaking. Navid was walking around the dance room on his hands, doing scissor kicks. Jacobi was practicing windmills, a classic power move he'd long ago perfected; he was trying now to turn his windmills into flares in the same routine. Carlos was watching him, hands on his hips, a helmet under his arm. Carlos could do head spins for days; he didn't even need the helmet. I felt at once excited and inferior as I stared at them. I was, by far, the least talented of the group. *Of course* they felt more comfortable performing in public. They were already so good.

Me, on the other hand, I needed a lot of work.

"You'll be fine," Bijan said to me, and nudged my arm.

I looked up at him.

"And you're not the only one who hates high school, you know? You didn't invent that."

I raised an eyebrow. "Yeah, I didn't think I did."

"Good." He glanced at me. "Just checking."

"So, hey," I said to him, "if you're only eighty percent gay, wouldn't that make you bisexual?"

Bijan frowned. Faltered a moment. "Huh," he said. "Yeah, I guess."

"You don't know?"

He tilted his head at me and said, "I'm still figuring it out."

"Do your parents know?"

"Uh." He raised his eyebrows. "What do you think?"

"I'm guessing no?"

"Yeah, and let's keep it that way, okay? I'm not interested in having that conversation right now."

"Okay."

"Maybe, like, on my deathbed."

"Whatever you want," I said, and shrugged. "Your eighty percent is safe with me."

Bijan laughed. He just looked at me. "You don't make any sense, you know that?"

"What? Why not?"

He shook his head. Stared out across the room. "You just don't."

I didn't have a chance to ask him another question. Navid was shouting at me to grab my bag, because our time in the dance room was up.

"I'm hungry as hell," he said, as he jogged over to us. "You guys want to get something to eat?"

It hadn't occurred to me that there might be something strange about me, a sophomore, hanging out with a bunch of senior guys all the time. I never thought about it that way. Navid was my brother, and these were his friends. This was a familiar habitat for me. Navid had been infesting my personal space—at home, at school—with his many guy friends since forever, and, generally, I didn't care for it. He and his friends were always eating my food. Messing with my stuff. They'd walk out of my bathroom and say, with zero self-awareness, that they'd cracked a window in there but if I had any interest in self-preservation I might want to use a different toilet for a while.

It was *gross*.

My brother's friends always started out vaguely good-looking, but all it took was a single week of focused observation before these dudes made me want to barricade myself in my room.

So it wasn't until we were leaving the dance studio that I was suddenly reminded that I was in high school, and that, for some reason, Navid and his friends were kind of cool. Cool enough that a cheerleader would be inspired to speak to me.

I'd begun noticing them, all the time now. The cheerleaders. They were always around, after school, and it took me an embarrassing length of time to realize that they were probably around all the time because they were getting together for practice every day. So when we ran into a group of girls as we were leaving, I was no longer surprised. What surprised me was when one of them waved me over.

At first I was confused. I thought she was having a conniption. And I was so certain that this girl was not waving at *me* that I ignored her for a full fifteen seconds before Navid finally nudged me and said, "Uh, I think that girl is trying to get your attention."

It was crazy, but she was.

"That's nice," I said. "Can we go?"

"You're just going to ignore her?" Jacobi looked amazed, and not in a good way.

"There is a one hundred percent chance that she has no good reason to talk to me," I said. "So, yes. I'm going to ignore her."

Bijan shook his head at me. He almost—*almost*—smiled.

Navid shoved me forward. "You said you were going to be nice."

"No I didn't."

But they all looked so disappointed in me that I finally gave in. I loathed myself the entire twenty-five-foot walk over to her, but I did it.

The moment I was close enough, she grabbed my arm.

I stiffened.

"Hey," she said quickly. She wasn't even looking at me; she was looking behind me. "Who's that guy over there?"

Wow, there was little I hated more than this conversation.

"Uh, who are *you*?" I said.

"What?" She glanced at me. "Oh. I'm Bethany. Hey, how are you even friends with these guys?"

This was it. This, right here. This was why I didn't talk to people. "Is this why you called me over here? Because you want me to hook you up with one of these dudes?"

"Yeah. That one." She gestured with her head. "The one with the blue eyes."

"Who? Carlos?" I frowned. "The guy with the curly black hair?"

She nodded. "His name is Carlos?"

I sighed.

"Carlos," I shouted. "Will you come over here, please?"

He walked over, confused. But then I introduced him to Bethany, and he looked suddenly delighted.

"Have fun," I said. "Bye."

Bethany tried to thank me, but I waved her away. I'd never been so disappointed in my own gender. The quality of this female interaction had been worse than abysmal. And I was just about to leave when I was suddenly distracted by a familiar face.

It was Ocean, exiting the gym.

He had that large gym bag strapped across his chest and he looked like he'd taken a shower; his hair was wet and his cheeks were pink. I saw him for only a second before he crossed the hall into another room and disappeared.

My heart sank.

I hadn't talked to Ocean in three days. I wanted to. I really, really wanted to, but I was trying to do what I thought was the right thing. I didn't want to lead him on. I didn't want him to think that there was potential here, between us. He tried, twice, to catch up with me after class, but I brushed him off. I did my best to avoid his eyes. I didn't go online. I kept our bio conversations as brief and boring as possible. I was trying not to engage with him anymore, because I didn't want to give him the wrong idea. But I could tell he was both hurt and confused.

I didn't know what else to do.

There was a small, cowardly part of me that hoped Ocean would realize on his own that I wasn't an option worth exploring. He seemed fascinated by me in a way that felt familiar but also entirely new, and I wondered if his fascination would wear off, like it always did in these kinds of situations. I wondered if he'd learn to forget about me. Go back to his friends. Find a nice blond girlfriend.

It was confusing, I know, how I'd gone from wanting a new friend in this school to suddenly wishing I could hit *undo* on the whole thing. Though, to be fair, I'd been looking for a platonic friend, preferably female. Not a boyfriend, not anything even close to that. I'd just wanted, like, a normal teenage experience. I wanted to eat lunch with friends, plural. I wanted to go to the movies with someone. I maybe even wanted to pretend to give a shit about the SATs. I don't know. But I was beginning to wonder if a normal teenage experience was even a thing.

"Hey, can we go? I'm starving." It was Navid, tapping me on the shoulder.

"Oh. Yeah," I said. But I was still staring at the door through which Ocean had disappeared. "Yeah. Let's get out of here."

SIXTEEN

I showed up to Mr. Jordan's class the next day, as promised, but my return was weirder than I'd expected. I hadn't realized that everyone would've known—or even noticed—that I'd walked out of class and hadn't been back most of the week. I didn't think anyone would care. But when I took my normal seat, the kids in my little cluster looked at me like I'd sprouted wings.

"What?" I said. I dropped my bag on the ground next to me.

"Did you really try to drop the class?" This, from one of the girls. Her name was Shauna.

"Yeah," I said. "Why?"

"Wow." The other girl, Leilani, was staring at me. "That's crazy."

Ryan, the fourth member of our group—a guy who always

talked *at* me and never looked me in the eye—chose that moment to yawn. Loudly.

I frowned at Leilani. "Why is that crazy? Mr. Jordan made me super uncomfortable."

Neither of the girls seemed to think this was an acceptable answer.

"Hey, why did Ocean follow you out the other day? What was that about?" Leilani again.

Now I was truly stunned. I couldn't begin to imagine why they cared about any of this. I hadn't even realized Leilani knew who Ocean was. This class was an elective, so there was flexibility in the roster—we weren't all in the same grade; Leilani and Shauna, for example, were juniors. "I don't know," I said. "I guess he felt bad."

Shauna was about to ask me another question when Mr. Jordan clapped his hands together, hard, and called out a greeting.

"All right everyone, we're switching things up today." Mr. Jordan was dancing the cha-cha in front of the room. He was so weird. I laughed, and he stopped, caught my eye. He smiled and said, "Good to see you again, Shirin," and people turned to stare at me.

I stopped laughing.

"So," he said. He was speaking to the class again. "Are you guys ready for this?" He paused for just a second before he said, "New groups! Everyone stand up."

The class groaned, loudly, and I agreed with the collective

sentiment. I definitely didn't want to meet any more new people. I hated meeting new people.

But I also understood that this was kind of the point.

So I sighed, resigned, as Mr. Jordan started sorting us into new clusters. I ended up across the room, sitting with three new girls, and we all avoided looking at each other for a few minutes.

"Hey."

I turned, startled.

Ocean was sitting, not next to me, exactly, but near me. In a different group. He was leaning back in his chair. He smiled, but his eyes looked wary, a little worried.

"Hi," I said.

"Hi," he said.

He had a pencil behind his ear. I didn't think people actually did that, but he currently had an actual pencil behind his ear. It was so cute. He was so cute.

"You dropped this," he said, and held out a small, folded piece of paper.

I eyed the paper in his hand. I was pretty sure I hadn't dropped anything, but then again, who knew. I took it from him, and, just like that, the worry in his eyes warmed into something else.

I felt my heart speed up.

Has anyone else figured out that you're always listening to music in class? Are you listening to music right now? How do you listen to music all the time without failing all your classes? Why did you delete your AIM profile that first time we talked?

I have so many questions.

I looked back at him, surprised, and he smiled so hard he almost laughed. He looked very pleased with himself.

I shook my head, but I was smiling, too. And then I deliberately pulled the iPod out of my pocket and hit play.

When I turned back around in my seat, I nearly jumped out of my skin.

The three other girls in my cluster were now staring blankly at me, looking possibly more confused by my existence than I'd expected.

"Don't forget to introduce yourselves," Mr. Jordan bellowed. "Names are important!" And then he picked up the large mason jar that sat on his desk every day and said, "Today's topic is"—he pulled a piece of paper out of the jar, read it—"the Israeli-Palestinian conflict! This one should be really good," he said. "Hamas! Terrorism! Is Iran complicit? Talking points will be on the board! Have fun!"

I dropped my head onto my desk.

It will probably surprise no one to hear that I was terrible at ignoring Ocean.

I pretended, really hard, to appear uninterested in him, but that's all it was. I was just really good at pretending. I'd denied myself permission to think about him, which somehow made it so that I thought about him all the time.

I noticed him too much now.

He seemed to be everywhere, suddenly. So much so that I started wondering if maybe I was wrong, if maybe it wasn't mere coincidence that kept bringing us together. Maybe, instead, he'd always been there, and maybe I'd only just begun to see him. It was like when Navid bought that Nissan Sentra; before Navid got the car, I'd never, ever noticed one of them on the road before. Now I saw old Nissan Sentras everywhere.

This whole thing was stressing me out.

I felt nervous, even just sitting in the same class with him. Our work in bio had become more difficult than ever, simply because I was trying to dislike him and it wasn't working; he was almost bionically likable. He had this really calming presence that always made me feel like, I don't know, like I could let my guard down when I was with him.

Which, somehow, only made me more nervous.

I thought being quiet—speaking only when I absolutely had to—would help defuse whatever tension existed between us, but it only seemed to make things more intense. When we didn't talk, some invisible lever was still winding a coil between our bodies. In some ways, my silence was more telling than anything else. It was a breathless sort of standoff.

I kept trying to break away, and I couldn't.

Today—it was now Monday—I only made it through thirty minutes of ignoring Ocean in bio. I was tapping my pencil against a blank page in my notebook, avoiding the dead cat between us and instead trying to think of things to hate about him, when Ocean turned to me, apropos of nothing, and said,

"Hey, am I saying your name right?"

I was so surprised I sat up. Stared at him. "No," I said.

"What? Are you serious?" He laughed, but he looked upset. "Why didn't you tell me?"

I shrugged. Turned back to my notebook. "No one ever says my name right."

"Well, I'd like to," he said. He touched my arm, and I looked up again. "How am I supposed to say it?"

He'd been pronouncing my name *Shi-reen*, which was better than most people; most people had been saying it in two hard syllables: *Shir-in*, which was very wrong. It was actually pronounced *Shee-reen*. I tried to explain this to him. I tried to tell him that he had to roll the *r*. That the whole thing was meant to be pronounced softly. Gently, even.

Ocean tried, several times, to say it correctly, and I was genuinely touched. A little amused.

"It sounds so pretty," he said. "What does it mean?"

I laughed. I didn't want to tell him, so I shook my head.

"What?" he said. His eyes widened. "Is it bad?"

"No." I sighed. "It means *sweet*. I just think it's funny. I think my parents were hoping for a different kind of kid."

"What do you mean?"

"I mean no one has ever accused me of being sweet."

Ocean laughed. He shrugged, slowly. "I don't know," he said. "I guess you're not *sweet* exactly. But"—he hesitated; picked up his pencil, rolled it between his hands—"you're, just, like—"

He stopped. Sighed. He wouldn't look at me.

And I didn't know what to do. I didn't know what to say. I definitely wanted to know what he was thinking but I didn't want *him* to know that I wanted to know what he was thinking, so I just sat there, waiting.

"You're so strong," he said finally. He was still staring at his pencil. "You don't seem to be afraid of anything."

I didn't know what I'd been hoping he'd say, exactly, but I was surprised. So surprised, in fact, that I was rendered, for a moment, speechless.

I so rarely felt strong. Mostly I felt scared.

When he finally looked up, I was already staring at him.

"I'm afraid of lots of things," I whispered.

We'd just been looking at each other, hardly breathing, when suddenly the bell rang. I jumped up, feeling unexpectedly embarrassed, grabbed my things, and disappeared.

He texted me that night.

what are you afraid of? he wrote.

But I didn't respond.

I walked into bio the next day, prepared to make the herculean effort to be an aloof, boring lab partner yet again, when the whole thing finally just fell apart. Collapsed.

Ocean ran into me.

I don't know what happened, exactly. He'd sidestepped too fast—someone had been rushing between the lab tables with a sopping dead cat in their hands—and he'd slammed into me just as I was walking up. It was like something out of a movie.

His body was hard and soft and my hands flew up, found purchase around his back and he caught me, wrapped his arms around me, said, "Oh— Sorry—" but we were still pressed together when instinct forced my head up, surprised, and I tried to speak but instead my lips grazed his neck, and for one second I could breathe him in, and he let go, too fast, and I stumbled; he caught my hands, and I looked at him, his eyes wide, deep, scared, and I pulled back, broke the connection, reeling.

It was the clumsiest production of physical interaction; the whole thing lasted no more than several seconds. I'm sure no one else even noticed it happen. But I saw him touch his neck where my mouth had been. I felt my heart stutter when I remembered his arms around me.

And neither of us spoke for the rest of the period.

I grabbed my bag when the bell rang, ready to run for my life, when he said my name and only the very basic rules of etiquette held me in place. My heart was racing, had been racing for an hour. I felt electric, like an overcharged battery. Things were sparking inside of me and I needed to go away, get away from him. Sitting next to him all through class had been profound and excruciating.

I'd had many unimportant, insignificant crushes on boys before. I'd had pathetic daydreams and silly fantasies and had devoted many pages in my journal to entirely forgettable people I'd known and quickly discarded over the years.

But I had never, ever touched someone and felt like this: like I was holding electricity inside of me.

"Hey," he said.

It took a lot of effort to turn around, but I did, and when I did, he looked different. Like maybe he was just as terrified as I was.

"Hi," I said, but the word didn't make much sound.

"Can we talk?"

I shook my head. "I have to go."

I watched him swallow, the Adam's apple moving up and down in his throat. He said, "Okay," but then he walked up to me, walked right up to me, and I felt something pop inside my head. Brain cells dying, probably. He wasn't looking at me, he was looking at the two inches of floor between us and I thought maybe he was going to say something but he didn't. He just stood there, and I watched the gentle motions of his chest as he breathed, in and out, up and down, and I felt a faint spinning in my head, and like my body had overheated, and my heart would not stop, could not stop racing and finally he whispered the words—without touching me, without even looking at me—he said, "I just need to know," he said, "are you feeling this, too?"

He looked up, then. Looked me in the eye.

I didn't say anything. I couldn't remember how. But he must've found something in my eyes because he suddenly exhaled, softly; he glanced, just once, at my lips, and he stepped back. Grabbed his bag.

And left.

I wasn't sure I would ever recover.

SEVENTEEN

I was a complete idiot at practice.

I couldn't remember how to do simple things. I kept thinking about the fact that Ocean and I had only touched *by accident* and what if we'd touched *on purpose* and wow, I wondered if my head would just explode. I also kept thinking that I didn't want to get my heart broken. I didn't know what could ever come of this, of us, or how we'd ever navigate these murky waters and I didn't know what to do.

I felt like I'd lost control.

Suddenly all I could think about was kissing him. I'd never kissed anyone before. A boy had been dared to kiss me once and he'd kissed me on the cheek and it was not repugnant, exactly, but the whole thing had been so awkward that even the memory bothered me.

I was, in this regard, woefully underprepared.

I knew my brother had kissed lots of girls. I didn't know what else he'd done, and I didn't ask. In fact, I'd had to tell him to shut up about it several times already because for some reason he always felt comfortable sharing these details with me. I think my parents had known about his many relationships, but I also think they were happy to pretend they didn't. I was also pretty sure my parents would've had simultaneous heart attacks if they knew I was even *thinking* about kissing a boy, which, surprisingly, did not at all factor into my considerations.

There was nothing about the idea of kissing Ocean that felt wrong to me. I just didn't see how kissing him would help anything.

Just then, my brother threw his water bottle at me.

I looked up.

"You okay?" he said. "You look sick."

I felt sick. Like maybe I had a fever. I was sure I didn't, but it was weird how hot my skin felt. I wanted to climb into bed and hide. "Yeah," I said, "I feel kind of weird. Do you mind if I cut out early? Head home?"

My brother came forward, collected his bottle. Pressed a hand against my forehead. His eyes widened. "Yeah. I'll take you home," he said.

"Really?"

He looked suddenly annoyed. "You think I'd let my sister walk home with a fever?"

"I don't have a fever."

"Yeah," he said. "You do."

He wasn't wrong. I'd gotten home earlier than usual, so my mom and dad weren't back from work yet. Navid brought me water, gave me medicine, and tucked me into bed. I didn't feel sick, though, I just felt strange, and I didn't know how to explain it. There was nothing apparently wrong with me except that my temperature had spiked.

Still, I slept.

When I awoke, the house was dark. I felt woozy. I blinked and looked around, parched, and grabbed the bottle of water Navid had left me. I drained the bottle, rested my hot head against the cool wall and wondered what the hell had happened to me. Only then did I notice my phone on my bedside table. I had five unread messages.

The first two were from six hours ago.

hey
how was practice?

There were three more messages, sent ten minutes ago. I checked the time; it was two in the morning.

you're probably asleep
but if you're not, will you call me?

(i'm sorry for using up all of your text messages)

I wasn't sure I was in the right headspace to call anyone at the moment, but I didn't think it through. I pulled up his number, called him right away—and then I burrowed under my covers, pulling the sheet up over my head to help muffle my voice. I didn't want to have to explain to my parents why I was wasting precious phone minutes talking to a boy at two in the morning. I had no idea what I'd say.

Ocean picked up on the first ring, which made me wonder if maybe he was hiding from his mom, too. But then he said "Hi," out loud, like a normal person, and I realized that no, it was just me whose parents were up her ass all the time.

"Hi," I whispered. "I'm hiding under my covers."

He laughed. "Why?"

"Everyone is asleep," I said quietly. "My mom and dad would kill me if they found me on my phone this late. Also, minutes are expensive."

He said, "Sorry," but he didn't sound sorry.

"I have a fever, by the way. I've been in bed this whole time," I explained. "I just woke up and saw your messages."

"What?" he said, alarmed. "What happened?"

"I don't know."

"Do you feel okay now?"

"I feel a little weird, but I'm okay, I think."

He was quiet just a beat too long.

"You still there?" I said.

"Yeah. I just—I didn't think about it until you said it, but I haven't been feeling great, either."

"Really?"

"Yeah," he said. "I just . . ."

I felt my head sparking again.

"Can we please talk about this?" His voice was soft, but scared. "I know you've been avoiding me but I don't know why and if we don't talk about this I just— I don't—"

"Talk about what?"

"Us," he said, the word a little breathless. "Us, *God*, I want to talk about us. I can't even think straight around you." And then, "I don't know what's happening anymore."

I felt my mind slow down even as my heart sped up. An awful, wonderful nervousness seized me around the throat.

I felt paralyzed.

I wanted so desperately to say something, but I didn't know what to say, how to say it, or whether I should even bother. I couldn't seem to decide. I was suddenly overthinking everything. And we'd been lost in the silence for several seconds when he finally said—

"Is it just me? Am I imagining this?"

The sound of his voice broke my heart. I had no idea how Ocean could be this brave. I had no idea how he could make himself this vulnerable. There were no games with him. There were no confusing, meandering statements with him. He just put himself out there, his heart exposed directly to the elements, and wow, I respected him for it.

But it scared me so much.

In fact, I was beginning to wonder whether my fever wasn't simply a consequence of this, of him, of this whole situation, because the more he spoke, the more delirious I felt. I felt my head swimming, my mind slowly evaporating.

I closed my eyes. "Ocean," I finally whispered.

"Yes?"

"I—I just—"

I stopped. Tried to steady my head. I could hear him breathing. I could feel him waiting for something, anything, and I could feel my heart ripping open and I realized there was no point lying about this. I thought he deserved to know the truth, at least.

"You're not imagining it," I said.

I heard his hard exhale. When he spoke, his voice was a little rough. "I'm not?"

"No. You're not. I feel it, too."

Neither of us said anything for a while. We just sat there in the silence, listening to each other breathe.

"So why are you pushing me away?" he said finally. "What are you afraid of?"

"*This*," I said. My eyes were still closed. "I'm afraid of this. There's nowhere for this to go," I said to him. "There's no future here—"

"Why not?" he said. "Because of your parents? Because I'm some random white guy?"

My eyes flew open and I laughed, but it made a sad sound. "No," I said. "Not because of my parents. I mean, it's true that my parents wouldn't approve of you, yeah, but not because you're a white guy. My parents wouldn't approve of *any* guy," I said. "In general. It's not just you. Anyway, I don't even care about that." I sighed, hard. "It's not because of that."

"Then why?"

I was quiet for too long, but he didn't push me to speak. He didn't say a word. He just waited.

Finally, I broke open the silence.

"You're a really nice person," I said to him. "But you don't know how complicated something like this would be. You don't know how different your life would be with me," I said. "You just don't know."

"What do you mean?"

"I mean the world is really awful, Ocean. People are super racist."

Ocean was quiet for a full second before he finally said, stunned, "*That's* what you're worried about?"

"Yes," I said quietly. "Yes."

"Well I don't care what other people think."

My head was overheating again. I felt unsteady.

"Listen," he said softly, "This doesn't have to be anything serious. I just want to get to know you better. I just— I mean I *accidentally* ran into you and I haven't been able to breathe straight for hours," he said, his voice tight again. "I feel kind of crazy. Like I can't— I mean— I just want to know what this is," he said finally. "I just want to know what's happening right now."

My heart was beating too hard. Too fast.

I whispered, "I've been feeling the same way."

"You have?"

"Yes," I said softly.

He took a deep breath. He sounded nervous. "Could we just—can we maybe just spend some time together?" he said. "Outside of school? Maybe somewhere far, far away from our disgusting lab assignment?"

I laughed. I felt a little dizzy.

"Is that a yes?"

I sighed. I wanted, so badly, to just say yes. Instead, I said, "Maybe. But no marriage proposals, okay? I get too many of those as it is."

"You're making jokes right now?" Ocean laughed. "You're, like, breaking my heart, and you're making jokes right now. Wow."

"Yeah," I sighed. I didn't know what was wrong with me. I was smiling.

"Wait—what did that *yeah* mean? Is that a yes to hanging out with me?"

"Sure."

"Sure?"

"Yes," I whispered. "I'd really like to hang out with you." I felt at once nervous and happy and terrified, but I could feel my temperature spiking again. I really felt like I might pass out. "But I should go," I said. "I'll call you later, okay?"

"Okay," he said. "Okay."

We hung up.

And I didn't get out of bed for three days.

EIGHTEEN

I was basically immobile the rest of the week. The fever finally broke on Friday, but my mom still made me stay home. I tried to tell her I was fine, that I had no other symptoms, but she didn't listen. I'd never developed a cold. I had no aches and pains in my body. I felt nothing but the heat in my head.

I felt a bit like my brain had been steamed.

Ocean had texted me, but I'd had so few moments of clarity that I never got around to texting him back. I figured he'd find out, one way or another, that I was still sick, but I never imagined he'd seek out my brother.

Navid came to visit me on Friday, after school. He sat down on my bed and flicked me in the forehead.

"Stop," I mumbled. I turned, buried my face in the pillow.

"Your boyfriend was looking for you today."

I turned back so fast I nearly snapped my neck. "Excuse me?"

"You heard what I said."

"He's not my boyfriend."

Navid raised his eyebrows. "Well, uh, I don't know what you did to this kid who is apparently not your boyfriend," he said, "but I'm pretty sure he's in love with you."

"Shut up," I said, and turned my face back into the pillow.

"I'm not kidding."

I flipped him off without looking.

"Whatever," Navid said. "You don't have to believe me. I just thought you should know. He's worried. Maybe you should call him."

Now I frowned. I readjusted slowly, folding a pillow under my neck, and stared at my brother. "Are you for real right now?"

Navid shrugged.

"You're not threatening to kick his ass?" I said. "You're telling me to *call* him?"

"I feel bad for the guy. He seems nice."

"Um." I laughed. "Okay."

"I'm serious," Navid said, and stood up. "And I'm only going to give you one piece of advice, okay? So listen closely."

I rolled my eyes.

"If you're not interested," he said, "tell him now."

"What? What are you talking about?"

Navid shook his head. "Just don't be mean."

"I'm not mean."

My brother was already at the door when he laughed. Hard. "You are *brutal*," he said. "And I don't want to see this dude get his heart shattered all over the place, okay? He seems so innocent. He clearly has no idea what he's getting himself into."

I stared at Navid, dumbfounded.

"Promise me," he said. "Okay? If you don't like him, let him go."

But I did like him. The problem wasn't knowing whether or not I liked him. The problem was that I didn't *want* to like him.

I could already see the future. I could imagine us going out somewhere, anywhere, and someone saying something awful to me. I could imagine his paralysis; I could imagine the awkwardness that would wash over us both, how we'd try to pretend it hadn't happened, even as I was filled slowly with mortification; I knew how such an experience would, inevitably, make him self-conscious about spending time with me, how he'd one day realize he didn't want to be seen with me in public. I could see him introducing me to the people in his world, see their thinly veiled disgust and/or disapproval, see how being with me would make him realize that his own friends were closet racists, that his parents were happy to make general pleasantries with the nonconforming among us so long as we never tried to kiss their children.

Being with me would puncture Ocean's safe, comfortable bubble. Everything about me—my face, my fashion—had become political. There was a time when my presence only confused people; I used to be just a regular weirdo, the kind of unfathomable entity that was easily disregarded, easily discarded. But one day, in the aftermath of a terrible tragedy, I'd woken up in the spotlight. It didn't matter that I was just as shaken and horrified as everyone else; no one believed my grief. People I'd never met were suddenly accusing me of murder. Strangers would scream at me in the street, at school, in the grocery store, at gas stations and restaurants to go home, go home, *go back to Afghanistan you camel-fucking terrorist.*

I wanted to tell them I lived down the block. I wanted to tell them I'd never been to Afghanistan. I wanted to tell them I'd only met a camel once, on a trip to Canada, and that the camel was infinitely kinder than the humans I'd met.

But it never mattered what I said anymore. People talked over me, they talked *for* me, they discussed me without ever asking my opinion. I'd become a talking point; a statistic. I was no longer free to be only a teenager, only a human, only flesh and blood—no, I had to be more than that.

I was an outrage. An uncomfortable topic of conversation.

And already I knew that this—whatever this was with Ocean—could only end in tears.

So I didn't call him.

NINETEEN

I didn't think I was doing the right thing by ignoring him again, I really didn't. I just didn't know what else to do. I didn't have all the answers. I cared about Ocean, and in my own, confusing way, I was trying to protect him. I was trying to protect the both of us. I wanted to go back to being acquaintances; I wanted us to be kind to each other and call it a day.

We were sixteen, I thought.

This would pass.

Ocean would go to prom with a nice girl with an easily pronounced name and I would move on, literally, when my dad inevitably got a higher-paying job elsewhere and would announce, proudly, that we'd be moving to an even better city, a better neighborhood, a better future.

It would be fine. Or something akin to fine.

The only trouble with my plan, of course, was that Ocean did not agree with it.

I showed up to Mr. Jordan's class on Monday, but I almost certainly failed that particular session because I said nothing, all period, and for two reasons:

1. I was still getting over the inexplicable heat in my head, and
2. I was trying not to draw attention to myself.

I didn't look at Ocean in class. I didn't look at anyone. I pretended not to pay attention because I hoped that Ocean would take the hint and stop talking to me.

It was a stupid plan.

I'd only just escaped the classroom, and I was darting down a deserted corridor when he found me. He caught my arm and I turned around. He looked nervous. A little pale. I wondered what I looked like to him.

"Hi," he whispered.

"Hi," I said.

He still hadn't let go of me; his fingers were wrapped around my forearm like a loose bracelet. I stared at his hand. I didn't actually want him to let go, but when he saw me staring he startled. Dropped my arm.

"I'm sorry," he said.

"For what?"

"For whatever I did," he said. "I did something wrong,

didn't I? I messed something up."

My heart sank. Flatlined. He was so nice. He was so nice and he was making this so hard.

"You didn't do anything wrong," I said. "I promise."

"No?" But he still looked nervous.

I shook my head. "I really have to go to class, okay?" I turned to go, and he said my name like a question. I looked back.

He stepped closer. "Can we talk? At lunch?"

I studied his eyes, the pain he was trying to hide, and I realized then that things had gone too far. I'd let things get too far and now I couldn't just ignore him and hope he would go away. I couldn't be that cruel. No, I'd actually have to tell him—in clear, focused sentences—what was about to happen. That we needed to stop this, whatever it was.

So I said okay.

I told him where my tree was. I told him to meet me there.

The thing I had no way of anticipating, of course, was that someone else would already be waiting for me.

Yusef was leaning against my tree.

Yusef.

Wow, I'd nearly forgotten about Yusef.

I still thought he was a really good-looking guy, and I'd be lying if I said I hadn't wondered about him once or twice in the last couple of weeks, but, for the most part, he'd slipped my mind. I had no reason to keep thinking about him, because I so rarely saw him around school.

And I had no idea what he was doing here.

I wanted him to leave, but Ocean hadn't yet arrived and I was already nervous enough about the conversation we were about to have; I didn't want to have to deal with asking Yusef to go somewhere else, too. Plus, it didn't seem fair for me to lay claim to public property. So I pulled out my phone, made a sharp left, and started texting Ocean to meet me elsewhere.

Yusef called my name.

I looked back, surprised, the unfinished text message still unsent. "Yeah?"

"Where are you going?" He walked over. He was smiling.

Maybe on a different day, at a different time, I would've been interested in his smile. Today, I was far too distracted.

"I'm sorry," I said, "I'm looking for someone."

"Oh," he said, and followed my gaze.

I was squinting out toward the quad, where most of the student body gathered for lunch every day. The quad was, as a result, a place I nearly always avoided, so I didn't really know what I was searching for as I looked around. But Yusef was still talking, and I was suddenly annoyed, which wasn't fair. Yusef couldn't have known the deep preoccupation of my mind. Nothing he'd said to me was offensive—it wasn't even unwelcome—it was just bad timing.

"I wanted to come back and check on my tree," he was saying. "I was hoping you'd be here."

"That's nice," I said, still frowning into the distance.

Yusef tilted his head into my line of sight. "Anything I can do to help?"

"No," I said, "I just—"

"Hey."

I spun around. My sudden relief was replaced, in an instant, by apprehension. Ocean had arrived, but he looked confused. He was staring at Yusef, who was standing too close to me.

I put five feet between us.

"Hey," I said, and tried to smile. Ocean turned in my direction, but he still seemed uncertain.

"This is who you were looking for?" Yusef again. He sounded surprised.

It took a concerted effort to keep from telling Yusef to go away, that this was obviously a bad time for small talk, that he clearly had no idea how to read social cues—

"Hey man, what's going on," Yusef said, the question almost like a statement, and reached forward to shake Ocean's hand. Except he didn't shake it, exactly. He did that thing that guys do sometimes, when they pull each other in and do a kind of hug-slap. "You know Shirin?" he said. "Small world."

Ocean allowed the gesture, accepting Yusef's friendly bro-hug involuntarily, and I was guessing only because he was a nice, polite person. His eyes, however, looked almost angry. Ocean didn't say a word to Yusef. Didn't offer an answer or an explanation.

"Hey, um," I said, "I need to talk to my friend alone, okay? We're going to go somewh—"

"Oh, okay," Yusef said. "I'll be quick, then. I just wanted to know if you'll be fasting next week. My family always throws a massive *iftar* on the first night and you and your brother—and your parents, if they're up for it—are welcome to come."

What the hell?

"How did you know I have a brother?"

Yusef frowned. "Navid is in most of my classes. I put two and two together after the last time we talked. He didn't tell you?"

"Okay, um"—I glanced at Ocean, who looked suddenly like he'd been punched in the gut—"yeah, I'll have Navid get in touch with you. I have to go."

I only vaguely remembered saying a proper goodbye after that. Mostly I remembered the look on Ocean's face as we walked away.

He looked betrayed.

I told Ocean I didn't know where to go, that I wanted to speak with him somewhere quiet and private but the library was the only place I could think of and you're not allowed to talk in there, not really, and he said, "My car is in the parking lot."

That was all he said. I followed him to his car in silence, and it wasn't until we were sitting inside, doors closed on our own little world, that he looked at me and said, "Are you"—he sighed and turned suddenly away, studied the floor—"are you dating that guy? Yusef?"

"What? No."

He looked up.

"*No*. I'm not dating anyone."

"Oh." His shoulders slumped. We were sitting in the back seat of his car, facing each other, and he leaned against the door behind him, rested his head against the window. He looked worn-out. He ran a hand down the length of his face, and finally, finally, he said, "What happened? What happened between now and the last time we talked?"

"I think maybe I had too much time to think about it."

He looked heartbroken. There was no other way to put it. And he sounded heartbroken when he said, "You don't want to be with me."

Ocean was so straightforward. Everything about him felt honest and decent and I really admired him for it. But right now his honesty was making this conversation harder than it needed to be.

I'd had a plan.

I'd had it all worked out in my head; I'd hoped to tell a story, paint a picture, illustrate very, very clearly why this whole thing was doomed, and why we should avoid hurtling toward the inevitable and painful dissolution of whatever it was we were building here.

But all my carefully thought-out reasons felt suddenly

small. Stupid. Impossible to articulate. Looking into his eyes had flipped tables in my head; my thoughts were now tangled and disorganized and I didn't know how else to do this but to throw my feelings at him in no particular order.

Still, I was taking too long. I was silent for too long.

I was fumbling.

Ocean sat up, sat forward. He leaned in and I felt my chest tighten. I could suddenly smell him—his particular, familiar scent—everywhere. I was sitting in his *car*, I realized, and it had only just occurred to me to look around, to get a sense of where we were, who he was. I wanted to catalog the moment, capture it in words and pictures. I wanted to remember this. I wanted to remember him.

I'd never wanted to remember anyone before.

"Hey," he said, but he said it softly. I don't know what he saw in my face, what he'd caught in my eyes or in my expression but he seemed suddenly different. Like maybe he'd realized that I'd fallen, hard, and that this wasn't easy for me, that I didn't actually want to walk away.

I met his eyes.

He touched my cheek, his fingers grazing my skin, and I gasped. Leaned back. It was unexpected. I overreacted. I was suddenly breathing too hard, my head full of fire again.

"I'm sorry," I said, "I can't do this."

"Why not?"

"Because," I said. "Because."

"Because why?"

"Because it won't work." I was flustered. I sounded stupid. "It just won't work."

"Isn't that up to us?" he said. "Don't we have control over whether or not this works?"

I shook my head. "It's not that simple. You don't get it. And it's not your fault that you don't get it," I said, "but you just don't know what you don't know. You can't see it. You can't see how different your life would be—how being with me, spending time with someone like me—" I stopped. Struggled for words. "It would be hard for you," I said, "with your friends, your family—"

"Why are you so sure that I care what other people think?"

"You're going to care," I said.

"No I won't. I already don't."

"You say that now," I said, shaking my head. "But you don't know. You're going to care, Ocean. You're going to care."

"Why can't you let me decide what I'm going to care about?"

I was still shaking my head. I couldn't look at him.

"Listen to me," he said, and he took my hands, and I didn't realize until that exact moment that my own hands were shaking. He squeezed my fingers. Tugged me closer. My heart felt wild.

"Listen to me," he said again. "I don't care what other people think. I don't care, okay?"

"You do," I said quietly. "You think you don't, but you do."

"How can you say that?"

"*Because*," I said, "because I always say that. I always say that I don't care what other people think. I say it doesn't bother me, that I don't give a shit about the opinions of assholes but it's not true," I said, and my eyes stung as I said it. "It's not true, because it hurts every time, and that means I still care. It means I'm still not strong enough because every time someone says something rude, something racist—every time some mentally ill homeless person goes on a terrifying rampage when they see me crossing the street—it *hurts*. It never stops hurting. It only gets easier to recover.

"And you don't know what that's like," I said. "You don't know what my life is like and you don't know what it'd be like to become a part of it. To tell the universe you're on my side. I don't think you understand that you'd be making yourself a target. You'd be risking the happy, comfortable world you live in—"

"I don't live in a happy, comfortable world," he said suddenly, and his eyes were bright, intense when he said it. "And if the life I've got is supposed to be some example of happiness then the world is even more messed-up than I thought it was. Because I'm not happy, and I don't want to be like my parents. I don't want to be like everyone else I know. I want to choose how to live my own life, okay? I want to choose who to be with."

I could only stare at him, my heart beating hard in my chest.

"Maybe you care about what other people think," he said, and his voice was softer now. "And that's fine. But I really, truly, don't."

"Ocean," I whispered. "*Please.*"

He was still holding my hands and he felt safe and real and I didn't know how to tell him that I hadn't changed my mind, not even a little bit, and that the more he spoke the more I felt my heart implode.

"Please don't do this," he said. "Please don't walk away from me because you're worried about the opinions of racists and assholes. Walk away from me because you hate me," he said. "Tell me you think I'm stupid and ugly and I swear this would hurt less."

"I can't do that," I said. "I think you're wonderful."

He sighed. He wasn't looking at me when he said, "That's not helping."

"I also think you have really beautiful eyes."

He looked up, surprised. "You do?"

I nodded.

And he laughed, softly. He took my hands and pressed them against his chest and he felt strong. I could feel his heart racing under my palms. I could feel the outline of his body under his shirt and it made me a little dizzy.

"Hey," he said.

I met his eyes.

"You don't have anything offensive you'd like to say to me? Maybe make me hate you a little bit?"

I shook my head. "I'm sorry, Ocean. I really am. For everything."

"I just don't understand how you can be so sure," he said, and his eyes were sad again. "How can you be *so sure* that this won't work that you won't even give it a chance?"

"Because I already know," I said. "I already know what's going to happen."

He said, "You don't know what's going to happen."

"Yes," I said, "I do. I already know how this story goes."

"No. You think you do. But you have no idea what's about to happen."

"Yes," I said, "yes, I—"

And he kissed me.

It wasn't the kind of thing I'd read about. It wasn't quick; it wasn't soft and simple. He kissed me and I felt actual euphoria, like all my senses had merged and I was reduced to breaths and heartbeats and repeating integers. It was nothing like I thought it would be. It was better, it was infinitely better, in fact it may have been the best thing that had ever happened to me. I'd never done this before but somehow I didn't need a manual. I collapsed into it, into him, and he parted my lips and I loved it, I loved how he felt, how he tasted sweet and warm and I felt delirious, I was pressed against the passenger

171

door and my hands were in his hair and I wasn't thinking about anything, I was thinking about nothing, nothing but this, but the impossibility of *this* when he broke away, gasping for air. He pressed his forehead against mine and he said *Oh*, he said, *Wow*, and I thought it was over and he kissed me again. And again. And again.

I heard the bell ring, somewhere. I heard it like I was hearing sound for the first time.

And then, suddenly, my mind was returned to me.

It was like a sonic boom.

I sat up too fast. My eyes were wild. I was nearly hyperventilating. "Oh my God," I said. "Oh my God, Ocean—"

He kissed me again.

I drowned.

When we broke apart we were both breathing hard, but he was staring at me and he said *Holy shit*, but softly, like he was speaking only to himself, and I said, "I have to go, I have to go" and he just looked at me, his mind not yet fully awake and I grabbed my backpack and his eyes widened, suddenly alert, and he said—

"Don't go."

"I have to go," I said. "The bell rang. I have to go to class."

This was obviously a lie, I didn't give a shit about class, I was just a coward, trying to run away, and I grabbed the handle, pushed the door open, and he said, "No, wait—"

And I said "Maybe we should just be friends, okay?" and I jumped out of the car before he could kiss me again.

I looked back, just once, and saw him staring at me through the window as I walked away.

He looked stunned.

And I knew I'd just made everything so much worse.

TWENTY

I ditched bio.

Our time with the dead cat had officially come to an end—we'd be resuming regular bookwork for a while until we received our next lab assignment—but I still couldn't face it. I didn't know what I'd do if I saw him again. Things were still too raw. My body felt like it was now made entirely of nerves, like muscle and bone had been removed to make room for all this new emotion.

Things between us had officially spiraled out of control.

I'd been touching my lips all afternoon, confused and amazed and a little suspicious that I'd imagined the whole thing. The heat in my head wouldn't abate. I had no idea what had happened to my life. But the insanity of the day only made me more anxious to get to practice. Breakdancing gave me focus and control; when I worked hard, I saw results. I liked how simple it was.

Straightforward.

"What the hell is going on with you?"

This was how my brother said hello to me.

I dropped my bag on the floor. Jacobi, Bijan, and Carlos were clustered in a far corner of the dance room, pretending not to stare at me.

"What?" I said, trying to read their faces. "What's wrong?"

Navid squeezed his eyes shut. Opened them. Looked up at the ceiling. Ran both hands through his hair. "I told you to *call* him," he said. "I didn't tell you to *make out* with him."

I felt suddenly paralyzed.

Horrified.

Navid was shaking his head. "Listen," he said, "I don't care, okay? I don't care about you kissing some dude—I never thought you were some kind of a saint—but you have to be careful. You can't just go around making out with guys like him. People notice."

I finally managed to pry my lips apart, but when I spoke, the words sounded like whispers. "Navid," I said, trying really hard not to have a heart attack, "what are you talking about?"

Navid looked suddenly confused. He was staring at me like he wasn't sure if my panic was real. Like he didn't know if I was only pretending to act like I didn't know how on earth he'd found out I'd kissed someone for the very first time today.

"Cars," he said, "have windows."

"So what?"

"So," he said, irritated, "people saw you two together."

"Yes," I said, "I understand that, but who cares?" I was nearly shouting at him, my panic transforming too quickly into anger. "Why would anyone care? Why would anyone tell *you*?"

Navid frowned at me, hard. He still couldn't seem to decide whether or not I was screwing with him. "Do you even know anything about this guy?" he said. "This Ocean kid?"

"Of course I do."

"Then I don't know why you're so confused."

I was breathing too hard. I wanted to scream. "Navid," I said carefully, "I swear to God if you don't tell me what the hell is going on right now I'm going to kick you in the crotch."

"Hey," he said, and cringed, "there's no need to get violent."

"*I don't understand*," I said, and I really was shouting now. "Why would anyone give two shits about who I do or don't decide to kiss? I don't know *anyone* at this school."

"Kid," he said, and suddenly he laughed. "You don't have to know anyone at this school. It's enough that he does. Your boyfriend is kind of a big deal."

"He's not my boyfriend."

"Whatever."

And then, panic creeping up my throat, squeezing—

"What do you mean," I said, "that he's kind of a big deal?"

"He's, like, their golden boy. He's on the varsity basketball team."

And I had to sit down, right there, my head suddenly spinning. I felt sick. Legitimately nauseous. I didn't know anything about basketball. I didn't care about sports, generally. I couldn't tell you shit about who did what with the ball or how to put it in a net or why it was so important to people that it did—but I'd learned one important thing about this school when I first got here:

They were obsessed with their basketball team.

They'd had a banner season the year prior and were still undefeated. I heard it every day over the morning announcements. I heard the constant, almost daily reminders about how the season was starting in just two weeks, that we should remember to support our team, we should make sure to attend local and away games, we should show up to pep rallies in school colors because school spirit was a thing, apparently. But I never went to pep rallies. I'd never been to a school game, not ever, not at any school. I only ever did the things I was absolutely required to do. I didn't volunteer. I didn't participate. I never joined the freaking Key Club. Just today I'd gotten an email reminding me that in fifteen days—on the day of the first basketball game of the season—everyone was supposed to dress head to toe in black; it was the school's idea of a joke: we were supposed to be pretending to attend the funeral of the opposing team.

I thought it was *ridiculous*.

And then—

"Wait," I said, confused. "How can he be on the varsity team? He's a sophomore."

Navid looked like he wanted to slap me upside the head. "Are you serious right now? How is it that I know more about this guy than you do? He's a freaking junior."

"But he's in two of my—" I started to say, and cut myself off.

Ocean was in my AP bio class. I was the one who was out of place there—I was actually a year ahead; normally AP bio was for juniors and seniors. The other class, Global Perspectives, was an elective.

Only freshmen weren't allowed to take it.

Ocean was a year older than me. This would explain why he seemed so certain about college when I'd asked him about it. He'd talked about choosing a school like it was a real thing; something to worry about, even. College was coming up for him. He'd be taking the SATs soon. He'd apply to schools next year.

He was a basketball player.

Oh my God.

I fell back, supine on the scuffed floor of the dance room,

and stared up at the recessed lighting. I wanted to disappear.

"Is it bad?" I said, and my voice sounded scared. "Is it really bad?"

I heard Navid sigh. He walked over to me, stared down. "It's not *bad*. It's just weird, you know. It's good gossip. People are confused."

"*Dammit*," I said, and squeezed my eyes shut.

This was exactly what I hadn't wanted.

TWENTY-ONE

When I got home that day I took comfort, for the very first time, in the fact that my parents never gave a shit about my school life. They were so oblivious, in fact, that I honestly wasn't sure my dad even knew where my school was. My coming home an hour late from a Harry Potter movie, now that—*that* was something to lose their heads over—but to imagine that my American high school might actually be scarier than the mean streets of suburbia? This leap seemed, somehow, impossible.

I could never get my parents to care about my life at school. They never volunteered for anything; they never showed up to school functions. They didn't read the newsletters. They didn't join the PTA or help chaperone school dances. My mom only ever set foot on campus to sign the papers for my registration. Otherwise, it just wasn't their thing. The only time they'd ever taken an interest was right after 9/11, when those guys pinned me down on my way home from school. Navid basically saved my life that day. He'd shown up with the cops just before those dudes could bash my head into the concrete. It had been a premeditated incident; someone had heard them talk, in class, about their plans to come after me, and tipped off Navid.

The cops never arrested anyone that day. The police lights had scared the guys enough to back off, so when the officers got out of the car I was sitting on the sidewalk, shaking, trying to untangle my scarf from around my neck. The cops sighed, told these two assholes to stop being stupid, and sent them home.

Navid was furious.

He kept telling them to do something, that those guys should be arrested, and the cops told him to calm down, that they were just kids, that there was no need to make this so dramatic. And then the officers walked over to me, where I was still sitting on the ground, and asked me if I was okay.

I didn't really understand the question.

"Are you *okay*?" one of the cops said again.

I wasn't dead, and for some reason I figured that must've meant I was okay. So I nodded.

"Listen," he said, "maybe you should reconsider this whole . . . getup." He gestured vaguely at my face. "Walking around like this all the time?" He shook his head. Sighed. "I'm sorry, kid, but it's like you're asking for it. Don't make yourself a target. Things are complicated in the world right now. People are scared. Do you understand?" And then, "Do you speak English?"

I remember shaking so hard I could barely sit straight. I remember looking up at the cop and feeling powerless. I remember staring at the gun holstered at his hip and being terrified.

"Here," he said, and offered me a card. "Call this number if you ever feel unsafe, okay?"

I took the card. It was a number for Child Protective Services.

That wasn't the beginning—this wasn't where my anger started—but it was a cauterizing moment I would never forget.

When I came home that day, still so stunned I hadn't figured out yet how to cry, my parents were transformed. It was the first time they'd ever seemed small to me. Petrified. My dad told me then, that day, that maybe I should stop wearing my scarf. If maybe it would be better for me that way. Easier.

I said no.

I told him I was fine, that everything would be fine, that they didn't need to worry, that I just needed to take a shower and I would be fine. It was nothing, I said. I told my parents I was fine because somehow I knew they needed the lie even more than I did. But when we moved away a month later, I knew it wasn't coincidence.

I'd been thinking about it a lot, lately. All the bullshit. The exhaustion that accompanied my personal choice to wrap a piece of cloth around my hair every day. I was so tired of dealing with this crap. I hated how that crap seemed to poison everything. I hated that I cared at all. I hated how the world kept trying to bully me into believing that I was the problem.

I felt like I could never catch a break.

I paused before pushing open the door to my house, my hand frozen on the handle. I knew my mom was cooking something because the crisp, cool air was infused with a delicious aroma. It was that perfect, perfect smell that would always take me back to the specific feeling of being a child: the scent of onions being sautéed in olive oil.

I felt my body relax.

I stepped inside, dropped my bag, and sank into a seat at the kitchen table. I leaned into the familiar, comforting sounds and smells of home, holding on to them like a lifeline, and I stared at my mom, who was, unquestionably, a human being of the superior variety. She dealt with so much. She'd survived so much. She was the bravest, strongest woman I'd ever known, and though I knew she faced all kinds of discrimination on a daily basis, she only rarely discussed it. Instead, she pushed through every obstacle, never complaining. I aspired to her levels of grace and perseverance. She worked all day long and came home just before my dad did, cooked up an amazing meal, and always had a smile, a slap to the back of the head, or a devastating piece of wisdom to impart.

Today, I wanted desperately to ask her what to do. But I knew I'd probably get the slap to the back of the head, so I reconsidered. Instead, I sighed. I looked at my phone. I had six missed calls and two text messages from Ocean—

> please call me
> please

—and I'd already looked at them about a hundred times. I kept staring at his words on my phone, feeling everything all at once. Just the memory of kissing him was enough to make me flush. I remembered him, every inch of him. My mind had recorded the moment in surprising detail, and I replayed it, over and over again. When I closed my eyes I could still feel him against my lips. I remembered his eyes, the way he'd looked at me, and my skin felt suddenly hot and electric. But when I thought about the fallout—the weirdness I would inevitably be forced to deal with at school the following day—I felt awful and embarrassed. I felt so dumb that I hadn't known his place in the hierarchy of this stupid school, I felt dumb that I'd never asked him what he did in his free time. I felt suddenly frustrated that I'd ditched all those pep rallies. I would've seen him when they paraded all the basketball players out into the center of the gym.

I would've known.

But I was now knee-deep in metaphorical cow shit, and I didn't know what to do. I didn't think ignoring Ocean was an option anymore—in fact, I'm not sure it ever was—but I also didn't know if talking to him would help, either. I'd already tried that. Today, in fact. That was the whole plan. I thought I was being mature by ending things in person. I could've been—in fact, would've preferred to have been—a coward who sent him a simple, unkind text message, telling him to leave me alone forever; but I'd wanted to do the right thing. I thought he deserved to have a proper conversation about it. But I'd somehow screwed everything up.

I dragged my feet that night. I stayed downstairs with my parents for far longer than I normally would. I ate dinner slowly, pushing my food around my plate long after everyone else had left the table and said, "I'm fine, just tired," to my parents' many concerned questions. Navid didn't say much to me except to shoot me a sympathetic smile, which I appreciated.

Nothing helped, though.

I was stalling for time. I didn't want to go up to my room where the closed door, the quiet, and the privacy would force me to make a decision. I was worried I would cave and call Ocean back, that I would hear his voice and lose my ability to be objective and then, inevitably, agree to *try*, to see what happens, to ultimately be alone with him on another, imminent occasion because wow, I desperately wanted to kiss him again. But I knew that this whole situation was hazardous to my health. So I put it off.

I managed to put it off until three in the morning.

* * *

I was lying in bed, wide-awake, completely incapable of shutting down either my brain or my body, when my phone buzzed on the table beside me. Ocean's message was at once simple and heartbreaking.

:(

I don't know why it was the sad-face emoticon that finally broke through my defenses. Maybe because it seemed so human. So real.

I picked up my phone because I was weak and I missed him and because I'd been lying there, thinking about him for hours already; my brain had succumbed long before he'd texted me.

Still, I knew better.

I clicked through to his number and I knew—even as I hesitated, my finger hovering over the call button—I *knew* that I was only inviting trouble. But I was also just, you know, a teenager, and my heart was still too soft. I was not a paragon of anything. I was definitely not a saint, as my brother had so clearly pointed out. Not a saint, not by a long shot.

So I called him.

Ocean sounded different when he picked up. Nervous. I heard him exhale, just once, before he said, "Hey."

"Hi," I whispered. I was hiding under my covers again.

He didn't say anything for a few seconds.

I waited.

"I really thought you weren't going to call me," he finally said. "Like, ever again."

"I'm sorry."

"Is it because I kissed you?" he said, and his voice was strained. "Was that—should I not have done that?"

I squeezed my eyes shut. This conversation was already doing things to my nerves. "Ocean," I said. "The kiss was amazing." I could hear him breathing. I could hear the way his breathing changed as I spoke. "The kiss was perfect," I said. "Kind of blew my mind."

He still didn't say anything.

And then—

"Why didn't you call me?" he whispered, and he sounded suddenly broken.

I knew then that this was it. Here it was. Here was the moment and I had to say it. In all likelihood it would kill me, but I had to say it.

"Because," I said. "I don't want to do this."

I heard the breath go out of him. I heard him turn away from the phone and swear and he said, "Is this because of the idiots at school? Because people saw us together?"

"That has a lot to do with it, yeah."

He swore again.

And then, quietly, I said, "I didn't know you were a basketball player."

It felt like a stupid thing to say, like it shouldn't have mattered what sport he played in his free time, but it had also begun to feel like a blatant omission on his end. He wasn't an average kid who'd decided to take up basketball in his spare time. He was a star player on the team. He'd apparently scored a lot of goals for someone his age. Baskets. Whatever. I'd looked it up online when I finally mustered the courage to lock myself in my room. There were articles about him in the local papers. Colleges were already circling him, talking about scholarships, talking about his potential, his future. I came across a few blogs and school-sponsored webcasts that were pretty illuminating, but when I dug deeper I discovered an anonymous LiveJournal account devoted only to him and his statistics over the years—a ton of numbers I couldn't understand about points and rebounds and steals—and I was suddenly confused.

Basketball was clearly a huge part of Ocean's life; it was obvious it had been for some time. And it had just occurred to me that, while yes, there was some fault on my end for not asking him more questions about himself, his omission was also strange. He'd never even *casually* mentioned basketball, not in a single one of our conversations.

So when he said, "I really wish you'd never found out," the whole thing began to make a little more sense to me.

And then—well, then he kind of broke open.

He said he started playing basketball after his parents split up, because his mom's new boyfriend was a youth basketball coach. He said he did it only because spending time with the new boyfriend seemed to make his mom happy. He played well, which made the boyfriend happy. Which made the mom happy. Which made him happy.

When his mom and the boyfriend split, Ocean was twelve. He tried to quit basketball, but his mom wouldn't let him. She said it was good for him. She said it made her happy to see him play so well. And then horribly, unexpectedly, his mom's parents died, he said, in this really tragic car accident, both of them at the same time, and his mom kind of lost her mind. But it was awful in two ways, he said. He said his mom was reeling from the emotional hit, but that she also, suddenly, didn't have to go to work anymore. Her parents had left everything to her—land, investments, all kinds of stuff—and he said it was all the money that eventually ruined his life.

He said he spent the next few years trying to keep his mom from crying all the time and that, eventually, they switched roles; one day he'd become the responsible one while she sort of collapsed inward and lost track of everyone but herself. When his mom finally pushed through the darkness, she became entirely about her social obligations. He said she became obsessed with finding another husband, and that it was awful and painful to watch.

"She never even notices when I'm not home," he said to me. "She's always out, always doing things with her friends or dating some new guy I have no interest in meeting. She's so convinced I'm going to be fine—she's always telling me I'm a good kid—and then she just disappears. She leaves money on the table and then, I don't know, I never know when I'm going to hear from her. She comes and goes. No schedule. Never commits to anything. She never even comes to my games. I left home for a week, once, just to see what would happen, and she didn't even call me. When I finally came home she seemed surprised to see me. She said she'd assumed I was away at basketball camp or something." He hesitated. "But it was the middle of the school year."

He said he kept playing basketball because his team had become a substitute for his family. It was the only one he had.

"But there's so much pressure," he said. "There's so much pressure to perform—and I'm really beginning to hate it. All of it. My coach is killing me every day, stressing me out about scouts and stats and these stupid awards and I don't know," he said. "I feel like I don't even know why I'm doing it anymore. I never played basketball because I loved it. It just became this thing that took over my entire life. It's like a parasite. And everyone is so *obsessed* with it," he said, anger bleeding into his voice. "It's like they can't even think about anything else. People only ever want to talk to me about basketball," he said. "Like it's all I am. Like it's *everything* I am. And it's not."

"Of course it's not," I said, but my voice was quiet. Sad. I understood too well what it was like to feel like you were defined by one superficial thing—to feel like you would never escape the box people had put you in.

It felt like you were going to explode.

"Ocean," I said, "I'm so sorry about your mom."

"I'm sorry I didn't tell you all of this sooner."

"It's really okay," I said. "I get it."

He sighed. "This is going to sound weird, I know—and really dumb—but I just—I loved how you never seemed to give a shit about who I was. You didn't know me. You didn't know *anything* about me. Like—not just that first day," he said, "but, like, for the next couple of months. I kept waiting for you to find out—I thought maybe you'd see me at a pep rally or show up to an event or something, I don't know, but you never did. You never even saw me after school."

"After school?" I said. But then I remembered, with a sudden moment of clarity, discovering him in the doorway of our dance room. And later, for a split second, leaving the gym. "What do you do after school?"

Ocean laughed. "See? This is exactly what I mean. I've been going to practice," he said. "We're always in the gym. I'd see you disappear into the dance room with those other guys and I always thought you'd, like"—he laughed again—"I don't know, I guess I thought maybe one day you'd walk by? See me in my basketball uniform? But it never happened. And I got so comfortable talking to you like this. Without the noise. It was like you actually wanted to get to know me."

"I did want to get to know you," I said. "I still do."

He sighed. "Then why walk away? Why throw this all away?"

"We don't have to throw anything away. We can just go back to being friends. We can still talk to each other," I said. "But we can have space, too. From each other."

"I don't want space," he said. "I've never wanted less space."

I didn't know what to say. My heart was hurting.

"Do you?" he said, and his voice was suddenly strained again. "Do you really want space from me? Honestly?"

"Of course not," I whispered.

He was quiet for a second or two. And when he next spoke, his words were soft. So sweet. He said, "Baby, please don't do this."

I felt a jolt of feeling flood through me. It left me a little breathless. The way he'd called me *baby*, the way he'd said it, it was nothing and everything all at once. There was so much emotion in the word, like he wanted me to be his, like he wanted us to belong to each other.

"Please," he whispered. "Let's just be together. Hang out. I want to spend more time with you."

He said he promised he wouldn't try to kiss me again and I wanted to say *don't you dare promise not to kiss me again* but I didn't.

Instead, I did exactly what I said I wouldn't do.

I gave in.

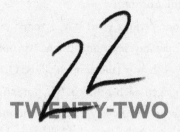

TWENTY-TWO

School was suddenly weird as hell.

I'd gone from being the kind of person people pretended they weren't staring at to being the kind of person who was openly gawked at. Some students didn't bother to hide the fact that they were talking about me as I passed. Some of them actually pointed at me as I walked by.

It was suddenly very good for me that I'd had so much practice ignoring faces. I stared at nothing as I walked; I looked at no one. Ocean and I had no plans; we hadn't discussed what today would look like simply because he was so certain it would be fine, that we were surrounded by idiots and none of it would matter. I knew he was wrong, of course, that all of it mattered, that we were actively swimming in the sewage that was high school and it wouldn't do us any good to pretend otherwise. I knew it was only a matter of time before it bubbled up into something ugly. But that first day, at least, was fairly uneventful. Sort of.

My first four periods were easy. I zoned out completely; hid earbuds under my scarf and listened to music while the world droned on. It was fine enough. Plus, Ocean and I had never really engaged each other in Mr. Jordan's class, so the whole thing was pretty low-key. Ocean found me after the bell rang, smiling so bright it lit up his whole face. He said hi. I said hi back. And then we split up. Our next classes were in different directions.

It was right around lunch when things hit peak weird.

This random girl cornered me. It was fast. Totally unexpected. She just about knocked me into one of the outdoor picnic benches.

I was stunned.

"Can I help you?" I snapped at her.

She was a beautiful Indian girl. She had long, dark hair, and really expressive eyes, and she was using those eyes today to express to me that she wanted to kill me. She looked livid. "You are a terrible role model for Muslim girls *everywhere*!" she said.

I was so surprised I actually laughed. Just once, but still.

I'd imagined today going badly in any number of different ways, but wow, wow, I had not been expecting *this*.

For a second, I thought she might be messing with me. I gave her a chance to take it back. To suddenly smile.

She didn't.

"Are you serious?" I said.

"Do you know how hard I have to work, every single day, to undo the kind of damage people like you do to our faith? To the image of Muslim women in general?"

Now I frowned. "What the hell are you talking about?"

"You are not allowed to go around kissing boys!" she cried.

I looked her over. "Have you never kissed a boy?"

"This isn't about me," she huffed, "this is about you. You wear *hijab*," she said. "You're disrespecting everything you're supposed to stand for."

"Um. Okay." I squinted at her. Half smiled. Flipped her off and kept walking.

She followed me.

"Girls like you don't deserve to wear hijab," she said, matching my pace. "It'd be better for everyone if you just took it off."

Finally, I stopped. Sighed. I turned to face her. "You are, like, everything that is wrong with people, you know? You," I said, "are what's wrong with religion. People like you make the rest of us look crazy, and I don't think you even realize it." I shook my head. "You don't know shit about me, okay? You don't know *shit* about how I've lived or what I've been through or why I choose to wear hijab and it's not your place to judge me or how I live my life. I get to be a fucking human being, okay? And you can go straight to hell."

Her jaw dropped open in such dramatic fashion that, for

a second, she looked like an anime character. Her eyes went impossibly wide, her mouth shaped into a perfect *o*.

"Wow," she said.

"Bye."

"You're even more horrible than I thought you'd be."

"Whatever."

"I'm going to pray for you."

"Thanks," I said, and started walking again. "I've got a test after lunch, so if you could focus your energy there, that'd be great."

"You are a terrible person!" she called after me.

I waved goodbye as I left.

Ocean was sitting under my tree.

He stood up when he saw me coming. "Hi," he said. His eyes were so bright—happy—in the sunlight. It was a beautiful day. It was the end of October; fall had officially arrived. There was a chill in the air, and I loved it.

"Hi," I said, and smiled.

"How was your day?" we both said at the same time.

"Weird," we answered in unison.

He laughed. "Yeah," he said, and ran a hand through his hair. "Really weird."

I tried hard not to say *I told you so*, because I didn't want to be that person, but I really had told him so, so I settled on a variation of the same thing and hoped he wouldn't notice. "Yeah," I said. "I, uh, figured it might be."

He grinned at me. "Yeah, yeah. I know."

"So," I said, and smiled back. "Are you sorry yet? Ready to call it quits?"

"No." He frowned, and looked, for a moment, genuinely upset. "Of course not."

"Okay." I shrugged. "Then let the shitshow begin."

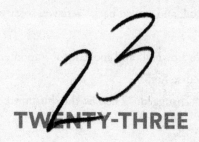

TWENTY-THREE

The first couple of weeks really weren't that bad, except for the fact that I'd started fasting, which just made me kind of tired. Ramadan was, honest to goodness, my favorite month of the year, despite how crazy that sounds. Most people weren't big fans of fasting for thirty days—each day from sunrise to sunset—but I loved it. I loved how it made me feel. It gave me a sharpness of heart and mind; I experienced clarity then as I rarely did during the rest of the year. Somehow, it made me stronger. After surviving a month of serious focus and self-discipline, I felt like I could overcome anything.

Any obstacle. Mental or physical.

Navid *hated* it.

All day long all he did was complain. He was never more annoying as a human being than he was during Ramadan. All he did was whine. He said fasting messed up his carefully balanced diet of simply grilled chicken breasts and staring at his abs in the mirror. He said it made him slow, that his muscles needed fuel, that all his hard work was being flushed down the toilet and he was losing too much weight, getting leaner every day and what about all the bulk he'd worked so hard to build? Besides, his head hurt, he was tired, he was thirsty; he'd stare at his abs again and make an angry noise and say, "This is such *bullshit*."

All day long.

Ocean was, unsurprisingly, curious about the whole thing. I'd stopped using the word *fascinated* to describe the way he engaged with me and my life, because the pejorative iteration of the word no longer seemed fair. In fact, his affection felt so sincere that I could no longer bring myself to even tease him about it. He was easily wounded. One day he'd asked me about Persian food again and I'd made a joke about how funny it was that he knew so little, how he'd really thought falafel and hummus were my thing, and he was suddenly so embarrassed he wouldn't even look at me.

So I tried to be gentle.

True to his word, Ocean really didn't seem to care about the general weirdness surrounding our situation. But then, we were also being really careful. Ocean's basketball commitments were even more intense than I'd expected—he was busy pretty much all the time. So we took it day by day.

We didn't do much at first.

I didn't meet his friends. I didn't go to his house. We didn't spend every moment together; we didn't even spend all our lunches together. To be clear, these were my suggestions, not his. Ocean wasn't thrilled about the distance I kept between us, but it was the only way I could do this—I wanted our worlds to merge slowly, without chaos—and he seemed resigned to accept it. Still, I worried. I worried about everything he'd have to deal with. What he might've already been dealing with. I'd check in with him daily, ask him if anything had happened, if anyone had said anything to him, but he refused to talk about it. He said he didn't want to think about it. Didn't want to give it oxygen.

So I let it go.

After a week, I stopped asking.

I just wanted to enjoy his company.

There was another breakdancing battle happening that next weekend, not long after Ocean and I first started, officially, spending time together, and I was excited. I wanted him to come with me, to see what it was like to attend one of these things in person, and, bonus: it was an outing that'd already been parent-approved, which would make any additional lies to my mom and dad much easier to believe. I had absolutely no interest in telling my parents the truth about Ocean, as I could imagine literally no scenario in which they would happily send me off into the night with a boy who wanted to kiss me, and I was very okay lying about it. My parents weren't the type to care about Ocean's race or religion; I already knew this about them. No, they would've disapproved no matter who he was. They just never wanted to believe that I was a normal teenager who liked boys, period. So it was kind of a relief, actually, not to tell them anything. This whole thing was dramatic enough without my involving my parents and their inevitable hyperventilations.

Ultimately, I thought I'd come up with a pretty solid plan; it would be a fun way to spend a Saturday night. Plus, Ocean could officially meet Navid and the other guys, and I could show him around this world I loved. But when I pitched it to Ocean, he sounded surprised. And then, polite.

"Oh," he said. "Okay. Sure."

Something was wrong.

"You don't like this plan," I said. "You think this is a bad plan." We were on the phone. It was late, really late, and I was whispering under my covers again.

"No, no," he said, and laughed. "It's a great plan. I'd love to see one of these battles—they sound so cool—it's just—" He hesitated. Laughed again. Finally, I heard him sigh.

"What?" I said.

"I kind of wanted to be alone with you."

"*Oh*," I said. My heart picked up.

"And you're inviting me to go out with you and, um, four other guys." I could hear the smile in his voice. "Which, I mean, is totally fine, if that's what you want to do, but, I just—"

"Wow," I said. "I'm so dumb."

"What? You're not dumb. Don't say that," he said. "You're

not dumb. I'm just selfish. I was looking forward to having you all to myself."

A pleasant warmth filled my head. Made me smile.

"Can we do both?" he said. "Can we go to the event and then, I don't know, do something afterward, just you and me?"

"Yeah," I said. "Definitely."

The event was late, long after sunset, so Navid and I had already broken our fasts and had dinner before we headed out. I drove over with Navid, and when we got there, Carlos, Jacobi, and Bijan found us in the parking lot. Ocean showed up soon after, but we had to find each other inside with the help of several text messages.

The place was packed.

I'd been to a few more battles since the first one I'd attended—we'd been going almost every weekend—and this one was, by far, the biggest. The crews here, tonight, were better; the stakes were higher. I looked around the room and realized my parents must not have known what kind of event they'd been approving all this time; I couldn't imagine them walking through here now and giving it the thumbs-up.

This wasn't really a scene for high school kids.

Nearly everyone around me looked like they were in college—or at the very least, nearly there—but even though they looked like kind of a rough crowd, I knew they weren't. There were looks you'd expect—piercings, tattoos, infinite hoodies and sweatpants—but then, it wasn't always obvious who was secretly the best. People would surprise you. I knew, for example, that the Korean dude in the far corner who rarely spoke and always showed up to these things in the same unassuming white shirt, cargo pants, and wire-framed glasses, would later strip down to a pair of metallic gym shorts and do air flares like nobody's business. There was always time, after the battle ended but while the music was still going strong, when people from the crowd would form cyphers— impromptu breaking circles—and blow your mind. There was nothing official about it. It was all adrenaline.

I *loved* it.

Ocean was taking in the room, his eyes wide. The crews were getting ready, the judges were taking their seats, and the DJ was hyping up the crowd, the bass so loud it made the walls vibrate. We had to shout to hear each other. "This," he said, "is what you do on the weekends?"

I laughed. "This, and homework."

The room was so tightly packed that Ocean and I were already pretty close to each other. He'd been standing behind me, because he didn't want to block my view, and it didn't take much for him to close the remaining inch of space between us. I felt his hands at my waist and I took a sudden breath; he tugged me backward, gently, pulling me close. It was a subtle move; I'm not sure anyone else even noticed it. The crowd was so loud and wild I could only barely make out Navid's head a couple of feet away. But I spent the rest of the night with my consciousness in two places at once.

The event was amazing. I always found these battles exhilarating. I loved watching people do things they were really good at, and the crews who came out like this were always at the top of their game.

But it wasn't the same for me this time. I was only half there.

The other half of me was focused, in every moment, on the warm, strong body pressed against me. It didn't seem possible that something so simple could've had such a profound effect on my cardiovascular system, but my heart never slowed its pace. I never relaxed, not really. I didn't know how. I'd never spent an hour standing this close to *anyone*. My nerves felt frayed, and it was all somehow more intense because we didn't really speak. I didn't know how to acknowledge, out loud, that this was insane, that it was crazy that any person could make another person feel so much with so little effort. But I knew Ocean and I were thinking the same thing. I could feel it in the subtle shifts of his body. I heard it in his sudden, slow inhalations. In the tightness in his breath when he leaned in and whispered, "Where the hell did you come from?"

I turned my head, just a little, just so I could see his face, and I whispered back, "I thought I told you I moved here from California."

Ocean laughed and pulled me, somehow, impossibly closer, wrapping both his arms fully around my waist, and then he shook his head and said, even as he was smiling, "That wasn't funny. That was a terrible joke."

"I know. I'm sorry," I said, and laughed. "You just make me so nervous."

"I do?"

I nodded.

I felt him inhale, his chest rising with the movement. He said nothing, but I heard the slight shake in his breath as he blew it out.

TWENTY-FOUR

Navid really came through for me that night.

He bought me an extra hour after the crowds cleared out so that I could go off on my own, somewhere, with Ocean.

"One hour, that's it," he said. "That's all I can swing. It's already late and if I get you home any later than eleven, Ma will kill me. Okay?"

I just smiled at him.

"Uh-uh. No," he said, and shook his head. "No smiling. I will be back here in exactly one hour, and no smiling. I want your happiness level to be, like, medium, when I come back here. If you have too much fun I'll end up having to kick someone's ass." He looked at Ocean. "Listen," he said, "you seem like a nice guy, but I just want to be clear: if you hurt her, I will fucking murder you. Okay?"

"*Navid*—"

"No, no, it's okay." Ocean laughed. "It's fine. I get it."

Navid studied him. "Good man."

"*Bye*," I said.

Navid raised an eyebrow at me. Finally, he left.

Ocean and I were suddenly alone in the parking lot, and though the moon was a mere crescent in the sky, it was beautiful and bright. The air smelled fresh and icy and like a particular type of vegetation I'd never learned the name of, but the scent of which seemed to come alive only in the late evenings.

The world felt suddenly full of promise.

Ocean walked me to his car and it was only after I was buckled in that I realized I'd never asked him where we were going. Part of me didn't even care. I would've been happy to just sit in his car and listen to music.

He told me then, without my asking, that we were going to a park.

"Is that okay?" he said, and glanced at me. "It's one of my favorite places. I wanted to show it to you."

"That sounds great," I said.

I rolled down the window when he started driving and leaned out, my arms resting on the open ledge, my face resting on my arms. I closed my eyes and felt the wind rush over me. I loved the wind. I loved the scent of the night air. It made me happy in a way I could never explain.

Ocean pulled into a parking lot.

There were gentle, grassy hills in the distance, their soft contours lit by dim uplights. The park seemed vast, like it went on and on, but it was clearly closed for the day. The thing that made the whole thing shine, however, were the bright lights from the adjacent basketball court.

It wasn't impressive. The court looked weathered, and the hoops were missing nets. But there were a couple of tall streetlamps, which made the space seem imposing, especially this late at night. Ocean turned off his car. Everything was suddenly black and milky with distant, diffused light. We were silhouettes.

"This was where I first learned to play basketball," he said quietly. "I come here when I feel like I'm losing my mind sometimes." He paused. "I've been coming back here a lot, lately. I keep trying to remember that I didn't always hate it."

I studied his face in the darkness.

There was so much I wanted to say, but this seemed like such a sensitive topic for him that I also wanted to be careful. I didn't know if what I wanted to say was the right thing to say.

Eventually, I said it anyway.

"I don't get it," I said, "why do you *have* to play basketball? If you hate it, can't you just—I don't know? Stop?"

Ocean smiled. He was looking straight out the windshield. "I love that you would even say that," he said. "You make it sound so simple." He sighed. "But people here are weird about basketball. It's more than just a game. It's, like, a lifestyle. If I walked away I'd be disappointing so many people. I'd piss off so many people. It would be . . . really bad."

"Yeah, I get that," I said. "But who cares?"

He looked at me. Raised his eyebrows.

"I'm serious," I said. "I don't know anything about bas-ketball, that's true, but it doesn't take much to see that people are putting pressure on you to do something you don't want to do. So why should you have to do this—put yourself through this—for someone else? What's the payoff?"

"I don't know," he said, and frowned. "I just, I *know* these people. Basketball is, like, the only thing I even talk to my mom about anymore. And I've known my coach forever—I knew him even before I started playing in high school—and he spent so much time helping me, training me. I feel like I owe him. And now he's relying on me to perform. Not just for him," Ocean said, "but for the whole school. These last two years—my junior and senior year—I mean, this is what we've been working toward. My team is counting on me. It's hard to walk away now. I can't just tell everyone to go to hell."

I was quiet a moment. It was becoming clear to me that Ocean's feelings about this sport were far more complicated than even he let on. And there was so much about this town and its interests that I still didn't understand. Maybe I was out of my depth.

Still, I trusted my gut.

"Listen," I said gently, "I don't think you should do any-thing that doesn't feel right to you, okay? You don't have to quit basketball. That doesn't have to be the solution. But I want to point out one thing. Just one thing I hope you'll think about the next time you're feeling stressed about all this."

"Yeah?"

I sighed. "You keep focusing on whether or not you'll disappoint all these people," I said. "Your mom. Your coach. Your teammates. Everyone else. But none of them seem to care that they're disappointing *you*. They're actively hurting you," I said. "And it makes me hate them."

He blinked.

"It isn't fair," I said quietly. "You're clearly in pain over this, and they don't seem to give a shit."

Ocean looked away. "Wow." He laughed. "No one's ever framed it for me like that before."

"I just wish you'd take your own side. You're so worried about everyone else," I said. "But I'm going to worry about you, okay? I get to worry about you."

Ocean went still. His eyes were inscrutable as he looked at me. And when he finally said, "Okay," it sounded like a whisper.

I faltered.

"I'm sorry," I said. "Was that mean? Everyone's always telling me how mean I am, but I don't really do it on purpose, I just wanted t—"

"I think you're perfect," he said.

We were both quiet on the drive back. We sat together in a comfortable silence until, eventually, Ocean turned on the radio. I watched him, his hands coated in moonlight, as he picked out a song, the contents of which I wouldn't hear and wouldn't remember.

My heart was far too loud.

He texted me, much later that night.

i miss you
i wish i could hold you right now

I looked at his words for a while, feeling too much.

i miss you too
so much

I was lying in bed, staring at the ceiling. My lungs felt tight. I was wondering about that, wondering why it was that feeling good made it so hard to breathe, when my phone buzzed again.

i really love that you'd worry about me
i was beginning to feel like no one ever worried about me

And something about his honesty broke my heart.
Then—

is that weird?

211

to want someone to worry about you?

not weird

just human

And then I called him.

"Hi," he said. But his voice was soft, a little faraway. He sounded tired.

"Oh— I'm sorry—were you sleeping?"

"No, no. But I'm in bed."

"Me too."

"Under the covers?"

I laughed. "Hey, it's this or nothing, okay?"

"I'm not complaining," he said, and I could almost see him smile. "I'll take whatever you're offering."

"Yeah?"

"Mm-hmm."

"You sound so sleepy."

"Yeah," he said quietly. "I don't know. I'm tired, but I feel so happy."

"You do?"

"Yeah," he whispered. "You make me so happy." He took a deep breath. Laughed a little. "You're like a happy drug."

I was smiling. I didn't know what to say.

"You there?"

"Yeah," I said. "I'm here."

"What are you thinking?"

"I'm thinking I wish you were here."

"Yeah?"

"Yeah," I said. "That'd be great."

He laughed and said, "Why?"

I had a feeling we were both thinking the same thing and neither one of us was saying it. But I'd wanted to kiss him all night. I'd been thinking about it a lot, actually. I'd been thinking about his body, the way it felt to have his arms around me, wishing we'd been alone longer, wishing we'd had more time, wishing for more. More of everything. I often daydreamed about him being here, in my room. I wondered what it would feel like to be wrapped up in him, to fall asleep in his arms. I wanted to experience all kinds of moments with him.

I thought about it, all the time.

Somehow, I knew he was hoping I'd say this to him. Out loud. Tonight. Maybe right now. It scared the crap out of me.

But then, he so often took that leap for me.

Ocean had always been so honest about his feelings. He told me the truth about how he felt even when everything was uncertain, when I otherwise would've stayed silent forever.

So I tried to be brave.

"I miss you," I said quietly. "I know I saw you a few hours ago but I already miss you. I want to see your face. I want to feel your arms around me," I said, and closed my eyes. "You feel so strong and you make me feel safe and I just— I think you're amazing," I whispered. "You're so wonderful that sometimes I honestly can't believe you're real."

I opened my eyes, the hot phone pressed against my flushed cheek, and he said nothing and I was relieved. I let the quiet devour me. I listened to him breathe. His silence made me feel like I was suspended in space, like I'd been dropped into a confessional.

"I really wanted to kiss you tonight," I said softly. "I wish you were here."

Suddenly, I heard him sigh.

It was more like a long, slow exhale. His voice was tight, a little breathless, when he finally said, "There's really no chance of you getting out of your house right now, is there?"

I laughed and said, "I wish. And trust me, I've thought about it."

"I don't think you've thought about it as much as I have."

I was smiling. "I think I should go," I said to him. "It's like three in the morning."

"Really?"

"Yeah."

"Wow."

I laughed again, softly.

We said good night.

And I closed my eyes and clutched my phone to my chest and felt the room spin around me.

TWENTY-FIVE

Ocean and I had managed to remain relatively drama-free for just over three weeks now. People were still occasionally staring, still wondering, but my rules about how we spent time together had kept things from getting out of hand. We talked most nights, saw each other as often as our schedules allowed, but kept our distance at school. Soon, most people had moved on, as there wasn't much news to report. I refused to feed the gossip. I didn't answer people's inane questions. Ocean really wanted to drive me to school in the mornings and I wouldn't accept his offer, no matter how badly I wanted to, because I didn't want to make a spectacle out of us.

He didn't love it. In fact, I think he really hated it, hated how I kept pushing him away. But the harder I fell for him, the more I wanted to protect him. And I was falling harder every day.

We'd stopped at my locker at lunch one day so I could switch out my books, and he waited for me, leaning against the wall of ugly metal units, occasionally peering into my open locker. Suddenly, his eyes lit up.

"Is that your journal?" he said.

He reached in and grabbed the weathered composition book and my heart seized so fast I thought I saw stars. I yanked it away from him and clutched it to my chest and felt, for a moment, truly horrified. I did not want him to read this, not *ever*. There'd be no way for me to maintain even a semblance of self-respect around him after he'd read my many pages-long descriptions of how it felt to be with him—to even be near him. It was way too intense.

He'd probably think I was crazy.

He was laughing at me, laughing at the look on my face, at the speed with which I'd yanked the thing out of his hands, and finally he just smiled. He took my hand. He was running his fingers along the inside of my palm and I swear that was really all it took, sometimes, to make my head spin.

He held my hand up against his chest. It was a thing he did with me a lot, pressed my hands against his chest, and I wasn't sure why. He never explained it and I didn't mind. I thought it was kind of adorable.

"Why don't you want me to read your diary?" he said.

I shook my head, eyes still too wide. "It's really boring."

He laughed out loud.

I remember it so clearly, the first time I saw him—it was

at that exact moment, right when Ocean laughed and I looked up at his face—that I felt someone staring straight through me. It was rare that I ever felt compelled to seek out the source of a stare, but this one felt different. It felt violent. And that was when I turned and saw his basketball coach for the very first time.

He shook his head at me.

I was so surprised I stepped back. I didn't actually know who the guy was until Ocean spun around to see what had startled me. Ocean's face cleared. He called out a hello, and though the guy—I learned then that his name was Coach Hart—nodded what seemed to be a pleasant hello in return, I caught the millisecond he took to catalog the details of my appearance. I saw him glance, just briefly, at my hand and Ocean's, intertwined.

Then he walked away.

And I felt a sudden, sick feeling settle in my gut.

TWENTY-SIX

Ocean came over for Thanksgiving.

My parents really loved Thanksgiving, and they did the thing really well. My mom also had a soft spot for strays; she'd always leave the door open for friends of ours who had nowhere to go, especially around the holidays. It was kind of our tradition. Every year our Thanksgiving table featured different guests; there was always someone—and usually they were friends of my brother—who didn't have family to spend the day with, or, alternatively, had family they hated and didn't want to spend the day with, and they'd always find refuge in our house.

This was how I'd convinced my parents to let Ocean come over.

I didn't tell them anything except that he was my friend from school, a friend I claimed had no one with whom to cook

a turkey on Thanksgiving, but also a friend who was very interested in Persian food.

This last bit delighted my parents to no end.

They lived for opportunities to teach people about Persian
everything. Whatever it was, Persian people had invented it,
and if they hadn't invented it, they'd almost certainly improved
it, and if you were able to explain in careful, thoughtful detail
that maybe there was something Persian people hadn't invented
or improved, well, then, my parents would say that whatever it
was probably wasn't worth having anyway.

The interesting thing about Thanksgiving this year was
that it fell almost right in the middle of Ramadan, so we'd be
breaking our fast and having Thanksgiving dinner all at the
same time. But we started our dinner preparations early, and
our guests were always invited to help.

Navid whined all day, even though he was given the sim-
plest task of making mashed potatoes. Ocean thought Navid
was hilarious, and I tried to explain that he wasn't doing a bit,
that Navid was really just, like, super annoying when he was
fasting, and Ocean shrugged.

"Still funny," he said.

I'm not sure whether it will surprise you to hear that my
parents loved Ocean. Maybe it was because he didn't argue
with them when they explained that Shakespeare, in Farsi, is
pronounced *sheikheh peer*, which means "old sheikh," and that
they felt this was definitive proof that Shakespeare was actually an old Persian scholar. Or maybe it was the way Ocean ate

everything they put in front of him and seemed to genuinely enjoy it. My parents had made sure to make an entirely separate, six-course meal for this friend of mine who'd never tried Persian food before, and they'd sat there and stared at him as he ate, and every time he said he liked what he'd eaten they would look up at me and beam, proud as peacocks, finding in Ocean further proof that Persian people had invented only the best things, including the best food.

Ocean sat patiently with my dad, who loved showing everyone his favorite videos on the internet, and never betrayed a hint of irritation, not even as my father made him watch video after video about the remarkable design and efficiency of European faucets. He went through phases, my dad did. That week was all about faucets.

Later, when all the food had been eaten and my mother had turned on the samovar, Ocean listened—attentively—as my parents tried to teach him how to speak Farsi. Except they didn't really teach; they would just *talk*. My mother was, for some inexplicable reason, convinced she could force an ability to speak Farsi directly into a person's brain.

She'd just said something really complicated, and nodded at Ocean, who she was certain would make a fine student, because why *wouldn't* he want to learn Farsi, Farsi was obviously the best language, and she repeated the phrase again. Then she gestured to Ocean.

"So," my mom said, "what did I just say?"

Ocean's eyes widened.

"That's not how you teach someone a language," I said, and rolled my eyes. "You can't just teach him Farsi through osmosis."

My mom waved me off. "He understands," she said. She looked at Ocean. "You understand, don't you? He understands," she said to my dad.

My dad nodded like this was the most obvious thing in the world.

"He does not understand," I said. "Stop being weird."

"We're not being weird," my dad said, looking affronted. "Ocean likes Farsi. He wants to learn Farsi." He looked at Ocean. "Don't you, Ocean?"

Ocean said, "Sure."

And my parents were thrilled.

"That reminds me," my dad said, his eyes lighting up, "of this poem I was reading the other night—"

My dad jumped up from the table and ran off to get his glasses and his books.

I groaned.

"We're going to be here all night," I whispered to my mom. "Make him stop."

My mom waved me down and said, "*Harf nazan.*" *Be quiet.*

And then she asked Ocean if he wanted more tea, and he said no, thank you, and she poured him more tea anyway, and my dad spent the rest of the night reading and translating really dense, old Persian poetry—Rumi, Hafez, Saadi—some of the absolute greats, and I wondered if Ocean would ever want to talk to me again. This particular ritual of my parents' was actually a thing I loved; I'd spent many nights sitting at the kitchen table with my parents, moved to tears by a particularly powerful line of verse. The problem was just that it took *forever* to translate old-world Farsi into English. Even a simple poem would take ages to get through because my parents would spend ten minutes translating the old Farsi into modern Farsi, and then they'd ask me to help them translate the modern Farsi into English, and twenty minutes later they'd just throw up their hands and say, "It's not the same. It's just not the same in English. It doesn't have the same flavor. You lose the heartbeat. You're just going to have to learn Farsi," they said to Ocean, who only looked at them and smiled.

It wasn't long before they'd started defending him over me. Every time I'd tell them to back off, to cut this short, they'd turn to Ocean for support. He, of course, very politely took their side, insisting that he didn't mind, and my mother asked him again if he wanted more tea and he said no, thank you, and she poured him more tea anyway, and she asked him if he wanted more food and he said no, thank you, and she filled four large Tupperware containers with leftovers and stacked them in front of him. But when he saw the food he seemed so genuinely grateful that by the end of the night my parents were half in love with him and perfectly ready to trade me in for a better model.

"He's so polite," my mother kept saying to me. "Why aren't you polite? What did we do wrong?" She looked at Ocean.

"Ocean, *azizam*," she said, "please tell Shirin she should stop swearing so much."

Ocean almost lost it for a second. I saw him about to laugh, hard, and he stifled it just in time.

I shot him a look.

My mom was still talking. She was saying, "It's always *asshole* this, *bullshit* that. I say to her, Shirin *joon*, why are you so obsessed with shit? Why everything is shit?"

"Jesus Christ, Ma," I said.

"Leave Jesus out of this," she said, and pointed the wooden spoon at me before using it to hit me in the back of the head.

"Oh my God," I said, waving her away. "Stop it."

My mom sighed dramatically. "You see?" she said. She was talking to Ocean now. "No respect."

Ocean only smiled. He looked like he was still failing to keep that smile from turning into a laugh. He pressed his lips together; cleared his throat. But his eyes gave him away.

Finally, Ocean sighed and stood up, stared at the stack of Tupperware containers set in front of him, and said he'd better call it a night. Somehow, it was almost midnight. I wasn't kidding about those endless faucet videos.

But when Ocean started saying goodbye, he looked at me like he didn't actually want to leave, like he was sorry he had to. I waved from across the room as he thanked my parents again, and, once I saw him walking toward the living room, I went upstairs. I didn't want to stick around too long and make a whole production of the goodbye. My parents were too smart;

I was pretty sure they'd figured out I had some kind of crush on this guy, but I didn't want them to think I was obsessed with him. But then I heard a soft knock at my bedroom door, not a moment after I'd closed it, and I was stunned to discover Navid and Ocean standing there.

Navid said, "You have fifteen minutes. You're welcome," and nudged Ocean into my bedroom.

Ocean was smiling, shaking his head. He ran a hand through his hair and sighed and laughed at the same time. "Your family is funny," he said. "Navid dragged me up here because he said he wanted to show me the bench press in his room. Is that even a real thing?"

I nodded. But I was kind of freaking out.

Ocean was standing in my bedroom and I had not been prepared for this. Not at all. I knew Navid was trying to do me a favor but I hadn't had a chance to tidy up my room, to make sure I didn't have any bras lying around or, to, like, I don't know, make myself seem cooler than I actually was, and I felt suddenly concerned that I had no idea what it would be like to see my bedroom through someone else's eyes.

But Ocean was staring.

My small, twin bed was in the right hand corner of the room. The comforter was mussed, the pillows stacked precariously. A few pieces of clothing had been thrown haphazardly on my bed—a tank top and shorts I'd worn to sleep. My phone was plugged into its charger, and it sat on the little bedside table. On the opposite wall was my desk, my computer perched on top, a stack of books sitting next to it. There was a dress form in another corner of the room, a half-finished pattern still pinned to the body. My sewing machine was on the floor nearby, and an open box full of all my other supplies—many spools of thread, pins and a pincushion, envelopes of needles—sat beside it.

In the middle of the floor was a small mess.

A handful of Sharpies were lying on the carpet next to an open sketch pad, an old boom box, and a pair of my dad's even older headphones. There wasn't much on the wall. Just a few charcoal pieces I'd done last year.

I'd scanned the whole space in a few seconds, and decided it would have to do. Ocean, on the other hand, was still staring; his assessment was taking a lot longer. I felt anxious.

"If I'd known you'd be coming in my room today," I said, "I would've, um, made it nicer."

But he didn't seem to hear me. His eyes were locked onto my bed. "This is where you talk to me at night?" he said. "When you're hiding under your covers?"

I nodded.

He walked over to my bed and sat down. Looked around. And then he noticed my pajamas, which seemed to baffle him for only a second before he said, "*Oh*, wow." He looked up at me. "This is going to sound so stupid," he said, "but it's only just occurred to me that you must take your scarf off when you get home."

"Um. Yeah," I said. I laughed a little. "I don't sleep like this."

"So"—he frowned—"when you're talking to me at night, you look totally different."

"I mean, not *totally* different. But kind of. Yeah."

"And this is what you're wearing?" he said. He touched the tank top and shorts on my bed.

"It's what I was wearing last night," I said, feeling nervous. "Yeah."

"Last night," he said quietly, his eyebrows raised. And then he took a deep breath and looked away, picking up one of my pillows like it might've been made of glass.

We'd been on the phone for hours last night, talking about everything and nothing, and just the memory of our conversation sent a sudden thrill through my heart. I didn't know exactly what time it was when we finally went to bed, but it was so late I remember only a weak attempt at shoving my phone under my pillow before happily dissolving into dreams.

I wanted to imagine that Ocean was thinking what I was thinking: that he, too, felt this thing between us building with terrifying, breathless speed and didn't know how or even whether to slow it down. But I couldn't know for certain. And Ocean had gone quiet for so long I started to worry. He didn't move from my bed as he scanned my room again, and my knot of nervousness grew only more wild.

"Too weird?" I finally said. "Is this too weird?"

Ocean laughed as he stood up, shook his head, and smiled. "Is that really what you think is going through my mind right now?"

I hesitated. Reconsidered. "Maybe?"

He laughed again. And then he glanced at the clock on my wall and said, "Looks like we only have a few minutes left." But he'd come forward as he spoke. He stood in front of me now.

"Yeah," I said softly.

He stepped, somehow, even closer to me. He slipped his hands into the back pockets of my jeans and I almost gasped and he pulled me tighter, pressed the lines of our bodies together and he leaned in, rested his forehead against mine. He wrapped his arms around my waist and just held me there, like that, for a moment. "Hey," he whispered. "Can I just tell you that I think you're really, really beautiful? Can I just tell you that?"

I felt my cheeks warm. He was so close I was sure he could hear my heart pounding. Our bodies seemed soldered together.

I whispered his name.

He kissed me once, gently, and lingered there, our lips still touching. My body trembled. Ocean closed his eyes.

"*This is crazy*," he said.

And then he kissed me desperately, without warning, and feeling shot through my veins with a searing, explosive heat. I felt suddenly molten. His lips were soft and he smelled so good and my mind had filled with static. My hands moved from his waist and up his back, and, in an accidental, unrehearsed movement, they slipped under his sweater.

I froze.

The sensation of his bare skin under my hands was so

unexpected. New. A little frightening. Ocean broke our kiss and smiled, gently, against my mouth.

"Are you afraid to touch me?" he said.

I nodded.

I felt his smile deepen.

But then I trailed my fingers along the smooth expanse of his back and he took a quick, sudden breath. I felt his muscles tighten.

Carefully, I traced the curve of his spine. I touched his waist, my hands moving around his torso. He felt so strong. The lines of his body were deeply, alarmingly sexy. And I was just beginning to get brave when he clamped his hands down on mine.

He took another unsteady breath and pressed his face into my cheek. Laughed, shakily. He didn't say a word. He just shook his head.

The pleasure of being this close to him was unlike anything I'd ever imagined. It was hyper-real. Impossible. His arms were around me now, strong and warm and pulling me close, and he just about lifted me off the floor.

There was a tiny part of my brain that knew this was a bad idea. I knew Navid could walk in here at any minute. I knew my parents were just moments away. I knew it, and somehow, I didn't care.

I closed my eyes and rested my head against his chest. Breathed him in.

Ocean pulled back, just a little. He looked me in the eye

and his own eyes were heavy, suddenly. Bright and deep and terrified.

He said, "What would you do if I fell in love with you?"

And my entire body answered his question. Heat filled my blood, the gaps in my bones. My heart felt suddenly alive with emotion and I didn't know how to say what I was thinking, what I wanted to say, which was—

Is this love?

—and I never had the chance.

Navid knocked on the door, hard, and we were like shrapnel, flying apart.

Ocean looked a little flushed. He took a second, looked around, looked at me. He didn't say goodbye, exactly. He just looked at me.

And then he was gone.

Two hours later, he texted me.

are you in bed?

yes

can i ask you a weird question?

I stared at my phone for a second. I took a deep breath.

okay

what does your hair look like?

I actually laughed out loud, before I remembered that my parents were sleeping. Girls never seemed to care about the state of my hair, but guys had been asking me this question forever. It was always the same question, and they never seemed to grow out of it.

it's brown. kind of long.

And then he called me.

"Hi," he said.

"Hi." I smiled.

"I like that I can imagine where you are now," he said. "What your room looks like."

"I still can't believe you were here today."

"Yeah, thanks for that, by the way. Your parents are amazing. That was really fun."

"I'm glad it wasn't excruciating," I said, but I felt sad, suddenly. I didn't know how to tell him that I wished his mom would get her shit together. "My parents are officially in love with you, by the way."

"Really?"

"Yeah. I'm sure they'd trade me in for you any day of the week."

He laughed. And then he didn't say anything for a while.

"Hey," I finally said.

"Yeah?"

"Is everything okay?"

"Yeah," he said. "Yeah." But he sounded a little out of breath.

"Are you sure?"

"I was just thinking about how your brother has terrible timing."

I was only a beat behind; it took me a second, but I suddenly understood what he was trying to say.

I'd never answered his question.

And I was suddenly nervous. "What did you mean," I said, "when you asked what I would *do*? Why did you phrase the question like that?"

"I guess," he said, and took a sharp breath, "I was just wondering if it would scare you away."

There was a part of me that adored his uncertainty. How he seemed to have no idea that I was just as far gone as he was.

"No," I said softly. "It wouldn't scare me away."

"No?"

"No," I said. "Not a chance."

TWENTY-SEVEN

Ramadan was over. We celebrated, we exchanged gifts, and Navid devoured the contents of our entire kitchen. The fall semester was quickly coming to a close. We were tipping over into the second week of December, and I'd managed to keep some level of distance in place between myself and Ocean for as long as either of us could bear it.

It had been almost two months since the day he'd kissed me in his car.

I couldn't believe it.

In the quiet, relative peace that surrounded our careful efforts to be inconspicuous, time sped up. Flew by. I'd never been so happy, maybe, ever. Ocean was *fun*. He was sweet and he was smart and we never ran out of things to talk about. He didn't have a lot of free hours, because basketball was a demanding extracurricular activity and a massive time-suck, but we always found a way to make it work.

I was happy with the compromise we'd made. It was safe here. Secretive, yes, but it was safe. No one knew our business. People had finally stopped gawking at me in the hallways.

But Ocean wanted more.

He didn't like hiding. He said it made it seem like we were doing something wrong, and he hated it. He insisted, over and over again, that he didn't care what other people thought. He didn't care, he said, and he didn't want a bunch of idiots to have this much control over his life.

Honestly, I couldn't disagree with him.

I was tired of hiding, too; I was tired of ignoring him at school, tired of always giving in to my cynicism. But Ocean was a lot more visible than even he knew or understood. Once I started paying closer attention to him—and to his world—the subtle gradations of his life began to come into focus. Ocean had ex-girlfriends at this school. Old teammates. Rivalries. There were guys who were openly jealous of his success, and girls who hated him for being uninterested. More important: there were people who'd built their careers on the back of the high school basketball team.

I knew by now that Ocean was really good at basketball, but I didn't know just how good until I started listening. He was only a junior, but he was outperforming his teammates by a wide margin, and he was, as a result, attracting a lot of attention; people were talking about how he might be good enough to win all kinds of state and national Player of the Year awards—and not just him, but his coach, too.

It made me nervous.

Ocean had this quintessential all-American look, the kind of look that made it easy for girls to fall in love with him, for scouts to know where to place him, for the community to think of him, always and forever, as a good boy with great potential and a bright future. I tried to explain why my presence in his life would be both complicated and controversial, but Ocean couldn't understand. He just didn't think it was that big of a deal.

But it wasn't something I wanted to fight over. So we compromised.

I agreed to let Ocean drive me to school one morning. I thought it would be a small, carefully measured step. Totally innocent. What I kept forgetting, of course, was that high school was home to infinite clichés for a reason, and that Ocean was, in some ways, still inextricable from his own stereotype. Even *where* he parked his car in the school parking lot seemed to matter. I'd never had a reason to know or care about this, because I was the weirdo who walked to school every day. I'd never interacted with this side of campus in the morning, never saw these kids or spoke to them. But when Ocean opened my door that day, I stepped out into a different world. Everyone was here. Here—in this school parking lot—this was where he and his friends hung out every morning.

"Oh, wow, this was a bad idea," I said to him, even as he took my hand. "Ocean," I said, "this was a bad idea."

"It's not a bad idea," he said, and squeezed my fingers. "We're just two people holding hands. It's not the end of the world."

I wondered, then, what it would be like to live in his brain. I wondered how safe and normal a life he must've lived in order to say something like that, so casually, and really, truly, believe it.

Sometimes, I wanted to say to him, for some people, it really was the end of the world.

But I didn't. I didn't say it because I was suddenly distracted. An unnerving quiet had just infected the groups of kids standing nearest to us, and I felt my body tense even as I looked forward and stared at nothing. I waited for something—some kind of hostility—but it never came. We managed to weave our way through the parking lot, eyes following our bodies as we went, without incident. No one spoke to me. Their silence seemed to be infused with surprise, and it felt, to me, like they were deciding what to think. How to respond.

Ocean and I had very different reactions to this experience.

I told him we should go back to arriving separately at school, that it was a nice try, but, ultimately, a bad idea.

He did not agree, not even a little bit.

He kept pointing out to me that it had been fine, that it was weird but it wasn't bad, and he insisted, most of all, that he didn't want their opinions to control his life.

"I want to be with you," he said. "I want to hold your hand and eat lunch with you and I don't want to have to pretend that I'm not, like"—he sighed, hard—"I just don't want to pretend not to notice you, okay? I don't care if other people don't like it. I don't want to worry all the time. Who gives a shit about these people?"

"Aren't they your friends?" I said.

"If they were my friends," he said, "they'd be happy for me."

The second day was worse.

On the second day, when I stepped out of Ocean's car, no one was surprised. They were just assholes.

Someone actually said, "Why're you fucking around with Aladdin over here, bro?"

This was not a new insult, not to me. For some reason people loved using Aladdin to put me down, which made me sad, because I really liked Aladdin. I loved watching that movie as a kid. But I'd always wanted to tell people that they were insulting me incorrectly. I wanted them to understand that Aladdin was, first of all, a guy, and that, second of all, he wasn't even the one who covered his hair. This wasn't even an *accurate* insult, and it bothered me that it was so lazy. There were so many better, meaner alternatives from the movie to choose from—like, maybe, I don't know, compare me to *Jafar*—but there was never a good time, during these types of situations, to bring it up.

Regardless, Ocean and I did not have the same reaction to the insult.

I was irritated, but Ocean was *angry*.

I could feel it then, in that moment, that Ocean was even stronger than he looked. He had a lean, muscular frame, but he felt, suddenly, very solid standing next to me. His whole body had gone rigid; his hand in mine felt foreign. He looked both angry and disgusted and he shook his head and I could tell he was about to say something when someone, very suddenly, threw a half-eaten cinnamon roll at my face.

I was stunned.

There was a moment of perfect silence as the sweet, sticky bun hit part of my eye and most of my cheek and then dragged, slowly, down my chin. Fell to the floor. There was icing all over my scarf.

This, I thought, was new.

Whoever threw the thing at me was suddenly laughing his ass off and Ocean just kind of lost it. He grabbed the guy by the shirt and shoved him, really, really hard and I wasn't sure what was happening anymore, but I was so mortified I could hardly see straight and I suddenly wanted nothing more than to just disappear.

So I did.

No one had ever thrown *food* at me before. I felt numb as I walked away, felt stupid and humiliated and numb. I was trying to make my way to the girl's bathroom because I really wanted to wash my face but Ocean suddenly caught up to me, caught me around the waist.

"Hey," he said, and he was out of breath, "Hey—"

But I didn't want to look at him, I didn't want him to see me with this shit all over my face so I pulled away. I didn't meet his eyes.

"Are you okay?" he said. "I'm so sorry—"

"Yeah," I said, but I was already turning around again. "I, um—I just need to wash my face, okay? I'll see you later."

"Wait," he said, "wait—"

"I'll see you later, Ocean, I swear." I waved, kept walking. "I'm fine."

I mean, I wasn't fine. I *would* be fine. But I wasn't there yet.

I got to the girl's bathroom and dropped my bag on the ground. I unwrapped my scarf from around my head and used a damp paper towel to scrub the icing off my face. I tried to clean my scarf the same way, but it wasn't as effective. I sighed. I had to try and wash parts of it in the sink, which just made everything wet, and I was feeling more than a little demoralized as I hung the slightly damp scarf around my neck.

Just then, someone else walked into the bathroom.

I was glad that I'd at least finished with the scrubbing of my face before she came in. I'd just pulled my ponytail free— I'd had to wash a little icing out of my hair, too, and I needed to retie the whole thing—when she walked over to the sink next to me. I knew I'd made myself super conspicuous in here, because I'd tossed my bag to the floor, disassembled myself, and was surrounded, at the moment, by little mountains of damp paper towels, but I hoped she wouldn't notice. Wouldn't ask questions. I didn't know who she was and I didn't care; I just didn't want to deal with any more people today.

"Hey," she said, and instinct forced my head up.

I'll always remember that moment, the way my hair fell around my face, how it shook out, in long waves, as I turned, the hair tie still wrapped around my wrist.

I looked at her, a question in my eyes.

And she took a picture of me.

"What the hell?" I stepped back, confused. "Why did y—?"

"Thanks," she said, and smiled.

I was dazed. She walked out the door and it took me a minute to find my head. It took me another few seconds to understand.

When I did, I was struck still.

And I suddenly felt so sick to my stomach I thought I might faint.

It had been a really shitty day.

Ocean finally found me in the hall. He took my hand and I turned around and at first he didn't say anything. At first he just looked at me.

"Some girl took a picture of me in the bathroom," I said quietly.

He took a tight breath. "Yeah," he said. "I know."

"You do?"

He nodded.

I turned away. I wanted to cry but I swore I wouldn't. I promised myself I wouldn't. Instead, I whispered, "What's going on, Ocean? What's happening right now?"

He shook his head. He looked devastated. "This is my fault," he said. "This is all my fault. I should've listened to you, I never should've let this happen—"

And just then some guy I'd never even seen before walked past us, slapped Ocean on the back and said, "Hey man, I understand—I'd hit that, too—"

Ocean shoved him, hard, and the guy shouted something angry and fell back, landing on his elbows.

"What the hell is wrong with you?" Ocean said to him. "What happened to you?"

They started yelling at each other and I just couldn't take it anymore.

I needed to leave.

I knew a little about digital cameras, but I didn't own one myself, so I couldn't, in that moment, understand how people were sharing photos of me so quickly. I only knew that someone had taken a photo of me without my scarf on—without my consent—and was now passing it around. It was a kind of violation I'd never experienced before. I wanted to scream.

It was *my* hair, I wanted to scream.

It was my hair and it was my face and it was my body and it was *my fucking business* what I wanted to do with it.

Of course, nobody cared.

I ditched school.

Ocean tried to come with me. He kept apologizing and he tried, so hard, to make it better, but I just wanted to be alone. I needed time.

So I left.

I walked around for a while, trying to clear my head. I didn't know what else to do. There was a part of me that wanted to go home, but I worried that if I locked myself in my bedroom I might never come out. I also really, really didn't want to cry.

I *felt* like crying. I felt like crying and screaming all at the same time, but I didn't want to give in to the feeling. I just wanted to push through this. I wanted to survive it without losing my head.

I knew, hours later, that things had gotten bad when Navid started texting me. If Navid had heard about this, things had to have blown up. And he was worried.

I told him I was okay, that I'd left campus. I'd ended up hiding in a local library. I was sitting in the horror section on purpose.

Navid told me to come to practice.

why?
because it'll help get your mind off things

I sighed.

how bad is it?

A few seconds later:

well, it's not great

I slipped back on campus only when I knew school was officially out. I went to my locker to grab my gym bag, but when I opened the door, a piece of paper fell out. I unfolded it to discover that there were two pictures of me, printed side by side. One with my scarf on, one without.

I looked confused in the latter of the two, but the photo wasn't otherwise unflattering. It was a perfectly okay picture. I'd always liked my hair. I thought I had nice hair. And it photographed well, actually, maybe better than it had looked in real life. But this revelation only made the whole thing more painful. It was more obvious than ever that this was never meant to be a silly stunt; the point here was never to make me look ugly or stupid. Whoever did this had wanted only to unmask me without my permission, to humiliate me by intentionally undermining a decision I'd made to keep some parts of me for just myself. They'd wanted to take away the power I thought I had over my own body.

It was a betrayal that hurt, somehow, more than anything else.

When I showed up to practice, Navid just looked sad.

"You okay?" he said, and pulled me in for a hug.

"Yeah," I said. "This school blows."

He took a deep breath. Squeezed me once more before letting go. "Yeah," he said, and exhaled. "Yeah, it really does."

"People are so fucked up," Bijan said to me, shaking his head. "I'm sorry you have to deal with this."

I didn't know what to say. I tried to smile.

Carlos and Jacobi were sympathetic.

"Hey, just point me in the right direction," Carlos said, "and I'll happily kick the shit out of someone for you."

I actually smiled, then. "I don't even know who did it," I said. "I mean, I saw the girl who took the photo of me, but I don't know anything else. I don't know anything about her," I said, and sighed. "I don't know people at this school."

And then Jacobi asked me what happened, how the girl had even managed to get the picture of me, and I told them that I'd been in the bathroom, cleaning up, because some guy had thrown a cinnamon roll at my face, and I tried to laugh about it, to make it seem funny, but all four of them went suddenly quiet.

Stone-faced.

"Some dude threw a cinnamon roll at your face?" Navid looked dumbstruck. "Are you fucking kidding me?"

I blinked. Hesitated. "No?"

"Who?" It was Jacobi now. "Who was it?"

"I don't know—"

"Son of a bitch," Carlos said.

"And Ocean didn't do anything?" Bijan, this time. "He just let some guy throw food at you?"

"What? No," I said quickly. "No, no, he, like, I don't know, I think he started fighting with him but I just walked away, so I didn't—"

"So Ocean knows who this guy is." Bijan again. He wasn't looking at me, he was looking at Navid.

"I mean, I think so," I said carefully, "but, like, it's really not—"

"You know what, fuck this shit," Navid said, and he grabbed his stuff. So did the other guys. They were all packing up.

"Wait—where are you going?"

"Don't worry about it," Carlos said to me.

"I'll see you at home," Navid said, squeezing my arm as he walked past me.

"Wait—Navid—"

"You'll be okay walking home today?" Jacobi now.

"Yeah," I said. "Yeah, but—"

"All right, cool. We'll see you tomorrow."

And they just left.

I heard, the next day, that they really had kicked the shit out of this guy, because the cops showed up at my house, looking for Navid, who shrugged it off. He told my horrified parents it was just a big misunderstanding. Navid thought it was hilarious. He said the only people who ever called the cops over a street fight were white people.

In the end, the kid didn't want to press charges. So they let it go.

Navid would be fine.

But things, for me, just kept getting worse.

TWENTY-EIGHT

It was one thing for me to have to deal with this sort of thing. I'd been here before. I knew how to handle these blows and I knew how to walk them off, even as they wounded me. And I took great care to appear so deeply, thoroughly unmoved by the whole photo debacle that the mess defused itself in a matter of days. I gave it no life. No power. And it withered easily.

Ocean, on the other hand, was new to this.

Watching him try to navigate the at once overwhelming and heartbreaking experience of the unmasked mob—

It was like watching a child learn about death for the first time.

People wouldn't leave him alone, suddenly. My face had become notorious overnight, and Navid kicking the crap out of one of these kids for throwing a pastry at my head had complicated everything. I mean, I didn't love Navid's methods, but I will say this: no one ever threw anything at me, not ever again. But kids now seemed terrified to even be near me. People were both angry *and* scared, which was possibly the most dangerous combination of emotions, and it made Ocean's association with me more outrageous than ever. His friends said awful things to him about me, about himself—things I don't even want to repeat—and he was forced into an impossible position, trying to defend me against slanderous statements about my faith, about what it meant to be Muslim, about what it was like to be *me*. It was exhausting.

Still, Ocean swore he didn't care.

He didn't, but I did.

I could feel myself pulling away, retreating inward, wanting to save him and myself by sacrificing this newfound happiness, and I knew he felt it happening. He could feel the distance growing between us—could see me shutting down, closing off—and I felt his panic. I could see it in the way he looked at me now. I heard it in his voice when he whispered *Are we okay?* on the phone last night. I felt it when he touched me, tentatively, like I might spook at any second.

But the more I pulled away, the steadier he became.

Ocean had made a choice, and he was so willing to stand by that choice that it made everyone angrier. He was alienated by his friends and he shrugged it off; his coach kept harassing him about me and he ignored it.

I think it was that he showed them no loyalty—that he seemed to care so little about the opinions of people he'd

known for far longer than he'd ever known me—that finally
pissed them off so much.

It was the middle of December, a week before winter break,
when it all got really ugly.

It was just a prank, in the end.

It was a stupid prank. Someone had wanted to mess with
Ocean and the whole thing spun so far out of control it threw
our entire world off its axis.

Some anonymous person hacked into the computer sys-
tems and sent out a mass email to the entire school district's
database. All the students and teachers in the entire county—
even the parents who were on school mailing lists—got this
email. The note was terrible. And it wasn't even about me. It
was about Ocean.

It accused him of supporting terrorism, of being anti-
American, of believing it was okay to kill innocent people
because he wanted access to seventy-two virgins. It called for
him to be kicked off the team. It said that he was a poor repre-
sentative of his hometown and a disgrace to the veterans who
supported their games. The note called him horrible names.
And the thing that made it even worse, of course, was that
there was a picture of the two of us holding hands at school.
Here was proof, it seemed to say, that he'd made friends with
the enemy.

The school started getting angry calls. Letters. Horrified
parents were demanding an explanation, a hearing, a town hall

meeting. I never knew people could care so much about the dramas surrounding high school basketball, but holy hell, it was apparently a very big deal. Ocean Desmond James was a very big deal, it turned out, and I don't think even he'd realized just how much until any of this happened.

Still, it wasn't hard for me to understand how we got here. I'd been expecting it. I'd been dreading it. But it was so hard for Ocean to stomach that the world was filled with such awful people. I tried to tell him that the bigots and the racists had always been there, and he said he'd honestly never seen them like this, that he never thought they could be like this, and I said yes, I know. I said that's how privilege works.

He was stunned.

We'd run out of places to find privacy—even just to talk about all that had transpired. We talked at night, of course, but we rarely had a chance to connect during the day, in person. The school was still so abuzz with all this bullshit that I couldn't even stop to speak to him in the halls anymore. Every class was an ordeal. Even the teachers looked a little freaked out. Only Mr. Jordan seemed sympathetic, but I knew there wasn't much he could do. And every day people I'd never once made eye contact with would lean over and say things to me when I took my seat.

"What does he have to do, exactly, to get the seventy-two virgins?"

"Isn't it against your religion to date white guys?"

"So are you, like, related to Saddam Hussein?"

"Why are you even here, if you hate America so much?"

I told them all to fuck off, but it was like a game of Whac-a-Mole. They just kept coming back.

Ocean blew off basketball practice one afternoon so that we could finally find a moment alone together. His coach was suddenly drowning the team in extra, unnecessary practices, and Ocean said it was because his coach was trying to keep him busy—that he was trying to keep the two of us apart. I knew that Ocean's decision to ditch practice would probably blow up in both our faces, but I was also grateful for the moment of peace. I'd been dying to see him, to speak to him in person and see for myself that he was okay.

We were sitting in his car in the parking lot at IHOP.

Ocean rested his head against the window, his eyes squeezed shut, as he told me about the most recent development in this shitstorm. His coach had been begging him to make the whole thing go away, and he'd said it would be easy: the school would issue a statement saying it was a stupid hoax, that the whole thing was nonsense, no big deal. Done.

I frowned.

Ocean looked upset, but I couldn't understand why. This didn't seem like a terrible idea. "That actually sounds like a great solution," I said. "It's so simple."

Ocean laughed then, but there was no life in it. And he finally met my eyes when he said, "In order for the statement to stick, I can't be seen with you anymore."

I felt like I'd been punched in the stomach. "Oh," I said.

In fact, it would be best, his coach had said, if Ocean were never publicly associated with me in any way, ever again. There was already school drama circling the two of us, and now this, the picture of us together, he said, was just too much. It was too political. All major news outlets seemed to indicate that we were about to go to war with Iraq, and the news cycle, though always insane, had been perhaps especially insane lately. Everyone was on edge. Everything was so sensitive. Ocean's coach wanted to tell everyone that the photo of us together was just another part of the prank, that it had been photoshopped, but this explanation would only have been believable if Ocean also promised to stop spending time with me. There could be no more photos of the two of us together.

"Oh," I said again.

"Yeah." Ocean looked exhausted. He ran both hands through his hair.

"So, do you"—I took a quick, painful breath—"I mean— I'd understand if y—"

"No." Ocean sat up, looked suddenly panicked. "No—no, hell no, fuck him, fuck all of them, I don't care—"

"But—"

He was shaking his head, hard. "*No*," he said again. He was staring at me in disbelief. "I can't believe you'd even— No, it's not even a discussion. I told him to go to hell."

For a moment, I didn't know what to say. I felt anger and heartbreak and even, suddenly, an immeasurable swell of joy, all in the same moment. It seemed impossible to know which emotion to follow, which one would lead me to the right decision. I knew that just because I wanted to be with Ocean didn't mean it would—or should—work out that way.

And my thoughts must've been easy to read, because Ocean leaned in and took my hands. "Hey, this isn't a big deal, okay? It seems like a big deal right now, but I swear this will blow over. None of this matters. They don't matter. This doesn't change anything for me."

But I couldn't meet his eyes anymore.

"Please," he said. "I don't care. I really don't. I don't care if they cut me from the team. I don't care about any of it. I never have."

"Yeah," I said softly. But I'd have been lying if I said I didn't think my presence in his life had only made things worse for him.

He didn't care.

But *I* did.

I cared. Things had been snowballing, fast, and I couldn't pretend I wasn't scared anymore. I cared that Ocean was about to be blacklisted by everyone in this town. I cared about his prospects. I cared about his future. I told him that if they cut him from the team he'd lose his chance at getting a basketball scholarship, and he told me not to worry about it, that he didn't even need the scholarship, that his mom had set aside some of her inheritance to pay for college.

Still, it bothered me.

I cared.

I was shaking my head, staring into my open hands when he touched my cheek. I looked up. His eyes were anguished.

"Hey," he whispered. "Don't do this, okay? Don't give up on me. I'm not going anywhere."

I felt paralyzed.

I didn't know what to do. My gut said *walk away*. Let him live his life. Even Navid told me that things had gone too far, that I should break things off.

And then, the next day, Coach Hart cornered me.

I should've known better than to talk to him alone, but he caught me in a crowd and managed to bully me, loudly, into coming into his office. He swore he just wanted to have a friendly chat about the situation, but the minute I stepped inside he started shouting at me.

He told me I was ruining Ocean's life. He said he wished I'd never moved to this town, that from the moment I'd shown up I'd been a distraction, that he'd known all along that it must've been me putting ideas in Ocean's head about quitting the team, causing trouble. He said that I'd shown up and made a mess of everything, of the entire district, and couldn't I see what I'd done? Parents and students across the county were in chaos, games had been postponed, and their reputation was on the line. They were a patriotic town, he said, with patriots among them, and my association with Ocean was destroying their image. This team mattered, he said to me, in ways that I could never understand, because he was sure that wherever I came from didn't have basketball. I didn't tell him that where I came from was California, but then, he never gave me a chance to speak. And then he said that I needed to leave Ocean the hell alone before I took away every good thing he had in his life.

"You end this, young lady," he said to me. "End it right now."

I really wanted to tell him to go to hell, but the truth was, he kind of scared me. He seemed violently angry in a way I'd never experienced alone in a room with an adult. The door was closed. I felt like I had no power. Like I couldn't trust him.

But this little chat had made things clearer for me.

Coach Hart was a complete asshole, and the more he screamed at me, the angrier I became. I didn't want to be bullied into making such a serious decision. I didn't want to be manipulated, not by anyone. In fact, I was beginning to believe that walking away from Ocean now, at a time like this, would be the greatest act of cowardice. Worse, it would be cruel.

So I refused.

And then his coach told me that if I didn't break up with him, that he would make certain that Ocean was not only kicked off the team but expelled for gross misconduct.

I said I was sure Ocean would figure it out.

"Why are you so determined to be stubborn?" Coach Hart shouted, his eyes narrowed in my direction. He looked like someone who screamed a lot; he was a stocky sort of guy with an almost permanently red face. "Let go of this," he said.

"You're wasting everyone's time, and it won't even be worth it in the end. He's going to forget about you in a week."

"Okay," I said. "Can I go now?"

Somehow he went redder. "If you care about him," he said, "then walk away. Don't destroy his life."

"I honestly don't get why everyone is this upset," I said, "over a stupid game of basketball."

"This is my career," he said, slamming the table as he stood up. "I've dedicated my entire life to this sport. We have a real shot at the playoffs this season, and I need him to perform. You are an unwelcome distraction," he said, "and I need you to disappear. *Now.*"

I hadn't realized, as I walked home from school that day, how far this craziness would go. I hadn't realized that his coach would be so determined to make this go away—to make *me* go away—that he'd actually be willing to hurt Ocean in the process. Here, with enough space between myself and his screaming coach, I was able to process the situation a little more objectively.

And, honestly, the whole thing was starting to freak me out.

It wasn't that I thought Ocean wouldn't recover from being kicked off the team; it wasn't even that I thought I couldn't tell Ocean what his coach had said to me, that he'd basically threatened me into breaking up with him. I knew Ocean would believe me, that he'd take my side. What scared me most, it turned out, weren't the threats. It wasn't the abusive rhetoric, the blatant xenophobia. No, what scared me most was that—

I guess I just didn't think I was worth it.

I thought Ocean would wake up, dizzy and destabilized by this emotional train wreck to discover that it hadn't been worth it, actually; that I hadn't been worth it. That he'd lost his chance to be a great athlete at a peak moment in his high school career and that, as a result, he'd lost his chance at playing basketball in college, at one day playing professionally. If this shitshow was to be believed, Ocean was good enough to be all this and more. I'd never seen him play—which seemed almost funny to me now—but I couldn't imagine that so many people would be *this* upset if Ocean weren't really, really good at putting a ball in a basket.

I felt suddenly scared.

I worried that Ocean would lose everything he'd ever known—everything he'd been working toward since he was a kid—only to discover that, eh, I wasn't even that great, in the end. Bad deal.

He would resent me.

I was sixteen, I thought. He was seventeen. We were just kids. This moment felt like an entire lifetime—these past months had felt like forever—but high school wasn't the whole world, was it? It couldn't have been. Five months ago I never even knew Ocean existed.

Still, I didn't want to walk away. I worried he'd never

forgive me for abandoning him, especially not now, not when he told me every day that this hadn't changed anything for him, that he'd never let their hateful opinions dictate how he lived his life. I worried that if I walked away he'd think I was a coward.

And I knew I wasn't.

I looked up, suddenly, at the sound of a car horn. It was relentless. Obnoxious. I was halfway down a main street, walking along the same stretch of sidewalk I followed home every day, but I'd been lost in my head; I hadn't been paying attention to the road.

There was a car waiting for me up ahead. It had pulled over to the side and whoever was driving would not stop honking at me.

I didn't recognize the car.

My heart gave a sudden, terrifying lurch and I took a step back. The driver was waving frantically at me, and only the fact that the driver was a woman gave me pause. My instincts told me to run like hell, but I worried that maybe she needed help. Maybe she'd run out of gas? Maybe she needed to borrow a cell phone?

I stepped cautiously toward her. She leaned out of her car window.

"Wow," she said, and laughed. "It's really hard to get your attention."

She was a pretty, older blond lady. Her eyes seemed friendly enough, and my pulse slowed its stutter.

"Are you okay?" I asked. "Did your car break down?"

She smiled. Looked curiously at me. "I'm Ocean's mom," she said. "My name is Linda. You're Shirin, right?"

Oh, I thought. *Shit shit shit.*

Oh shit.

I blinked at her. My heart was beating a staccato.

"Would you like to go for a ride?"

TWENTY-NINE

"Listen," she said, "I want to get this out of the way right upfront." She glanced at me as she drove. "I don't care about the differences in your backgrounds. That's not why I'm here."

"Okay," I said slowly.

"But your relationship is causing Ocean a real problem right now, and I'd be an irresponsible mother if I didn't try to make it stop."

I almost laughed out loud. I didn't think this was the thing that would turn her into an irresponsible mother, I wanted to say.

Instead, I said, "I don't understand why everyone is having this conversation with *me*. If you don't want your son to spend time with me, maybe you should be talking to *him*."

"I tried," she said. "He won't listen to me. He's not listening to anyone." She glanced in my direction again. I suddenly realized I had no idea where we were going. "I was hoping," she said, "that you would be more reasonable."

"That's because you don't know me," I said to her. "Ocean is the reasonable one in the relationship."

She actually cracked a smile. "I'm not going to waste your time, I promise. I can tell that my son genuinely likes you. I don't want to hurt him—or you, for that matter—but there are just things you don't know."

"Things like what?"

"Well," she said, and took a deep breath, "things like—I've always relied on Ocean getting a basketball scholarship." And then she looked at me, looked at me for so long I worried we'd crash into something. "I can't risk him getting kicked off the team."

I frowned. "Ocean told me he didn't need a scholarship. He said that you had money set aside for him, for college."

"I don't."

"What?" I stared at her. "Why not?"

"That's really none of your business," she said.

"Does Ocean know about this?" I said. "That you spent all his money for college?"

She flushed, unexpectedly, and for the first time, I saw something mean in her eyes. "First of all," she said, "it's not his money. It's my money. I am the adult in our household, and for as long as he lives under my roof, I get to choose how we live. And second of all"—she hesitated—"my personal affairs are not up for discussion."

I was floored.

I said, "Why would you lie about something like that? Why wouldn't you just tell him that he has no money for college?"

Her cheeks had gone a blotchy, unflattering red, and her jaw was so tight I really thought she might snap and start screaming at me. Instead, she said, very stiffly, "Our relationship is strained enough as it is. I didn't see the point in making things worse." And then she pulled to a sudden stop.

We were in front of my house.

"How do you know where I live?" I said, stunned.

"It wasn't hard to find out." She put the car in park. Turned in her seat to face me. "If you get him kicked off the team," she said, "he won't be able to go to a good school. Do you understand that?" She was looking me full in the face now, and it was suddenly hard to be brave. Her eyes were so patronizing. Condescending. I felt entirely like a child. "I need you to tell me you understand," she said. "Do you understand?"

"I understand," I said.

"I also need you to know that I don't care where your family is from. I don't care which faith you practice. Whatever you think of me," she said, "I don't want you to think I'm a bigot. Because I'm not. And I never raised my son to be that way, either."

I could only stare at her now. My breaths felt short; sharp. She was still talking.

"This is about more than taking a stand, okay? If you can

believe it, I still remember what it was like to be sixteen. All those emotions," she said, waving a hand. "It feels like the real deal. I actually married my high school sweetheart. Did Ocean tell you?"

"No," I said quietly.

"Yes," she said, and nodded. "Well. You see how well that worked out."

Wow, I really hated her.

"I just want you to understand," she said. "That this isn't about you. This is about Ocean. And if you care about him at all—which I'm pretty sure you do—then you need to let him go. Don't cause him all this trouble, okay? He's a good boy. He doesn't deserve it."

I felt suddenly impotent with rage. I felt it dissolving my brain.

"I'm really glad we had this talk," she said, and reached over me to push open my door. "But I'd be grateful if you didn't tell Ocean it happened. I'd still like to salvage a relationship with my son."

She sat back, the open door screaming at me to get out.

I felt then, in that moment, the insubstantial weight of my sixteen years in a way I'd never felt before. I had no control here. No power. I didn't even have my driver's license. I didn't have a job, I didn't have my own bank account. There was nothing I could do. Nothing I could do to help, to make this better. I had no connections in the world, no voice anyone would listen to. I felt at once everything, *everything*, and nothing at all.

I didn't have a choice anymore. Ocean's mother had taken my options away from me. She'd screwed up, and now it was my fault that Ocean would have no money for college.

I'd become a convenient scapegoat. It felt too familiar.

Still, I knew I had to do it. I'd have to drive a permanent wedge between us. I thought Ocean's mom was awful, but I also knew that I could no longer let him get kicked off the team. I couldn't bear the weight of being the reason his life was derailed.

And sometimes, I thought, being a teenager was the worst thing that had ever happened to me.

THIRTY

It was horrible.

I didn't know how else to do it—it'd been so hard for us to find time alone together—so I texted him. It was late. Very late. Somehow, I had a feeling he'd still be up.

hey
i need to talk to you

He didn't respond, and for some reason I knew it wasn't because he hadn't seen my message. I thought he knew me well enough to know that something was wrong, and I often wondered if he knew right then that something terrible was about to happen.

He texted me back ten minutes later.

no

I called him.

"Stop," he said, when he picked up. He sounded raw. "Don't do this. Don't have this conversation with me, okay? I'm sorry," he said, "I'm so sorry about everything. I'm sorry I put you in this situation. I'm so sorry."

"Ocean, please—"

"What did my mom say to you?"

"What?" I felt thrown off. "How did you know I talked to your mom?"

"I didn't," he said, "but I do now. I was worried she was going to try to talk to you. She's been on my ass all week, begging me to break up with you." And then, "Did she do this? Did she tell you to do this?"

I almost couldn't breathe.

"Ocean—"

"Don't do it," he said. "Not for her. Don't do this for any of them—"

"This is about *you*," I said. "Your happiness. Your future. Your life. I want you to be happy," I said, "and I'm only making your life worse."

"How can you say that?" he said, and I heard his voice break. "How can you even think that? I want this more than I've ever wanted anything. I want everything with you," he said. "I want all of it with you. I want *you*. I want this forever."

"You're seventeen," I said. "We're in high school, Ocean. We don't know anything about forever."

"We could have it if we wanted it."

I knew I was being unkind, and I hated myself for it, but I had to find a way to get through this conversation before it killed me. "I wish this were simpler," I said to him, "I wish so many things were different. I wish we were older. I wish we could make our own decisions—"

"Don't—baby—don't do this—"

"You can go back to your life now, you know?" And I felt my heart splinter as I said it. My voice shook. "You can be normal again."

"I don't want normal," he said desperately. "I don't want whatever that is, why don't you believe me—"

"I have to go," I said, because I was crying now. "I have to go."

And I hung up on him.

He called me back, about a hundred times. Left me voice mails I never checked.

And then I cried myself to sleep.

THIRTY-ONE

I had two weeks off for winter break and I drowned my sorrows in music, I stayed up late reading, I trained hard, and I drew ugly, unimpressive things. I wrote in my diary. I made more clothes. I threw myself into practice.

Ocean wouldn't stop calling me.

He texted me, over and over again—

I love you
I love you
I love you
I love you

Part of me felt a little like I'd died. But here, in the silent explosion of my heart, was a quiet that felt familiar. I was just me again, back in my room with my books and my thoughts.

I drank coffee in the mornings with my dad before he left for work. I sat with my mom in the evenings and binge-watched episodes of her favorite TV show, *Little House on the Prairie*, after she'd found the DVD box sets at Costco.

But I spent most of my days with Navid.

He'd come into my room, that first night. He'd heard me crying and he sat down on my bed, pulled the covers back, pushed my hair out of my face, and kissed me on the forehead.

"Fuck this town," he said.

We hadn't really talked about it since then, and not because he hadn't asked. I just didn't have the vocabulary. My feelings were still inarticulate, comprising little more than tears and expletives.

So we practiced.

We didn't have access to the dance rooms at school over winter break, and we were really sick of the cardboard boxes we'd used on weekends, so we splurged on an upgrade. We went to Home Depot, purchased a roll of linoleum, and jammed it into Navid's car. It was easy to unfurl the linoleum in deserted alleys and parking lots. Sometimes Jacobi's parents let us use their garage, but it didn't really matter where we were; we'd just set up our old boom box and breakdance.

I'd mastered the crab walk pretty well, believe it or not. Navid had started teaching me how to do the cricket, which was a level of difficulty slightly higher than that, and I was getting better every day. Navid was *thrilled*—but only because he had a personal stake in my progress.

Navid was still really invested in the school talent show—something I no longer cared even a little bit about—but he'd been planning it for so long that I didn't have the heart to tell him I didn't want to do it anymore. So I listened to his ideas about choreography, the songs he wanted to mix for the music, which beats were best for which power moves. I did it for him. I officially hated this school more than any other school I'd ever been to, and had absolutely zero interest in making an impression. But he'd trained me so patiently all these months; I couldn't turn back now.

Besides, we were getting really good.

The first week of winter break seemed to crawl by. It was impossible to deny, despite all empirical evidence to the contrary, that there wasn't a massive cavity in my chest where my emotions used to be. I felt numb, all the time.

I stared at Ocean's text messages before I fell asleep, hating myself for my own silence. I wanted desperately to text him back, to tell him that I loved him, too, but I worried that if I reached out to him, I wouldn't be strong enough to walk away again. So many times, I thought, I'd tried to draw a line in the sand, and I was never strong enough to keep it there.

If only I had.

If only I'd told Ocean to go away after he followed me out of Mr. Jordan's class. If only I hadn't texted him later that night. If only I'd never agreed to talk to him at lunch. If only I'd never gone with Ocean to his car maybe he never would've kissed me and maybe then I wouldn't have known, I wouldn't have known what it was like to be with him and none of this would've happened and God, sometimes I really wished I could go back in time and erase all the moments that led to this one. I could've saved us both all this trouble. All this heartache.

Ocean stopped texting me on week two.

The pain became a drumbeat; a rhythm I could write a song to. It was always there, stark and steady, rarely abating. I learned to drown out the sound during the day, but at night it screamed through the hole in my chest.

THIRTY-TWO

Yusef had become a good friend of Navid's, and I'd been completely unaware of this until he started showing up to our breakdancing practices. Apparently Navid had sold him on the art of breakdancing, and he was now interested in learning.

We were practicing in the far corner of a rarely frequented Jack in the Box parking lot when Yusef first showed up, and I was upside down when I saw him. Navid had been in the middle of teaching me to spin on my head, and when he let go of my legs to say hi, I fell over on my ass.

"*Oh my God,*" I shouted, "What the hell, Navid—"

I shucked off my helmet, readjusted my scarf, and tried to sit up with some dignity.

Navid only shrugged. "You have to work on your balance."

"Hey," Yusef said, and smiled at me. His eyes lit up; his

whole face seemed to shine. Smiling was an objectively good look for him. "I didn't know you'd be here, too."

"Yeah," I said, and tugged absently at my sweater. I tried to smile back but wasn't really feeling it, so I waved. "Welcome."

We spent the rest of the week together, all six of us. It was nice. Carlos and Bijan and Jacobi had somehow become my friends, too, which was comforting. They never really talked to me about what happened with Ocean, even though I knew they knew, but they were kind to me in other ways. They told me they cared without ever saying the words. And Yusef was just—cool. Friendly.

Easy.

It was kind of amazing, actually, not to have to explain everything to him all the time. Yusef wasn't terrified of girls in hijab; they didn't perplex him. He didn't require a manual to navigate my mind. My feelings and choices didn't require constant explanations.

He was never weird with me.

He never asked me dumb questions. He never wondered aloud whether or not I had to shower with that thing on. One day, last year—at a different high school—I was sitting in math class and this guy I barely knew wouldn't stop staring at me. At all. Fifteen minutes passed and finally I couldn't take it anymore. I spun around, ready to tell him to go to hell, when he said,

"Hey, okay, so—what if you were having sex and that thing just, like, fell off your head? What would you do then?"

Yusef never asked me questions like that.

It was nice.

He started hanging out at our house all the time, actually. He'd come over after practice to eat and play video games with my brother and he was always really, really nice. Yusef was the obvious choice for me, I knew that. I think he knew that, too, but he never said anything about it. He'd just look at me a little longer than most people did. He'd smile at me a little more than most people did. He waited, I think, to see if I'd make a move.

I didn't.

On New Year's Eve I sat in the living room with my dad, who was reading a book. My dad was always reading. He read before work in the mornings and every evening before bed. I often thought he had the mind of a mad genius and the heart of a philosopher. I was staring at him that night, and staring into a cold cup of tea, thinking.

"Baba," I said.

"Hmm?" He turned a page.

"How do you know if you've done the right thing?"

My dad's head popped up. He blinked at me and closed his book. Removed his glasses. He looked me in the eye for only a moment before he said, in Farsi, "If the decision you've made has brought you closer to humanity, then you've done the right thing."

"Oh."

He watched me for a second, and I knew he was saying, without speaking, that I could tell him what was on my mind. But I wasn't ready. I still wasn't ready. So I pretended to misunderstand.

"Thanks," I said. "I was just wondering."

He tried to smile. "I'm sure you've done the right thing," he said.

But I didn't think I had.

THIRTY-THREE

We went back to school on a Thursday, my heart lodged firmly in my throat, but Ocean wasn't there. He didn't show up for either of the classes we had together. I didn't know if he'd gone to school that day, because I never saw him, and I suddenly worried that maybe he'd transferred classes. I couldn't blame him if he had, of course, but I'd been hoping for a glimpse of him. Of his face.

School was, otherwise, anticlimactic. I'd become a photo-shopping error, and our two weeks away on break had given everyone some kind of amnesia. No one cared about me anymore. There was new gossip now, gossip that didn't concern me or my life. As far as I could tell, Ocean had been returned to his former status. There was no longer any need to panic, as I'd been surgically removed from his life.

Everything was fine.

People went back to ignoring me in the way they always had.

I was sitting under my tree when I saw that girl again.

"Hey," she said. Her long brown hair was tied up into a ponytail this time, but she was still unmistakably the same girl who told me I was a terrible person.

I wasn't sure I wanted to say hi to her.

"Yes?"

"Can I sit down?" she said.

I raised an eyebrow, but I said okay.

We were both silent for a minute.

Finally, she said, "I'm really sorry about what happened. With that picture. With Ocean." She was sitting cross-legged on the grass, leaning against my tree, and staring out toward the quad in the distance. "That must've been really awful."

"I thought you said I was a terrible person."

She looked at me, then. "People in this town are so racist. Sometimes it's really hard to live here."

I sighed. Said, "Yeah. I know."

"I kind of couldn't believe it when you showed up," she said, and she was looking away again. "I saw you on the first day of school. I couldn't believe you were brave enough to wear hijab here. No one else does."

I broke off a blade of grass. Folded it in half. "I'm not brave," I said to her. "I'm scared all the time, too. But whenever

I think about taking it off, I realize my reasons have to do with how people treat me when I'm wearing it. I think, it would be easier, you know? So much easier. It would make my life easier not to wear it, because if I didn't wear it, maybe people would treat me like a human being."

I broke off another blade of grass. Tore it into tiny pieces.

"But that seems like such a shitty reason to do something," I said. "It gives the bullies all the power. It would mean they'd succeeded at making me feel like who I was and what I believed in was something to be ashamed of. So, I don't know," I said. "I keep wearing it."

We were both quiet again.

And then—

"It doesn't make a difference, you know."

I looked up.

"Taking it off," she said. "It doesn't make a difference." She was staring at me now. Her eyes were full of tears. "They still treat me like I'm garbage."

She and I became friends after that. Her name was Amna. She invited me to have lunch with her and her friends, and I was genuinely grateful for the offer. I told her I'd look for her around school tomorrow. I thought maybe I'd ask her to go to the movies sometime. Hell, I might even pretend to give a shit about the SATs when she was around.

It sounded nice.

* * *

I saw Ocean for the first time the next day.

I'd gotten to the dance room a little early, and I was waiting outside for Navid to arrive with the key when Yusef showed up.

"So this is where the magic happens, huh?" Yusef was smiling at me again. He was a big smiler. "I'm excited."

I laughed. "I'm glad you like it," I said. "Not many people even know what breakdancing is, which is kind of heartbreaking. Navid and I have been obsessed with it for, I don't know, forever."

"That's really cool," he said, but he was smiling at me like I'd said something funny. "I like how much you like it."

"I do like it," I said, and I couldn't help it—I smiled back. Yusef was so buoyant all the time; his smiles were occasionally contagious. "Breakdancing is actually a combination of kung fu and gymnastics," I said to him, "which I think will work out well for you, because Navid said you used to fi—"

"Oh—" Yusef looked suddenly startled. He was staring at something behind me. "Maybe"—he glanced at me—"should I go?"

I turned around, confused.

My heart stopped.

I'd never seen Ocean in his basketball uniform before. His arms were bare. He looked strong and toned and muscular. He looked so good. He was so gorgeous.

But he looked different.

I'd never gotten to know this side of him—the basketball

player version of him—and in his uniform he looked like someone I didn't know. In fact, I was so distracted by his outfit that it took me a second to realize he looked upset. More than upset. He looked upset and angry all at once. He was frozen in place, staring at me. Staring at Yusef.

I started to panic.

"Ocean," I said, "I'm not—"

But he'd already left.

I found out on Monday that Ocean had been suspended from the team. He'd gotten into a fight with another player, apparently, and he'd have to sit out the next two games for disorderly conduct.

I knew this, because everyone was talking about it.

Most people seemed to think it was funny—it was almost like they thought it was cool. Getting into a fight on the court seemed to give Ocean some kind of street cred.

But I was worried.

The second week was just as bad. Awful. Stressful. And it wasn't until the end of the week that I realized Ocean had not, in fact, switched any of his classes.

He was just cutting class. All the time.

I realized this when I showed up in bio on Friday, and he was there. Sitting in his chair. The same one he always sat in.

My heart was suddenly racing.

I didn't know what to do. Did I say hi? Did I ignore him?

Would he want me to say hi? Would he prefer that I ignore him?

I couldn't ignore him.

I walked up slowly. Dropped my bag on the floor and felt something in my chest expand as I stared at him. Emotions, filling the cavity.

"Hey," I said.

He looked up. He looked away.

He didn't say anything to me for the rest of the period.

THIRTY-FOUR

Navid had been working all of us harder than we'd ever worked in practice. The talent show was in two weeks, which meant we were practicing until really late, every night. Every day it seemed increasingly stupid to me that I'd be performing in a talent show for this terrible school, but I figured we'd just see it through. Get it over with. Breakdancing had been my only constant through everything this year, and I was so grateful for the space it gave me to just be, to breathe, and to get lost in the music.

I felt like I owed Navid this favor.

Besides, the stakes were higher than I thought they'd be. It turned out that the talent show was a really big deal at this school—bigger, it seemed, than at any of the other schools I'd been to, because it took place during the actual school day. They shut down classes for this. Everyone came out. Teachers, students, all the staff. Moms and dads and grandparents were already standing around the gym, anxiously snapping pictures of nothing important. My own parents, on the other hand, had no idea what we were doing today. They weren't here cheering us on, holding bouquets of flowers in sweaty, nervous hands. My parents were so generally unimpressed with their own children that I really believed I could, I don't know, win something like a Nobel Peace Prize, and they'd only reluctantly attend the ceremony, all the while pointing out that lots of people won Nobel Prizes, that, in fact, they gave out Nobel Prizes every year, and anyway the peace prize was clearly the prize for slackers, so maybe next time I should focus my energy on physics or math or something.

My parents loved us, but I wasn't always sure they liked us.

Mostly, the vibe I got from my mom was that she thought I was a dramatic, sentimental sort of teenager whose interests were cute but useless. She loved me, fiercely, but she also had very little tolerance for people who couldn't sack up and get their shit together, and my occasional lapses into deep, emotional holes made her think I was still uncooked. She was always waiting for me to grow up.

She'd been getting ready to leave for work this morning when, as she was saying goodbye, she caught a glimpse of my outfit. She shook her head and said, *"Ey khoda. Een chiyeh digeh?"* *Oh God. What is this?*

I was wearing a newly altered, totally revamped military-style jacket with epaulets and brass buttons, and I'd embroidered the back, by hand; it read, in a loose script, *people are strange*. It was not only an homage to one of my favorite songs by the Doors—but it was a statement that deeply resonated with me. The whole thing had taken hours of work. I thought it was amazing.

My mom cringed and said, in Farsi, "Is this really what you're going to wear?" She craned her neck to read the back of my jacket. "*Yanni chi people are strange?*" And I didn't even have a chance to defend my outfit before she sighed, patted me on the shoulder, and said, "*Negaran nabash.*" *Don't worry.* "I'm sure you'll grow out of it."

"Hey," I said, "I wasn't worried—" But she was already walking out the door. "Hey, seriously," I said, "I actually like what I'm wearing—"

"Don't do anything stupid today," she said, and waved goodbye.

But I *was* about to do something stupid.

I mean, I thought it was stupid, anyway. Navid thought this talent show was awesome. It was apparently a big deal that we even got to perform; some committee had whittled down a stack of submissions and chosen, of the many, only ten acts to be onstage today.

We were up fourth.

I hadn't realized how serious this was until Navid explained it to me. Still, there were, like, a couple thousand kids at our school, and they'd all be sitting in the audience, watching us— and nine other performances—and I didn't understand how this could turn out to be a good thing. I thought it was dumb. But I reminded myself that I was doing it for Navid.

We were waiting in the wings with the other performers—mostly singers; a couple of bands; there was even a girl who'd be performing a solo on the saxophone—and for the first time, I was the only one in our group who appeared to have retained any level of chill. We'd changed into matching silver windbreakers, gray sweatpants, and gray Puma suedes—and I thought we looked good. I thought we were ready. But Jacobi, Carlos, Bijan, and Navid seemed super nervous, and it was weird to see them like this. They were normally so cool; totally unflappable. I realized then that the only reason I didn't share their nerves was because I genuinely didn't care about the outcome.

I felt deflated. Kind of bored.

The guys, on the other hand, wouldn't stop pacing. They talked to each other; they talked to themselves. Jacobi would start saying, "So, like we all walk— Yeah, we all walk out at the same—" and then he'd stop, count something out on his fingers, and then nod, only to himself. "Okay," he'd say. "Yeah."

And every time a new act went up, I felt them tense. We listened to the thuds and squeaks that meant they were prepping the stage for a new performance; we heard the slightly muted cheers following the introduction; and then we sat, very quietly, and listened to our competitors. Carlos was always wondering aloud whether or not the other performers were any good. Bijan would assure him that they sucked. Jacobi would disagree. Carlos would agonize. Navid would look up at me and ask, on five different occasions, whether I'd gotten the right music to the AV tech.

"Yeah, but, remember—we changed the mix at the last minute," he said. "Are you sure you got him the new one?"

"Yes," I said, trying not to roll my eyes.

"You're sure? It was the CD that said *Mix Number Four* on it."

"Oh," I said, feigning surprise. "Was it mix number four? Are you su—"

"Oh my God Shirin don't mess with me right now—"

"*Calm down*," I said, and laughed. "It's going to be fine. We've done this a thousand times."

But he wouldn't sit still.

In the end, I was wrong.

The show wasn't dumb at all. Actually, the whole thing was kind of awesome. We'd done this routine so many times I didn't even have to think about it anymore.

We started out with all five of us doing a fully choreographed dance routine, and as the music changed, so did we. We broke apart and took turns taking center stage, each of us performing a different combination of moves; but our performances were fluid—they talked to each other. The whole thing was meant to breathe, like everything we did was part of a larger heartbeat. The boys killed it.

Our choreography was fresh; our moves were tight and perfectly in sync; the music was mixed beautifully.

Even I wasn't too bad.

My uprock was the best it'd ever been; my six-step was spot-on, and I dropped into a crab walk that morphed, briefly, into a cricket. The cricket was a similar move; my body weight was still balanced on my elbows, which I'd tucked into my torso; the difference was that you moved around in a circle. The whole thing was pretty fast. I felt strong. Totally stable. I ended with a rise up, and then fell forward into a handstand, only to arch my back and let my legs curve behind me, never touching the ground. This was a pose called hollowback, and it was a move that might've been, for me, even harder than the crab walk. I'd been working on it forever. After a few seconds, I let gravity pull me down, slowly, and I jumped back up again.

It was my one routine. I'd practiced it a million times.

Bijan ended the whole set by doing four backflips across the stage, and when our performance was over we all had about half a second of quiet to look at each other, still catching our breaths. Somehow we knew, without speaking, that we'd done okay.

What I hadn't been expecting, of course, was for the rest of the school to agree. I hadn't been expecting them to suddenly stand up, to start screaming, to generally lose their shit at our performance. I hadn't been expecting the cheers, the thunder of applause.

I hadn't been expecting us to *win*.

* * *

Mostly, I was happy for my brother. He'd built this moment; he'd spearheaded this mission. And when we were handed a plastic trophy and a fifty-dollar gift certificate to the Olive Garden, Navid looked like he'd been handed the moon. I was so happy for him.

But then, I don't know—

School became suddenly ridiculous.

For a full week after the talent show I couldn't get to class without incident. People started chasing me down the hall. Everyone wanted to talk to me. Kids began waving at me as I walked by. I was cutting across the quad one day and one of the janitors saw me, said, "Hey, you're that girl who spins on her head!" and I was legitimately freaked out.

I hadn't even spun on my head.

I mean, I was happy they weren't calling me towelhead anymore, but the sudden and abrupt transition from nasty to nice was giving me whiplash. I was confused. I couldn't believe people thought I'd forget that just over a month ago they were treating me like an actual piece of shit. My teachers, who, post-Ramadan—when I'd wanted to take a day off to celebrate literally the biggest holiday in the Muslim calendar—had said to me, "We're going to need a note from your parents to make sure you're missing school for a real thing," were now congratulating me in front of the whole class. The politics of school popularity were baffling. I didn't know how they could change gears like this. They'd all seemed to have abruptly forgotten that I was still the same girl they'd tried to humiliate, over and over again.

Navid was experiencing a similar issue, but, unlike me, he didn't seem to mind. "Just enjoy it," he said.

But I didn't know how I could.

By the end of January I had an entirely different social status than I'd had just weeks prior. It was *insane*.

I opened my locker and five invitations to five different house parties all fell out, onto my face. I was sitting under my tree at lunch, reading a book, when a group of girls shouted at me, from across the quad, to come sit with them. Guys had started talking to me in class. They'd come up to me after school, ask me if I had plans, and I'd say *yes, I have big plans to get the hell out of here*, and they didn't get it. They'd offer to drive me home.

I wanted to scream.

I'd somehow, inadvertently, done something that'd given the population at this school permission to put me in a different kind of box, and I didn't know how to deal with it. It was more than confusing—it *killed* me to discover the depth of their spinelessness. Somehow, I wasn't a terrorist anymore. I'd leveled up. They now saw me as some kind of exotic-looking breakdancer. Our performance had deactivated their alarms.

I was deemed cool. Safe.

Threat Level Green.

And it wasn't until Coach Hart passed me in the hall,

tipped his basketball hat at me and said, "Nice job the other day," that I felt suddenly certain I'd spontaneously combust.

I'd broken up with Ocean over this.

I'd walked away from one of the most amazing people I'd ever known because I'd been bullied into it by his coach, by his peers, by his own mother. My face, my body, my general image in his life had been hurting him. Had been a threat to his career. To his prospects.

What about now?

What if Ocean had fallen for me *now*? Now, when the students didn't find me so scary anymore. Now, when people looked in my direction and smiled; now, when I couldn't walk down the hall without someone trying to talk to me; now, when my teachers stopped me after class and asked me where I'd learned to dance like that.

Would the timing have made a difference?

The breathtaking levels of their hypocrisy had given me a migraine.

I saw Ocean again on a Wednesday.

I was at my locker long after the final bell rang, swapping my things out in preparation for practice—the talent show was over, but we still had a lot more we wanted to do—when Ocean found me. I hadn't spoken a single word to him since the day I'd seen him in bio, and for the first time in a month, I had a real opportunity to study him. To look into his eyes.

But what I saw only made me feel worse.

He looked tired. Worn-out. He looked thinner. He never really showed up to class anymore, and I wasn't sure how he was getting away with it.

"Hi," he said.

I felt frozen at just the sound of his voice. Overwhelmed. A little bit like I wanted to cry.

"Hi," I said.

"I don't"—he looked away, ran a hand through his hair— "I don't actually know what I'm doing here. I just—" He stopped and looked up, off into the distance. I heard him sigh.

He didn't have to explain.

It was the middle of February. The halls had been plastered with Cupid cutouts and paper hearts. Some club on campus was selling Valentine's Day candy grams and the violently pink posters assaulted me everywhere I went. I'd never needed an excuse to think about Ocean, but Valentine's Day was only two days away, and it was hard not to be constantly reminded of what I'd lost.

Finally, he looked at me.

"I never got to tell you that I saw you," he said. "In the talent show." His mouth threatened to smile, and then, didn't. "You were great," he said softly. "You were so great."

And I could no more control the words I said next than the earthquake he'd left in my bones. "I miss you," I said. "I miss you so much."

Ocean flinched, like I'd slapped him. He looked away and when he looked up again I swore I saw tears in his eyes. "What am I supposed to do with that?" he said. "What am I supposed to say to that?"

I don't know, I said, I'm sorry, I said, never mind, I said, and my hands were shaking, and I dropped my books all over the floor. I scrambled and Ocean tried to help me but I told him I was fine, it was fine, and I stacked the books in my locker, I said a clumsy goodbye, and the whole thing was so awful that I didn't realize I'd forgotten to spin the combination—that I'd forgotten to make sure my locker was even closed—until long after I'd finished practice.

When I came back to check, I breathed a sigh of relief. Everything was still there. But I was just about to close it back up when I realized that my journal, which I'd always, always hidden at the bottom of my locker, had suddenly moved to the top.

THIRTY-FIVE

I spent the whole rest of the night feeling vaguely terrified.

Was I imagining it? Had I managed to move my journal when I was reshuffling everything? Was it coincidence or accident?

And then—

What if I *hadn't* imagined it? What if Ocean actually read my journal?

I'd been gone for under two hours, so I didn't think there was any danger of him having read the whole thing, but even small portions of my diary were extremely sensitive to me.

I grabbed it from its current hiding place in my bedroom and starting reading in reverse. I figured if Ocean had started reading my journal, he'd have been most interested in the things I'd written recently, and I only had to scan the page for a second before I felt suddenly awash with mortification. I squeezed my eyes shut. Covered my face with one hand.

I had a dream about Ocean last night, the contents of which were extremely intense. This was, wow. This was terrible. I sat down on my bed, cringing through another flush of embarrassment, and kept turning pages, going backward in time.

> My anger at how other students treated me now; how
> they pretended their original cruelty had never
> happened.
> My thoughts on seeing Ocean in his uniform; my fear
> that he'd think I was interested in Yusef.
> The agony of coming back to school; worrying about
> Ocean, worrying about his suspension.
> My conversation with my father; my worries that I'd done
> the wrong thing.
> Reflections on conversations with Yusef; how I never had
> to explain myself to him.
> Pages and pages trying to capture how I felt about
> Ocean's absence in my life; how much I missed him;
> how terrible I felt about everything that'd happened.
> A single page that read—
> I love you, too, so much, so much

It went on like this through the last few weeks. Mostly it was just me, chronicling heartbreak the only way I knew how.

I exhaled a long, shaky breath and looked up at the wall. My mind was at war with itself.

There was a part of me that felt true horror at the idea of Ocean having read any of this. It felt like an intrusion, a betrayal. But there was another part of me that understood why he might've been looking for answers.

I hated how things had ended between us. I hated how I was forced to walk away from him, hated that he didn't know the truth, hated that he told me he loved me and I'd just ignored him. Especially after everything—after everything we'd been through, after everything he'd said to me and how hard he'd fought to be with me—

He told me he loved me and I'd just ignored him.

Just thinking about it broke my heart all over again. And suddenly, I hoped he really had read these pages. Suddenly, I wished he would. I wished he knew.

Suddenly, I wanted to tell him everything.

The more I thought about it, the more the prospect of Ocean discovering these pages felt a bit like freedom. I wanted him to know that I loved him, but I knew I couldn't say it to him now, not in person, not without an explanation about the way things ended between us. It was embarrassing, in so many ways, to imagine him reading my personal thoughts. In other ways, it was kind of liberating.

Still, I didn't know for sure if he'd read any of it.

It was then that I noticed one of the pages in the journal had been torn, just a little. I flipped to it. It was dated that last day of school, just before winter break. The day I'd ended things with Ocean.

The first part was all about his coach, cornering me. All the awful things he'd said about me. How he'd threatened to expel Ocean if I didn't break up with him. And then more, later, about his mother. How she'd lost his money for school. How she'd asked me never to tell him anything about our conversation.

And then, at the end, how, regardless of all the threats, I just didn't think I was worth the sacrifices he was making for me.

I closed the book. I was breathing too fast.

THIRTY-SIX

The next day at school was insane.

Ocean was expelled.

I was sitting with Amna under my tree when I heard the commotion. Kids in the quad were shouting—people were scrambling—and a few of them were screaming, "Fight! Fight!"

I felt a sudden, horrible feeling tighten in my gut.

"What do you think is happening?" I said.

Amna shrugged. She stood up, walked out several feet, and looked out into the distance. She'd come by today to give me a bag of ginger candies her mother had made, and I remembered this because when she spun around, her eyes wide, she dropped the little ziplock bag to the ground.

Ginger candies spilled out over the grass.

"Oh my God," she said, "it's Ocean."

He'd punched his coach in the face. I ran into the quad

just in time to see two guys trying to break up the fight and Ocean started fighting them, too. People were screaming at each other.

Ocean was shouting, "You're all a bunch of hypocrites," and someone tried to haul him away and he said, "Don't touch me—don't you fucking touch me—"

He'd quit the team.

He was expelled later that day. He'd apparently broken Coach Hart's nose pretty badly; he'd need to have surgery.

And I wasn't sure I'd ever see Ocean again.

THIRTY-SEVEN

My mornings were always something like this:

Navid and I fought over who got to shower first in our shared bathroom, because he always managed to make everything wet, and after he finished shaving he'd leave these tiny little hairs all over the sink and it didn't matter how many times I told him how gross it was, he never seemed to take the hint. Still, he usually won the right to take the first shower because he had to be at school an hour earlier than me. My parents would then force the both of us to come downstairs and eat breakfast, during which time my mother would ask us if we'd done our morning prayers and Navid and I would spoon cereal into our mouths and lie that we had, and my mom would roll her eyes and tell us to make sure we at least did our afternoon prayers, and we'd lie that we would, and my mom would sigh, heavily, and then Navid would leave for school. My parents left for work shortly thereafter, and I usually had the house to myself for at least thirty glorious minutes before I began my hike to the panopticon.

It hadn't occurred to me that this information—information I'd shared with Ocean when he wanted to drive me to school for the first time—would continue to be useful to us.

I'd just finished locking the door when I turned around to discover Ocean standing in front of my house. He was in front of his car, in front of my house. Looking at me.

I almost couldn't believe it.

He lifted his hand in an approximation of a wave, but he seemed uncertain. I walked over, my heart beating out of my chest, until I was standing right in front of him and somehow, this seemed to surprise him. He'd been leaning against his car; he suddenly stood up straighter. He shoved his hands in his pockets. He took a deep breath and said, "Hey."

"Hi," I said.

The air was cold—icy, even—and it smelled the way early mornings always smelled to me: like dead leaves and the dregs of unfinished cups of coffee. He wasn't wearing a jacket, I realized, and I didn't know how long he'd been standing out here. His cheeks were pink. His nose looked cold. His eyes were brighter in the morning light; more blues, sharper browns.

And then—

"I'm so sorry," we said at the same time.

Ocean laughed, looked away. I merely stared at him.

Finally, he said, "Do you want to skip school with me today?"

"Yeah," I said. "Yeah."

He smiled.

I watched him while he drove. Studied his profile, the lines of his body. I liked the way he moved, the way he touched things, the way he held his head up with such casual dignity. He always seemed so comfortable in his own skin, and it reminded me of what I loved about the way he walked: he had this really steady, certain step. The way he moved through the world made me think it had never occurred to him, not once, not even on a really rough day, to wonder whether he might've been a bad person. It was obvious to me that he didn't dislike himself. Ocean didn't dissect his own mind. He never agonized over his actions and he was never suspicious of people. He never even seemed to experience embarrassment the way that I did. His mind seemed, to me, like an extremely peaceful place. Free from thorns.

"Wow," he said, and when he exhaled it was a little uneven. "I don't, um, want to tell you to stop, like, looking at me, exactly, but all this uninterrupted staring is really making me nervous."

I sat back, suddenly mortified. "I'm sorry."

He glanced in my direction. Attempted a smile. "What are you thinking about?"

"You," I said.

"Oh." But it sounded more like a breath.

And then, suddenly, we were somewhere else. Ocean had parked his car in the driveway of a house I didn't recognize but felt fairly certain was his own home.

"Don't worry, my mom isn't here," he said, after he'd turned off the car. "I just really wanted to talk to you somewhere private, and I didn't know where else to go." He met my eyes and I felt panic and peace all at the same time. "Is this okay?"

I nodded.

Ocean opened my door for me. He took my backpack and slung it over his shoulder and walked me toward his house. He looked a bit apprehensive. I *felt* a bit apprehensive. His house was big—not too big—but big. Nice. I wish I'd noticed more when we walked inside, but the morning had already been punctuated by moments so intense that its details seemed to be rendered in watercolor. Soft and a little blurred. All I really remember was his face.

And his bedroom.

It wasn't a complicated space. In fact, it was reminiscent of my own room. He had a bed, a desk, a computer. A bookshelf that was filled not with books but with what appeared to be basketball-related awards. There were two doors in here, which made me think he had his own bathroom, and a maybe a walk-in closet. The walls were white. The carpet was soft.

It was nice. There was no clutter.

"Your room is so clean," I said to him.

And he laughed. "Yeah," he said, "well, I actually hoped you'd be coming over today. So I cleaned it."

I looked at him. I didn't know why I was surprised. It was obvious that he'd made a kind of plan to come get me today. To talk to me. But there was something about imagining him cleaning his room in anticipation of my possible visit that made me adore him. I suddenly wanted to know what he'd done. What he'd removed. I wanted to know what his room looked like before he'd organized it.

Instead, I sat on his bed. His was a lot bigger than mine. But then, he was also a lot taller than me. My bed would've squished him.

Ocean was standing in the middle of his room, watching me as I looked over the details of his life. It was all very spare. His comforter was white. His pillows were white. His bed frame was made of a dark brown wood.

"Hey," he said gently.

I looked up.

He sounded suddenly close to tears. "I'm so sorry," he said. "About everything."

He told me he'd read my journal. He apologized, over and over again. He said he was sorry, he was so sorry, but he'd just wanted to know what had happened with his mom—what she'd said to me to cause all this—because he didn't think I'd ever tell him. He said he'd asked his mom a thousand times what she'd said to me that day but that she refused to answer any of his questions, that she'd shut him out completely. But then, in the process of searching for the parts about his mother, he'd seen everything else, too. How his coach had bullied me. Screamed at me. All the awful things that'd happened to me at school. All of it.

"I'm so sorry," he said. "I'm so sorry they did this to you. I'm sorry I didn't know. I wish you'd told me."

I shook my head. Toyed with the comforter under my hands. "It's really not your fault," I said to him. "It's my fault. I messed this up."

"What? No—"

"Yes," I said. I met his eyes. "I shouldn't have let this happen. I should've told you what your mom said to me. I just—I don't know. She made me feel so stupid," I said. "And she said you had no money for college, Ocean, and I just couldn't let you—"

"It doesn't matter," he said. "I'll figure it out. I'll call my dad. I'll take out a loan. It doesn't matter anymore."

"I'm so sorry," I said. "I'm sorry about all of it."

"Don't worry," he said. "Really. I'll figure it out."

"But what are you going to do now?" I said. "About school?"

He exhaled heavily. "I have a hearing in a week. They haven't *officially* expelled me yet," he said, "but I'm pretty sure they will. Until then I'm suspended. I might end up having to go to school in a different district."

"Really?" My eyes widened. "Oh my God."

"Yeah," he said. "Unless, you know, I manage to convince everyone at the hearing that I was actually doing them a *favor* by breaking my coach's nose. Though I'm guessing the chances are slim."

"Wow," I said. "I'm so sorry."

"Don't be. I was happy to punch that piece of shit in the face. I'd do it again in a heartbeat."

We were both quiet a moment, just staring at each other.

Finally, Ocean said, "You have no idea how much I missed you."

"Um, I think I do," I said. "I think I'd win that competition."

He laughed, softly.

And then he walked over, sat beside me on his bed. My feet didn't touch the floor. His did.

I was suddenly nervous. I hadn't been this close to him in so long. It was like starting over again, like my heart had to have these heart attacks all over again and my nerves were sparking, my head was filling with steam all over again and then, very gently, he took my hand.

We said nothing. We didn't even look at each other. We were looking at our hands, entwined, and he was drawing patterns along my palm, and I could hardly breathe as he left trails of fire along my skin. And then, all of a sudden, I noticed that his right hand was bruised. The knuckles on his right fist looked like they'd been destroyed, actually.

Gingerly, I touched the torn skin. The wounds had only barely begun to heal.

"Yeah," he said, in response to my unspoken question. His voice was tight. "That's, um . . . yeah."

"Does it hurt?" I asked.

We both looked up. We were sitting so close together that when we'd lifted our heads our faces were only inches apart. I could feel his breath against my skin. I could smell him—his faint cologne, the scent that was entirely his own—

"It—yeah," he said, and blinked, distracted. "It kind of"—he took a sharp, sudden breath—"I'm sorry," he said, "I just—"

He took my face in his hands and he kissed me, kissed me with such intensity that I was flooded, at once, with feelings so painful I made a sound, an involuntary sound that was almost like crying. I felt my mind blur. I felt my heart expand. I touched his waist, tentatively, ran my hands up his back and I felt something break open inside me, something that felt like surrender. I got lost in the feel of him, in the heat of his skin, in the way his body shook when he broke away and I felt like I was dreaming, like I'd forgotten how to think. *I missed you*, he kept saying, *God, I missed you,* and he kissed me again, so deeply, and my head was spinning, and he tasted, somehow, like pure heat. We broke apart, fighting to breathe, holding on to each other like we were drowning, like we'd been lost, left for dead in a very large expanse of sea.

I pressed my forehead to his and whispered, "I love you."

I felt him tense.

"I'm sorry I didn't say it sooner," I said. "I wanted to. I wish I had."

Ocean didn't say a word. He didn't have to. He was gripping my body like he'd never let me go, like he was hanging on for dear life.

THIRTY-EIGHT

In the end, the thing that broke us apart wasn't all the hatred. It wasn't the racists or the assholes.

I was moving again.

Ocean and I had two and a half months of perfect happiness before my dad broke the news, in the beginning of May, that we'd be leaving town as soon as Navid graduated. We'd be gone by July.

The weeks in the interim passed in a sweet, strangled sort of agony. Ultimately, Ocean hadn't been expelled. His mother had hired a lawyer for the hearing and—in a twist that surprised only Ocean—it turned out that he was just too well-liked. The school board agreed to suspend him for an extra week and call it a day. They tried to convince him to rejoin the basketball team, but Ocean refused. He said he never wanted to play basketball competitively, not ever again. In some ways, he seemed so much happier.

In other ways, not at all.

We were always acutely aware of our fast-approaching expiration date, and we spent as much time together as we could. My social status had changed so dramatically—climbing only higher after news broke that Ocean had punched his coach in the face because of me—that no one even blinked at us anymore, and we were both stunned and confused, all the time, at the perfect ridiculousness of high school. Still, we took what we could get. We were wrapped up in each other, feeling happy and sad all at once, pretty much all the time.

Ocean's mom realized that pushing me out of her son's life had only fractured her own relationship with him, so she let me back in. She tried to get to know me and did a mediocre job of it. It was fine. She was still kind of weird, but for the first time in a long time, she was actively involved in Ocean's life again. His near-expulsion actually seemed to shake something loose in her brain; she was maybe more surprised than anyone that Ocean had voluntarily broken someone's nose, and, suddenly, she was asking him questions. She wanted to know what was happening in his head. She started showing up for dinner and staying home on weekends and it made him so happy. He loved having his mom around.

So I smiled. I ate her potato salad.

School was always weird. It never really settled into anything normal. Slowly, after a great deal of soul-searching, my classmates dug deep and found the intestinal fortitude to speak to me about things besides breakdancing and that thing on my head, the results of which turned out to be both entertaining and illuminating. The more I got to know people, the more I realized we were all just a bunch of frightened idiots walking around in the dark, bumping into each other and panicking for no reason at all.

So I started turning on a light.

I stopped thinking of people as mobs. Hordes. Faceless masses. I tried, really hard, to stop assuming I had people figured out, especially before I'd ever even spoken to them. I wasn't great at this—and I'd probably have to work at it for the rest of my life—but I tried. I really did. It scared me to realize that I'd done to others exactly what I hadn't wanted them to do to me: I made sweeping statements about who I thought they were and how they lived their lives; and I made broad generalizations about what I thought they were thinking, all the time.

I didn't want to be that person anymore.

I was tired of focusing on my own anger. I was tired of focusing only on my memories of terrible people and the terrible things they'd said and done to me. I was tired of it. The darkness took up too much valuable real estate in my head. Besides, I'd moved enough times now to know that time was a fleeting, exhaustible thing.

I didn't want to waste it.

I'd wasted so many months pushing Ocean away and I wished so much, every day, that I hadn't. I wished I'd trusted him sooner. I wished I'd savored every hour we had together. I wished for so much. For so many things with him. Ocean had made me want to find all the other good people in the world and hold them close.

Maybe it was enough, I thought, that I knew someone like him existed in this world. Maybe it was enough that our lives had merged and diverged and left us both transformed. Maybe it was enough to have learned that love was the unexpected weapon, that it was the knife I'd needed to cut through the Kevlar I wore every day.

Maybe this, I thought, was enough.

Ocean had given me hope. He'd made me believe in people again. His sincerity had rubbed me raw, had peeled back the stubborn layers of anger I'd lived in for so long.

Ocean made me want to give the world a second chance.

He stood in the middle of the street when our cars pulled away on that sunny afternoon. He stood there, motionless, and watched us go, and when his figure was finally swallowed up by the space between us, I turned back around in my seat. Caught my heart as it fell out of my chest.

My phone buzzed.

don't give up on me, he wrote.

And I never did.

EXCLUSIVE
Bonus
CHAPTERS
KEEP READING TO HEAR FROM OCEAN JAMES

ONE

I heard it before I even made it downstairs:

The sound of the television.

The volume had been turned down enough that the sound seemed more like a vibration, an unintelligible mess of white noise. This was how she liked it. She said she couldn't fall asleep without it. And I knew my mom well enough to know that when I walked into the living room I'd find her passed out on the couch. She'd be dressed in yesterday's clothes—her shoes kicked off, onto the floor—and her bag would be tossed on the kitchen table, keys and receipts and old packs of gum spilling out. The sight of her, splayed on the couch like that, always left a pit in my stomach.

Worse, it had given me a complex.

It didn't matter where I was anymore; the soft, ambient

sounds of television always transported me back to this exact moment, and this moment always made me feel like shit.

Which meant that most mornings made me feel like shit.

I sighed, shook my head. I couldn't wait to get the hell out of here. Away from this. Her. Everything.

I moved quietly through the house—leaving the lights off and the shades drawn—trying not to wake her as I grabbed my bio book and the binder I'd left on the dining table last night. I never actually wanted to be here at night, but I was too practical to stay out late indefinitely, and when I was home, I did my work downstairs. I wasn't sure why; I had a perfectly good desk in my bedroom. But sometimes, when I was willing to be honest with myself, I wondered if the truth was that I was still waiting up for her. For a chance to see her.

Waiting for my mommy.

Jesus.

I shook my head, embarrassed by my own thoughts, and grabbed a protein bar from the pantry. I ripped it open and took a bite, chewing as I pulled on my sneakers, and took a final glance around the kitchen. Take-out boxes and unopened cutlery kits littered the counter. Dirty bowls were stacked in the sink, greasy forks and spoons sitting in the basin. I almost couldn't believe how quickly she'd made this mess. I'd just cleaned the kitchen last night.

I could feel something tensing inside me—a mix of anger and frustration—and I knew I needed to leave before things got worse. She had to do so little to piss me off these days that I couldn't even tell when I was overreacting anymore. But just as I was about to slip out the door, I heard her tired, croaky voice.

"Hey, honey."

My shoulders gave out. Slowly, I turned to face her.

She was trying to sit up, her movements unsteady. Mascara was smudged under her eyes. Her dress was rumpled.

"Where are you going?" she said, and smiled. "Don't you want to make your mom a cup of coffee?"

"I wish I could, but"—I nodded at the door—"I'm running late."

"For what?"

"School."

She cringed, tapping her fist against her forehead. "Oh, honey," she said, and laughed. "I'm sorry. I don't know why I thought today was Saturday."

"It's Wednesday."

Her smile vanished at the harsh sound of my voice, and I felt bad instantly. I sighed. I was about to say something when—

"Well. If it's *Wednesday*," she said, the warmth gone from her eyes, "then you better get going."

"Mom, I wasn't—" I hesitated. Looked away. I was staring at the front door, studying its bland design, when I said quietly, "Where were you last night?"

"I was out."

I looked up.

She was finger-combing her hair, yanking a little when she met resistance.

3

"Out?" I said. "That's it?"

She met my eyes then. Looked annoyed. "I didn't think I needed to tell my teenage son every detail of my life."

"That's not what I meant."

She got to her feet. "I'm going to take a shower. We can talk later, okay?"

"When?"

She glanced at me, confused. "What do you mean?"

"When will we talk?" I said, the anger creeping back into my voice. "When will I see you? Will you be here when I get home from school?"

She waved an absent hand at me. "Oh, honey, I don't know. Don't you have basketball practice after school?"

My eyes widened. Then narrowed. "Are you serious? We're not even in season right now."

She crossed her arms. Shot me an unkind look. "What is this, an interrogation? I know you're not having official practices yet, but I also know Coach Hart well enough to know that you're supposed to be training, even in the off-season."

I felt suddenly, inexplicably sad.

Every day I felt like we were drifting farther apart, like the earth had fissured open between us and it was only a matter of time before we lost each other forever. I kept begging her to jump, to meet me here before the distance between us grew impassable, and every day she ignored me, too busy being busy to realize that one day I might leave and never look back.

I stared at her now, trying to understand, and, failing that,

I looked away. There were a thousand things I wanted to say—wanted to shout at her—and didn't. Finally, I laughed. Quietly.

She didn't like that. "And what, exactly, is so funny?"

"Nothing." I felt suddenly tired. "Nothing is funny. I have to go."

"Then go."

I nodded without looking at her.

I hated how much I cared, hated how much I wanted her to give a shit about me, hated how much she didn't.

So I muttered a quiet, "whatever," and left.

I didn't even slam the door behind me.

TWO

It was true, what my mom said.

We were in the off-season, but I still spent a lot of time training. Running. Hitting the gym. And even though I had another couple of weeks before we entered more serious pre-season conditioning, Coach rarely let me rest. This year, I would be one of the youngest shooting guards to play for the varsity team. Ever.

I should've been celebrating. Hell, I should've been *happy*. Instead, I spent the summer feeling lost. Confused. I didn't even know if a basketball career was what I wanted. But I'd been playing ball for so long that I never even had a chance to consider something else. This was it. This was what everyone wanted for me.

Apparently it was the only thing I was good at.

I stepped out of my car and into the school parking lot,

slinging my backpack over my shoulder as I slammed the door closed behind me. It was the middle of September, and the heat had died down enough for the morning air to feel just right. The breeze was crisp. The sun was bright. I turned my face up to the sky and closed my eyes.

I knew I was being ungrateful.

Basketball had done so much for me. Changed my life. My team had become the family I never had, given me friends and a support system I didn't know what I'd do without. But there had always been this small, nagging voice in my head that insisted that, maybe, basketball didn't have to be everything, all the time, forever.

Maybe I could be good at something else, too.

And then, suddenly—

Josh Henson slammed into me with both hands, laughing like a drunk idiot. I didn't think he was actually drunk; it wasn't even eight in the morning. Still, I was irritated.

I shoved away from him. "What the hell, man—"

"What the *fuck*, James?" Josh was still laughing, and I stifled the impulse to roll my eyes. My oldest friends loved pretending they couldn't tell the difference between my first and last names—both of which are, technically, first names. I couldn't remember how it started, but they'd been doing it for so long I didn't know how to tell them to stop. "I didn't know you and Cynthia broke up," he said.

I shot him a confused look. "That's old news."

"Not to me."

I shrugged and walked away.

He grabbed my arm. "Hey," he said, but his voice had mellowed a bit. "I was wondering—"

I already knew what he was going to ask, so I shook him off and kept walking. I needed to get to my locker before class, and I'd been running later than usual this morning, so I was short on time. "You can ask her out," I said. "I don't care."

"For real?"

I stopped. Turned to face him. "We split up, like, two months ago."

Josh just stared at me.

"What?" I said, feeling newly irritated.

"Why did you break up with her?"

"I never said I broke up with her."

"Jesus Christ," he said softly. His eyes were wide, stunned. "What is *wrong* with you?"

"There's nothing wrong with me," I said, looking away. "She's just not my type."

"How the fuck is Cynthia Johnson not your type? Are you fucking blind?"

And I couldn't help it. I laughed. "Listen, do you need something from me? Because I have shit to do."

"Me?" He pointed at his chest. "No. I don't need anything. You, on the other hand, might need to seek medical attention."

I laughed again. "And on that note."

"Wait— So— You really wouldn't mind if I, like, asked Cynthia to homecoming?"

I shook my head as I walked away. "You can ask Cynthia to marry you for all I care. It's not my business."

"The fuck is wrong with you, bro?" Josh called after me. "I never said anything about marriage."

By the end of the day I was more than exhausted, I was pissed. And there was so much to be irritated about, I didn't even know where to direct my frustration. My mom was the obvious choice, I knew that, but Coach had become a close second. He'd asked me to meet him in his office at lunch. He wanted to discuss the training program he'd designed for the next two months of my life—but that training program turned out to be more like abject torture. It was the kind of intensive training that was usually reserved for remedial players. I didn't understand why he was putting so much pressure on me, but it was obvious he'd chosen to whip me into shape for something— maybe his ticket to fame—and I didn't like it. I didn't like what was happening to us. Our relationship used to mean something; once upon a time, he'd been like a pseudo-parent to me.

But lately all he ever wanted to talk about was basketball. It didn't seem to matter if I was foaming at the mouth or bleeding from the gut, as long as I could make the shot.

I sighed.

My entire conversation with him had left me with a raging headache, which had been made worse by the shit I'd had to deal with when Cynthia cornered me, like, five minutes ago.

She was apparently pissed off because I'd told Josh I'd broken up with her—she'd made it very clear when we split that she didn't want people to know she was the one who'd been dumped—and I tried to explain that I hadn't actually said those exact words to anyone, and even if I had, Josh shouldn't have been stupid enough to repeat them to her, but my response only seemed to make things worse.

She screamed at me.

Literally screamed at me—in a single, angry breath—her fists clenched dangerously at her sides. For a moment I thought she might hit me. But then, thankfully, she stormed off.

It felt like people had been screaming at me nonstop today, and I was grateful the day was nearly over. My last class was AP bio, and I was looking forward to only pretending to care about the molecular diversity of life. The minute I sat down, I dropped my head in my hands. There was a dull ache pressing behind my eyes, so I squeezed them shut. I barely even heard my teacher as she announced that we'd be beginning our first lab assignment that day, and I looked up, confused, when she called my name. But then she called someone else's name, too.

And then she declared us partners.

I stiffened. I was realizing, a little slowly, that the name my teacher had called out—Shirin Jafari—was the name of the girl who sits in front of me. I blinked at the back of her head, surprised. She was generally hard to miss. I wasn't sure if she was the only Muslim kid at our school, but I knew for a fact that she was the only one who wore that head thing. And even though she was in two of my classes, I'd only spoken to her once, on the first day of school. I'd accidentally knocked her shoulder with my bio book, and she'd seemed really angry about it, which felt like an overreaction.

But then, maybe she'd been having a rough day.

I was with a group of kids last week when I saw her walk by, and someone asked her why she was in school. He said—

"Isn't it, like, against your religion for women to read?"

She only glanced at him—with no expression on her face—and kept walking.

"So I guess you don't understand English, huh?" he shouted after her.

People laughed.

I'd said nothing.

And now, as I stared at her, I felt a sudden stab of guilt. I probably should've said something. But the truth was, I didn't know anything about her, and I didn't even know if she needed defending. She never seemed to care. She seemed to float in and out of campus every day, untethered to anything. I never saw her with anyone. I'd never even heard her talk in class.

And I realized I was suddenly very curious to hear her speak.

I waited for her to turn around, to say hi or, I don't know, acknowledge the fact that we'd been paired up for this assignment, but she didn't move. Most of the kids were out of their chairs already, animatedly discussing the dead cat we were supposed to dissect, but Shirin didn't even seem to notice. I stood up slightly to get her attention, but when I peered over her shoulder, I saw her sketching, with great concentration, in her notebook.

It looked like some kind of street graffiti.

I frowned.

Finally, I slid out of my chair and tapped her on the shoulder. She jumped nearly a foot in the air.

Her pencil fell to the floor—it rolled to a stop at my feet—and she looked up at me with such deep, intense eyes, I took a sudden step back.

"*What?*" she said.

She was angry again, and I was instantly nervous. I didn't know what I'd done wrong. "We're— We're lab partners," I said. "Mrs. Cho just paired us up."

"Oh."

She was staring at me when she exhaled the single word, and for the briefest, strangest moment, I felt my heart speed up. She had such a focused, piercing gaze that making direct eye contact with her was close to terrifying. But then she looked away, and the connection between us severed so fast that I blinked, bewildered by the whiplash.

Finally, she stood up.

She didn't seem to notice that I was still looking at her, and I caught an unexpectedly intimate glimpse of her lower torso when she lifted the hem of her sweater, tugged free the iPod tucked into the waistband of her jeans, and hit pause.

My eyes widened.

I wanted to ask her about that, about whether or not she

spent all day listening to music under her head thing, but I didn't want to push it. She already seemed kind of pissed, and, besides, I'd asked her about that iPod once, that first day, and she didn't seem interested in discussing it.

So I said nothing.

Actually, neither of us said much. In fact, Shirin seemed so completely uninterested in my company that I began to feel self-conscious about it. I introduced myself when we got to our lab station, and other than staring at me, wide-eyed, when I told her my name was Ocean, she said literally nothing. I tried to laugh, tried to explain my name by telling her my parents were weird, and she only shrugged.

I wanted to say something else to fill the awkward silence growing between us, but I wasn't sure what to say. She was so strange. She was wearing a pale yellow hoodie—the hood pulled up over her head thing—that literally said *stranger*, right across the front, in bright blue letters. It almost looked like the letters had been stitched by hand.

I frowned.

I opened my mouth to ask about her sweater, and then changed my mind. Instead, I glanced at her while we worked. The minutes ticked by and I waited, patiently, for her to look at me. To say something. To seem even a little bit curious about this assignment, or maybe her lab partner.

She didn't.

I'd never thought of myself as a conceited person, but I wondered, suddenly, if I was. I'd have been lying if I said I hadn't thought she'd be a little excited to be my partner. I was so used to people in this town—and in this school—knowing everything about me that I guess I thought she knew something about me, too. Maybe I thought she'd be impressed.

The realization made me hate myself a little.

And then I wondered, in possibly my lowest moment, if maybe she really didn't understand English. That answer made the most sense; it would explain her silence, her general disinterest, the way she never seemed to be aware of what was happening around her. But then, not half a second later, I felt awful for thinking it. I squeezed my eyes shut as a fresh stab of guilt speared me through the gut.

Jesus.

Of course she understood English. This was an AP bio class. I knew she was a sophomore—that much was made clear on the first day of school, when people were trying to figure out where she'd come from—which meant there was no way she was in this class by accident. In fact, it probably meant that she was super smart.

Wow, I thought. I had no idea I was such an asshole.

I didn't know when I'd become this person—the kind of guy who was so sure girls would be falling over themselves to talk to him that, barring an inability to speak English, he couldn't imagine why they wouldn't. I looked away, ran a hand through my hair and felt, suddenly, thoroughly ashamed of myself. Hell, maybe the conclusion was something so much more obvious. Maybe she was just shy.

I glanced at her face again, but this time, she looked up, too.

I took a sharp breath. *Shy* was definitely the wrong assessment. This girl might've been quiet, but she was definitely not shy. She was looking at me right now like she knew, knew I'd been watching her this whole time, and she was warning me to knock it off. I felt my skin prickle with embarrassment, but, somehow, I couldn't look away. So when she finally narrowed her eyes at me, looking both angry and disappointed, I coughed and averted my gaze, but not before I felt a flush of heat rush up my neck.

She didn't look at me again after that. Didn't even turn her head in my direction.

I spent the rest of the period distracted.

I'd never known anyone like her before. I'd never even seen, in person, anyone like her before. And the experience was so far from what I thought it might be that I almost didn't know what to do with myself. I'd have to work with this girl for two months, and right now I couldn't even get her to look at me, and I couldn't figure out why. Or why I cared.

In fact, I was so preoccupied trying to figure out what was going on with her that I did a shitty job being her lab partner. The hour was nearly up and we still hadn't finished the work; I couldn't believe it. But what surprised me even more was that when I glanced at the clock I felt—not sadness, exactly—but something like—

Disappointment.

I hadn't realized how much I'd wanted to hear her say something until it hit me that it wasn't going to happen. She clearly had no interest in being my friend. But we still needed to figure out how to get the rest of the work done before tomorrow, so I'd have to bite the bullet and talk to her again.

"So," I said, trying to smile, "I don't think we're going to be able to finish this before the bell rings."

She was still cutting into the cat, carefully separating skin from muscle, and she was so focused on what she was doing that I wondered if she'd even heard me. But then she finished the section she'd been working on, and her face relaxed. She blinked, hesitating as she flipped the scalpel over in her hand, and I wondered, for no reason at all, if she had any idea how pretty she was.

And then I sank back in my seat, startled by my own thoughts.

Wow, not helpful.

I tried again, this time offering to stay late to finish the assignment. "I can't stay long," I said, purposely keeping my eyes on my lab sheet, "but I have a little time after school."

She looked up suddenly, as if startled out of a trance. "Excuse me?"

This girl was so weird. Her body was here, but her brain seemed to live on another planet. It was confusing, because she didn't strike me as a silly, airheaded sort of person, and it made me wonder if she did this on purpose—if she purposely tuned out the people and experiences she didn't like.

God, I had a thousand questions.

Instead, I said, "We still have to write a report for today's findings." I glanced again at the clock. "But the bell is about to ring. So we should probably finish this after school, right?"

"Oh," she said, and hesitated. "Well. I can't meet after school."

And then, all at once, I felt stupid.

I could feel it—could feel the heat rising up my neck again—and I wondered if I'd just offended her by even asking. Maybe her parents were super strict about this sort of thing. Maybe she wasn't even allowed to talk to guys. What the hell did I know?

"Right," I said. "I get it." But I was so embarrassed I couldn't even look at her. "Are you— I mean, are you not allowed, to, like—"

"*Wow.*"

I looked up at the sharp sound of her voice. She was staring at me like I was an actual idiot, and I felt my stomach flip in the worst way.

I froze.

"Wow," she said again, this time quietly. She shook her head and turned away, but not before I saw the pained look on her face.

That was a bad sign.

I had no idea what had just happened, but I knew enough to understand that I'd done something wrong. I kept waiting for her to explain, to tell me what I'd done to upset her, but she was patently ignoring me now, and I almost couldn't help it when I said—

"Wow what?"

She finished washing and drying her hands before she looked me directly in the eye. Her own eyes were bright with feeling, deep and unflinching, and I felt it again—a sudden, swift kick in my heart.

Jesus, I was nervous.

"Listen," she said, "I don't know what you've already decided about what you think my life is like, but I'm not about to be sold off by my parents for a pile of goats, okay?"

Shit.

Panic bloomed in my chest. I'd fucked this up. I'd definitely fucked this up and I didn't know what to do to fix it.

The idiot in me made a joke.

"Herd of goats," I said. "It's a herd—"

"Whatever the hell kind of goats," she said, her eyes flashing. "I don't care. I just happen to have shit to do after school."

"Oh."

"So maybe we can figure this out some other way," she said. "Okay?"

Panic was quickly expanding inside of me. It must've been panic. I didn't know how else to explain my sudden inability to be articulate. I felt frozen, immobilized by guilt and nervousness and the sudden, strange thrill I felt when she looked at me. This girl was genuinely terrifying.

I floundered.

"Oh," I said. "Okay." And then, because I felt a desperate

need to fill the silence with something normal, I said, "What, uh, what are you doing after school?"

She'd been packing her things away when I spoke, and her spine stiffened as she looked at me. Her eyes narrowed, suspicious.

"What?" she said. "Why do you care?"

I almost swore out loud.

I couldn't seem to get this right. Everything I said struck a nerve with her. Everything I said was exactly wrong. Even this, just now—

I didn't know what to do.

I felt myself giving up the fight as I said quietly, "I don't know."

And she went still.

Slowly, she tugged the hood of her sweater back. Her hair was still covered, but her face seemed suddenly more open. Her head was tilted to the side, her lips slightly parted, as her eyes traveled my face, my neck, the length of my body. I was standing up—we both were—because we'd been packing our things, and I felt like I couldn't move. She was studying me openly, unselfconsciously, and it made me feel naked. I was suddenly overcome by a need to know what she was thinking. I wanted to know what she was deciding about me, and I wondered if she'd find me lacking. And then I wondered at how quickly I'd gone from barely registering this girl's existence to—*this*. Whatever this was. Whatever I was doing now.

I was staring at her again.

I couldn't help it. She was looking at me full in the face, and I didn't know where else to look. The two seconds she spent scanning me for errors seemed to multiply in the silence between us.

I had time to study her, too.

And wow, I couldn't help but notice that she was really beautiful. Scary beautiful. Her eyes were sharp and clear. She seemed completely unafraid of the world.

And then, suddenly, I seemed to pass a test.

Her expression softened. Her eyes warmed a little. And her voice was close to something like happiness when she said, "I'm joining a breakdancing crew."

I was sure she was messing with me. I nearly laughed out loud. I waited for her to laugh, too, to tell me the truth, but she said nothing.

I smiled. "Is that a joke?"

She rolled her eyes. The bell rang. And in an instant her face had closed off again.

Shit.

"I have to go," she said, the words hollow.

My heart sank, like a stone, into the pit of my stomach.

"But what about the lab work?" I said.

She sighed, obviously disappointed, but finally wrote something down on a piece of paper and handed it to me.

"You can text me," she said. "We'll work on it tonight."

I stared at the piece of paper. Of all the things I thought might happen today, I never thought I'd be going home with this girl's phone number.

"But be careful with that," she said suddenly. "Because if you text me too much, you'll have to marry me. It's the rules of my religion."

I felt my face freeze.

I didn't know her well enough to be able to tell if she was joking. Just a moment ago I thought she was making a joke and I turned out to be very wrong. Maybe this girl never joked. How would I know? I didn't know anything about her religion. And as far as I was aware, her being married off to some guy she barely knew sounded like it might've been within the realm of possibility.

"Wait," I said. "What?"

She almost smiled, but I didn't know what that meant. And when she said, "I have to go, Ocean," I thought maybe I'd missed a beat.

I just wanted to be sure.

I'd heard about Muslim girls having arranged marriages. I'd watched the news. Maybe this was a real thing.

"Wait," I said. "No, seriously— You're joking, right?"

I got my answer in the form of a long, sad sigh. She shook her head, said, "Wow," one last time, and left.

She didn't even glance back as she said goodbye.

And I couldn't get her out of my head for the rest of the night.

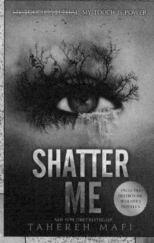